VALERIUS EVERREIGNING
The Valerian Chronicles – Volume 3

T. R. Rankin

VALERIUS EVERREIGNING
The Valerian Chronicles – Volume 3

DOUBLE DRAGON

ISBN 978-1-78695-656-9
Double Dragon
is an imprint of
Fiction4All

This Edition Published 2021
Fiction4All
www.fiction4all.com

Cover art by Ken Vaudrain

DEDICATION

In Memory of May Caister,
Who would have been pleased

Cast of Characters

Asperides-- Viceroy of Palmeria, son of Armagon

Baneluc-- Unsuccessful candidate for Steward of Thule

Bartolome-- Valerius' household servant at Zagorbia

Beryl -- Midwife who attends Eomer

Bokmar-- Resistance leader in Cartho

Boltar-- Captain of Elusive

Brendel-- Thorngere's sister

Burmac-- Old friend of Valerius who dies at Zagorbia

Caramon-- King of Falkan under old regime, killed by Fantar

Carmen-- Ambassador of Fantar who appears at Zagorbia

Chad-- Servant of Volkmir who accompanies Vahla

Colinus-- Fantar's prisoner, former Commander of the Kantaran Guard

Corloc-- Elder of Gan, a fishing village near Thorngere's home

Curio-- Left in charge at Falkan by Vincipius

Daemon-- Flotilla Commander for Valerius, originally from Palmeria

Daneloc-- Thorngere's brother-in-law

Emaus-- Young soldier of Vincipius rescued by Valerius

Eomer-- Valerius' wife, daughter of Reuters

Fantar-- Regicide and self-proclaimed Emperor

Fargo Cimmeon-- New King of Falkan, nephew of Caramon

Gainor-- Captain of Valerius' forces, originally from Bangorum

Gamlarch-- Resistance leader at Balac, former commander of Valerian Guard

Glaucon-- Leader of Fantar's forces at Battle of Kantar

Gormlath-- Commander of Fantar's Imperial Guard

Grumwald-- Admiral of Valerius' fleet

Haradin-- Renegade Iblis leader

Karghan-- Scythian leader

Koltar-- King of Kantar in the Hidden Valley

Kundar-- Chief Scout for resistance in Palmeria, speaks Scythian

Markus Vincipius-- Head of army attacking Zagorbia.

Oracle-- Oracle of Cartho

Owen of Rodale-- Ambassador Fantar sends to Oracle

Panella-- Thorngere's mother

Quamous-- Burghermeister of Cartho

Ragnar-- Leader of the free forces of Zagorbia

Reuters-- King of Dulcai

Rondo-- Ambassador from Dulcai to Valerius at Zagorbia

Thornalon-- Thorngere's father

Thorngere-- Valerius' friend and second in command

Uban-- Captain of a supply vessel captured at Zagorbia

Vahla-- Valerius' sister and an Enchantress

Vauhna-- Vahla's mother's name, alias Vahla uses in Palmeria

Valerian-- Son and heir to Valerius Everreigning

Valerius-- High King of Valeria and all the Inland Sea

Vaxagores-- General for Asperides at Palmeria

Volkmir-- Mage of Valeria

Whitman-- Sergeant who tries to rape Vahla

Zenemahr-- Viceroy of the Telos Military District

Zimlait-- Naval Commander for Valerius, originally from Cobanos

PROLOGUE

In a cave, high in the mountains south of Zagorbia, an ancient Mage shivered before an open fire. By his side, a woman tucked a blanket closer about his chin, while a servant added another log to the fire. It was not winter, nor even particularly cold-though at that altitude the nights often were-and the opulently furnished cave was certainly comfortable. But the mage had not been well, and that very afternoon had begun to show signs of fever. He sat now, tightly swaddled in a pillowed armchair, his wispy white beard spilling down the blanket like corn silk, and gazed into the fire with moist, fever-bright eyes.

"Come here and sit by me, girl," he commanded. "There are some matters we must discuss, signs I have seen."

"Can it not wait, Volkmir?" the woman protested, but nonetheless sat down on a stool by his side. "The hour grows late and you need your rest."

"No, the time is ripe now, Vahla my girl, and I will have rest soon enough. Chad..."

The servant was a small, dark-complected man who moved like a shadow. At the mage's nod, he sprinkled a spoonful of powder over the fire. Instantly, a cloud of thick green smoke boiled up, filling the chamber with a sweet, pungent smell. The girl felt it catch in the back of her throat and swallowed hard not to cough. As the smoke began to clear, Chad added more powder, pouring a thin trickle this time, and the smoke, as if following instruction, rose up straight in a narrow column and formed a small, vaguely round cloud above the flames. Here it hovered, throbbing and pulsing like a wispy balloon on an insubstantial string, occasionally augmented by fresh powder from Chad.

"Look deep, Vahla," said the mage, "for herein we should see something of the signs I mentioned- of a new power rising in the east to rival the claim of King Valerius."

Vahla looked close, squinting with concentration, but could see only smoke, swirling and churning like an impenetrable curtain. "Another of Fantar's minions?" she asked, darting a quick glance at the mage.

"I know not," said Volkmir, "nor yet what events the signs portend. Surely, Fantar reigns in the east, but whether this Asperides is a scion of his line, an anointed of his, or someone entirely new, I know not. I only sense his force and am drawn to it, like iron to lodestone."

Beside the fire, Chad deftly added more powder, rose tinted this time, and bands of pink and red began to swirl within the smoky orb. Both mage and assistant leaned forward now, peering intently at the moiling cloud. Vahla swallowed again. Her mouth was thick and dry, and she felt like some of the cloud had entered her brain. She coughed suddenly and Chad handed her a cup of wine. She drank deeply, thinking, 'I feel like a cat with a hairball.' It was funny, that thought, and she was very aware of her mouth curling upwards in a smile. But then, something caught her eye in the fire.

It was like a spark, but it wasn't. It was blue, and looked like a tiny picture that flashed in the fire, then floated swiftly upward into the smoke and disappeared. It happened so fast she was not sure she had actually seen it, and was just thinking she hadn't when something flashed again, in the cloud this time. Suddenly, the cloud filled with an image of the sea at night, under a clear, full moon, and she could see the yellow light rippling off the waves. Then it was just cloud again and she started to exclaim. But the mage hushed her, for the smoke had once more become sea.

It was a quiet sea, a round ball of sea floating like a painting above the fire, yet so clear and close she felt she could reach out and touch it. Then a boat sailed by, very fast, and she jerked back as if it would burst from the cloud and run her down. "What was that?" she said.

"Hush, girl," said the mage. "It looked like a boat."

"I thought you said this was going to be the east?"

"Hush, I said! We see what we are given to see. From that we try to understand."

Vahla hushed and the sea image began to move. It slipped backwards, as if the eye, or whatever it was, were moving along behind the boat. Then it soared up, like a bird, away from the surface, and fixed on the boat, bright in the moonlight. It was a twin-hulled craft with a bridge deck, sailing swiftly

13

along across a light evening breeze. A man stood at the helm and several others lined the weather pontoon. Another figure-half the size of the helmsman-stood forward by the mast, peering ahead into the darkness.

"Why, that's the catumaran-Lord Koltar's invention!" Vahla exclaimed. "And that must be Colinus there by the mast. He's supposed to be with Valerius in Zagorbia. What's he doing here?"

"Valerius sent him east as a military envoy," Volkmir whispered. "He's been using the boat for courier duty because it's so fast. But why Colinus is aboard now, I know not. Perhaps he brings the message we seek."

"But he seems to be looking for something."

"Hush now!" Volkmir hissed. "Your breath will distort the skein."

The image above the flames had indeed begun to shimmer, but now, as the two observers quieted, it too settled, and zoomed in on the half-sized man by the mast, the one called Colinus. He was looking at something, his round, boyish face thrust forward, his eyes squinting. And he was obviously concerned about the bright light of the moon for he kept glancing back at it, a look of irritation crossing his face. He signaled the helmsman to alter course a bit and pointed in the direction he wanted to go. As if on cue, the image above the flames shifted, too, and followed his hand. The image panned to a shore where, on either hand, thousands of campfires stretched away into the darkness, and as they drew

14

closer, dark shapes along the shelving beach resolved themselves into ships.

"It's an army!" said Vahla.

"And if I'm not mistaken," said Volkmir, studying the scene intently, "that stretch of beach is along the coast east of Zagorbia. Yes, there! See that stream? And that lone stand of trees inland? Chad and I used to land there years back, didn't we Chad?"

"Yes, Master," said Chad, stepping back from the fire and glancing into the image cloud for the first time. "Chad row long way. Trees where we hid boat."

"That's no more than a day's march east of the headland behind the city."

"But what can it mean?" Vahla wanted to know. "Whose army is it?"

"Whose army I know not, my dear-unless our friend Colinus here can discover that for us-but I suspect it means your brother, Valerius, is in for some unpleasantness. But let's see what else portends."

The image showed the boat sailing along parallel to the shore now, and Colinus busily counting the ships, his face hard with alarm and concentration. Suddenly, a shower of arrows fell about them, some thudding into the deck, some splashing along side, and one narrowly missing Colinus himself. Quickly, the craft turned and headed back out to sea, but two more flights reached them before they were out of range, a shaft from the last one piercing the helmsman's right calf.

As he fell, Colinus ran back to grab the tiller-the bar shoulder high on him which the wounded man had guided with his hip.

Back on shore, a group of armed men swarmed down the beach and in moments, two ships were launched in pursuit, their oars digging the black waters into phosphorescence under the brilliant moon. Large square sails dropped from their yards and the two galleys surged ahead, froth bubbling at their bows. Colinus watched them as he steered and ordered minor adjustments to the set of his own sail. Another flight of arrows was launched from the first ship, but it fell well short, and as Colinus left the loom of the land, the sea breeze freshened. His strange craft heeled, lifted its windward pontoon, and began to fairly fly across the waters. Spray dashed back into Colinus' face, and as he leaned back against the increasing pull of the tiller, his teeth bared in a feral grin.

Quickly, the pursuing craft lost ground and soon, the second of the two turned back. But the first kept on, hoping some mischance would yet bring them up with their prey. On and on they raced under the yellow moon, the 'catumaran' skipping along like a white stone, the oared galley walking the waters like some amphibious centipede, the gap between them widening steadily.

"They'll never catch him now," Vahla started to say, but before the words were out, the scene in the shimmering cloud shifted yet again, this time shooting forward across the rippled sea as if it were an arrow, and settled on a dark, sodden shape, a

16

large tree trunk, awash in the black quickness of the sea. "What's that?" she shouted. "Oh, no!"

The view pivoted to show the onrushing catamaran. Vahla screamed. At the last instant, Colinus looked up as if he had heard her voice and their eyes locked across imaginary space. Then the pontoon hit and he was catapulted into the sea.

The cloud screen went blank. Where an instant before was life and tragedy, now there was only roiling smoke. Vahla looked about wildly, the familiar surroundings registering as if she herself had just been dropped into the room. Then she saw Volkmir. He had collapsed, and lay sprawled in the chair like a carelessly flung doll.

"Volkmir!" she yelled, reaching out and lifting him. His eyes were rolled back but he still had breath, a feeble wind that rattled in his throat. "Volkmir! Come back! Are you all right? Volkmir!"

The mage's eyelids fluttered and his head shook. He inhaled sharply, then groaned. His eyes focused on her. "Are you all right?" she asked, more softly this time.

"You must go," he said, his voice little more than a whisper.

"Go? Go where? To warn Valerius?"

"You will know."

"Know what?" she asked. "What does this mean?"

Volkmir shook his head. His breathing was a bit steadier now. He lay back in the crook of her arm and closed his eyes as if to sleep. But she would have none of that and gave him a little shake.

"What do you mean?" she insisted.

"I don't know," he said.

"But you must," she stammered, "You're the mage!"

Volkmir chuckled, a raspy, hollow sound like the scraping of dry leaves. "Vahla, my dear," he said, "you've been with me for nearly a year now. Have you not yet seen that I'm a fraud?"

"But..." said Vahla, indicating the swirling cloud that still hung above the fire.

"A parlor trick, merely. Like most of my magic. Anyone can make the smoke. What it shows is the Gods' will. I do no more than observe."

"But..."

"No," said the mage, "it's true. I can advise you no better than your own heart. Probably less well. All I know is that you are called, and that you must go. The moon was full in that image. That means you have just over a week. Chad will guide you."

Vahla stared down at him, her mouth searching for words.

"Look!" said Volkmir. "At the cloud."

Vahla looked back. The surface had cleared again, showing a clear darkness now, and a tiny, distant light. As she watched, a figure entered from near at hand and walked slowly towards the light. It was Volkmir. Quickly she looked down at the old man in her arms. He was dead.

Chapter 1
VISIONS

The town of Zagorbia lay on the western side of a peninsula that thrust itself northward like a wedge into the narrow, twenty-mile wide channel separating the Inland Sea from the Outer Ocean. Along its spine, a bony ridge reared up to form a rocky promontory a thousand feet high before plunging, sheer, into the sea. Along this ridge, in the already sweltering, pre-dawn heat, ran Valerius Everreigning, Rightful High King of Valeria and all the Inland Sea-and a man in exile.

He was a massive figure, heavily muscled, and fairly covered with thick, black hair that had just recently begun to show traces of gray. Naked, but for a loin cloth and sandals, he ran with a feral grace, his feet steady on the worn, brown path, his eyes scanning the ground ahead of him. As he reached the final ascent, where the path wound upwards among white rocks, he picked up his pace and chugged along with a powerful, chopping stride, arms pumping, breath quickening with effort. Nearing the summit, he began to sprint, his huge thighs driving him up the final few feet of barren rock to the peak. There, he staggered and reeled drunkenly, gasping loudly in the sticky air.

Awakened by his arrival, two sentries scurried away down the path, terrified that the king had caught them napping. Oblivious of them, Valerius bent with his hands on his knees, his chest heaving, until his heart stopped hammering and his breathing subsided. That was better, he thought, straightening up and pacing about. He had been doing this trek every other morning now for the past month or so, and this was the first time he had been able to run the entire slope. It wasn't much, of course; in his youth, he could have run the whole two miles from town and back without breaking sweat. Still, between this and the regular drills with his troops, he felt he was beginning to get in shape-enough so he wouldn't embarrass himself when it came to hard fighting. He did not want a repeat of his performance during the Battle of Kantar, when he had nearly dropped from exhaustion. Dying an honorable death in battle was one thing; being struck down because you couldn't lift your sword was quite another!

Around him, the sun had just broken from the earth's rim and cast its golden net across the shimmering blue of the sea. As he walked about, Valerius scanned the horizon. He was expecting word from his envoy in the east, but the sea in that direction was clear of ships. To the north, across the strait, the distant land lay like a blue shadow. But the waters were empty between. To the west and south, from where he was daily expecting a fleet from Kantar, the Outer Ocean spread clear to the still dark horizon. Directly south, the ridge fell away quickly to the massive walls of the Palace, below which-and out of sight from his position-lay the town. Beyond, the mainland was low and swampy, thickly forested and crisscrossed with bogs and streams, until it reached the eastern shoreline that was lost in the glare of the rising sun.

From a small pouch at his waist, Valerius pulled a large red gem on a golden chain. Placing the chain carefully about his neck, he raised the gem to his eye and scanned the horizon again, looking through the stone as one would a spyglass. He did a complete sweep, avoiding only the harsh glare of the sun, and then lowered the gem and shook his head. He saw nothing.

Nothing again. For months now he had been repeating this ritual, looking for some sign, but with the same result. The stone was the famed Eye of Valeria, vision stone of the Rightful High King, and a symbol of his power. With it, according to legend, the High King-who bore the name "Valerius Everreigning" from generation to generation-could see into the future and into the hearts of men. But in all the time since he had reclaimed it-which was close to three years now-there had only been two occasions when he had seen anything at all. And even those "things" had been so vague and insubstantial that he sometimes feared they were mere imaginings. Still, he remained convinced of the Stone's powers, and believed that if he was unable to use them, it was because he had never learned how.

His father had claimed not to believe in the Eye and had never used it-a claim that, in Valerius' opinion, had cost him his head, the Eye, and his empire, in that order. And that, in turn, had cost young Valerius fifteen years of exile before he was able to regain the Stone and begin the work of wresting the empire back from Fantar, the regicide-and his own half-brother-who had usurped it. The old Mage, Volkmir, had said the stone's powers were in the hands of the gods, that they gave and withheld them at their whim. It was he who had recovered the Eye after Fantar burned out his eye with it and flung it into the sea. But despite having been the official Mage of Valeria, and heir to a line as long as the King's, Volkmir, too, knew little of the stone's use. Apparently, the secrets of the stone were so profound that the succession of Kings Valerius Everreigning had thought it prudent not to share them with their wizards.

Valerius wished now that had not been the case. For the past year he had been amassing forces at Zagorbia and planning an amphibious assault on Valeria, the heart of Fantar's Empire. That assault now awaited only the contingent from Kantar and the completion of another dozen or so ships being refitted along the shore. But was Fantar aware of what he was up to? Did he know that a scant two hundred miles from his famed walls lay an army of nearly twenty thousand, and a fleet large enough to transport them? And if he knew, what was he doing to prepare? Had he called up his reserves? Was Valeria a ripe plum or an armed fortress? And Valerius' planned landing at Balac, a fishing village a few days' march east of the city-was that still the best option? Or had Fantar foreseen that, too, and moved to forestall him? These and a hundred other questions plagued him, and he fretted that the power to answer them was supposedly resting in his very hand, mute.

Disgusted, he turned on his heel and started back down towards the palace, when something caught his eye: rounding the point that formed the western edge of Zagorbia's harbor was a galley, crawling under oars like a bug across the sea. As it turned and headed in towards the shore, a snippet of morning breeze caught the banner at its masthead and revealed the royal Panthers of Kantar. Valerius started to run.

At the palace, Valerius sent a page running to summon his council, then sluiced himself down with a bucket of water and hurried in to his private chambers to dress. Eomer, his Queen, lay still asleep and as he toweled himself dry, he watched her face, so peaceful and childlike in the morning light, so radiant and beautiful. As if moved by his scrutiny, Eomer stirred and rolled to her back, revealing under the linen sheet, a belly large with child. Struck by this, Valerius stood for a moment- naked to the world, the damp towel hanging limp from his hand-while an image, as clear and bright as the morning itself, flashed through his mind. It was of a young man, tall and strong, standing before the throne at Valeria. At first, Valerius thought it was himself as a youth, standing before his father. But then, with dreamlike prescience, he realized it was not himself but another young man-this child, perhaps, whose fetal shape was before him? - and that the presence on the throne was not his father but... But who? Was that himself or another? And were those bracelets on the young man's wrists, or chains?

Suddenly, Valerius was gripped by a deep, wrenching fear and he shuddered and shook himself to clear it. Turning away quickly, he pulled on a clean toga and grabbed the Eye. But as he started to slip the chain over his head, the stone caught a shaft of light from the window and shot a searing red flash directly into his eyes. It stung as though someone had flung a glass of wine in his face, and sent a shock through his entire body. Then, in the afterglow, another vision transfixed him. It was not a specific image this time, but a sea of them, swirling through his brain like a whirlpool, full of shape and sound and dark forebodings, of armies on the march and ships menacing dark seas. It was a fearful thing, like something awakened from a nightmare and it howled through his soul like a dark wind.

In a moment it passed, but it left him staggered and weak, and he dropped onto a chair, his face bleak and weary. On the bed, Eomer still slept quietly, stretched on her back, the mound of his unborn child rising from her middle. On this his eye settled and his face slowly tightened in fear and pain. But then, like a subtle wind shift at sea presages a change in the weather, his face cleared and he sat upright: what had seemed so dire moments before, faded away quickly, like memories of a dream in the morning sun, and he was filled with a driving sense of urgency. Rising quickly, he left the room, his face set and determined.

Thorngere leaned on the massive battlements of the palace; his chin sunk in his palm, and watched the morning light sparkle across the harbor as an early breeze ruffled the crowded waters. Among the sleek war galleys anchored there, he could see his own little scow, Elusive, moored just off the beach. She looked very plain and pedestrian among so many great warships, but she tugged against her mooring nonetheless, as if eager to pluck up and go. Soon, he hoped, she would get that chance. The fleet had been standing ready for the better part of a month now, and as soon as the Kantaran cavalry arrived, Valerius was sure to announce his plans. That a trip for Thorngere would be among them was as sure as the day.

And none too soon, either, for Thorngere was not pleased with his recent stay in Zagorbia, and not pleased with himself, either. Too much leisure was bad for a man. Nothing to do left too much time to think, and too many opportunities to run afoul of one's own best interests. Better to be at sea, where the air was clear and clean, and where the needs of the ship commanded one's mood. That, or making the rounds of resistance leaders about the Inland Sea, compiling reports and studying the dispositions of the foe. That was work for a man! That would keep his thoughts in trim... and himself from foolishness.

Across the harbor, the shore curved around and extended out into a long, rocky point with a headland that provided shelter from the south and west, the only protection the harbor had to offer.

Idly, he watched as a small galley came to anchor in its lee and sent a boat in towards the white adobe town that curled around the harbor and splashed upwards against the hills like sea foam.

Zagorbia was a prosperous town, and from Thorngere's vantage point on the walls of the massive and heavily fortified palace, it looked neat and well kept. Unlike many of its neighbors, Zagorbia had been spared the more serious ravages of Fantar's war. Last to fall of all the cities around the Inland Sea, it was here that the great wave of Fantar's conquest spent itself, and here where many of his most hardened veterans-including Tarpon, his most hated general-had settled after their fifteen-year, three thousand mile odyssey. In their wake, an empire had been crushed, and many of its defenders put to the sword.

It was also here, in the labyrinth of mud and jungle on the mainland to the south, that the first effective resistance had formed under the leadership of Ragnar, and here, with the arrival of his fleet from Kantar, that Valerius had achieved his first major victory in his efforts to win back that empire.

But it was not thoughts of Zagorbia that Thorngere wished to avoid. Or of Ragnar's heroics in winning it, though he had been regaled again the night before with tales of those very escapades by Ragnar himself. No, it was the other thing that had happened later: that was why he wished to be at sea.

The sun suddenly felt hot on the back of his neck and he could feel the beginnings of a dull headache, the result of too much un-watered wine.

They had been in a tavern in the lower town, a somewhat less than respectable place. Ragnar had been celebrating the birth of his son, and Thorngere had been helping. What else, Ragnar had loudly admonished, were good friends for?

What else indeed? Perhaps he had helped too much. Perhaps that was it, although he knew it was not. And Ragnar had thought he was helping Thorngere, too. That was no doubt why he brought the wench over. "Here he is, girl," he had announced, thrusting the supple, soft-scented thing onto his lap, "Lord Thorngere himself-most famous swordsman in the land, and brother to His Majesty the High King!" Then, in an aside to Thorngere, "Here's one to drive the gloom from your thoughts, lad... You're all she's talked of this long day!"

But what would she be talking of now, the little minx? How the famous swordsman had lain like a sack on his bed, his great 'sword' shriveled in its sheath? Thorngere pounded his fist on the russet stone of the battlement. Here was the great Lord Thorngere indeed, moping about like some mournful wretch, as useless to himself as he was to the world, clutching to the memory of another like a man impaled on a spear, afraid either to yank it free or drive it home, yet dying all the while of guilt and shame.

In truth, it was love Lord Thorngere wished to flee; a love as potent as it was forbidden. It plagued him constantly and had turned his once boisterous mien into a sodden, sullen thing. But would the sea affect a cure? Not in this life, he thought, though in the clear breeze and distant sky, he thought he might yet be able to breathe.

Starting from his reverie, Thorngere turned to find a small page tugging at his robe. "Beg pardon, my Lord, but it's the King. He's called the Council and bade me fetch you right away."

28

Chapter 2
A COUNCIL OF THE KING

The Council Chamber was situated high in the inner palace, and opened onto a wide veranda with a panoramic view of the harbor and the glistening sea. It had been designed, in more opulent days, so that those who toiled least in this tropical land could benefit most from the cool breezes of the sea. But of those who assembled this morning, there were none who had not seen hard toil in plenty, and few for whom the view signified more than clear sailing. They were hard-bitten, tenacious men, these advisors to King Valerius-military men for the most part, men who had fought most of their lives in a cause few thought they could ever win.

There were perhaps fifteen present this morning, lounging about a long, polished marble table and awaiting the arrival of the King. They hailed from all around the Inland Sea, from towns like Bangorum and Durumkai, Telos and Dunskol, and from Zagorbia itself. There was even a newly arrived ambassador from Dulcai, which rested far to the south along the coast of the Outer Ocean. They represented the last remnants of the free forces of their respective cities. Each, in his turn, had fought against Fantar and lost as that power-mad regicide had ravaged his way from city to city all around the Inland Sea, beginning with the conquest of his native Valeria, and the killing of his own father, the former High King.

Fantar was also thought, at that time, to have killed young Valerian, his half-brother and the legitimate heir to the High King's name and throne. But Valerian had not died. He had escaped, and lived under an assumed name for many years-even fighting beside many of these same men as comrade in arms-before being able to reveal himself and crystallize a movement to regain his throne. In the past few years, this movement had gained momentum, first with the establishment of a secure base of operations in the Hidden Valley of Kantar and supported by an underground network of resistance fighters set up by Thorngere. Then, in a series of stunning victories the previous summer, Valerius had destroyed Fantar's naval forces in Dulcai, crushed an army sent to corner him in Kantar, and with the aid of Ragnar's resistance, had captured Zagorbia itself. Now, with word of his successes spreading throughout the empire, and with fresh recruits and resources flooding in to him, the stage was set for his next move.

But what move? For months now, these men had been training and waiting, expecting any day to be ordered aboard their ships. But where they would sail when that order came, and where they would land, they had no idea. There were rumors, of course; there are always rumors in an army waiting for battle. Some said Valerius planned to march eastward and take the empire back one city at a time. Others said he would sail east, to the end of the Inland Sea, and there cut the empire in half by taking Palmeria. Still others said north, that he would gather the unconquered tribal chieftains there and sweep down on Valeria from the mountains, just as Fantar himself had done. But of his actual plans, King Valerius had said nothing.

All they knew was that couriers came and went almost daily and that many late nights showed candles burning in Valerius' special map room high in the palace. They knew, too, that the season was advancing, especially in the north, and that another few months lost would see the fall rains begin. And they knew that this council, whatever it portended, was not a scheduled meeting, and that the galley which had entered the harbor only an hour before flew the royal banner of Kantar.

But it was not thoughts of Valeria, or even directly of Fantar, that occupied Valerius as he paced restlessly about in an adjoining chamber, awaiting the arrival of Thorngere. With him was another of royal rank, a tiny, dark-featured man, not half the size of Valerius, who sat quietly on a bench against the wall, tugging gently at his beard and watching the pacings of his massive companion with quick, inquisitive eyes.

"I must say, I'm surprised at your reaction, Your Majesty," said this one.

"Eh?" said Valerius, the words obviously breaking in on his thoughts. "Oh, I beg your pardon, Koltar. I guess I'm not being much of a host this morning. What did you say?"

"What I meant, Your Majesty, was that you seem unduly distracted by this news. I would not have thought that a few unruly Iblis would occasion so much concern."

"Oh, it's not just Haradin-though I can't help but notice that you, my friend, have deemed his depredations serious enough to come here yourself. And it's not that I disagree, mind-it's just that the interruption is so frustrating. I've near fifteen thousand men here and a fleet, manned and ready to move, and now this!"

"You're convinced he's not acting on his own, then?"

"On the contrary, I'm almost sure that he is. I can't see the Iblis allying with anyone. But I can't take that chance, you see? Once we launch our assault in the north, we could be tied up for months. Our support lines must be clear. If there's any chance Haradin's in league with Fantar, or if there is even a chance that a significant force is lurking among the Fortunate Isles, I have to take care of it now, even though it means a delay."

"Well, I can't say I relish the prospect of leaving Kantar undefended with him on the wild either," said Koltar. "But what if you catch him?" The little man was sitting very erect now, his head cocked, and an eyebrow raised.

"Oh ho," Valerius laughed ruefully. "This time the bugger will hang. We've given old Haradin more than enough rope before now, wouldn't you say? It's time we used it."

Koltar seemed to relax when he heard this. "I would say he has more than earned the distinction hanging would confer, though I doubt the example would improve his people."

Just then, a breathless and embarrassed Thorngere hurried in from the side door, muttering apologies as he came. But when he saw Koltar, his face lit up with delight. "Koltar!" he grinned, grasping the tiny man's hand. "I mean, Your Majesty! What are you doing here?"

"Koltar has brought some very disturbing news about our friend Haradin in the Fortunate Isles," said Valerius. "But, there's no time for explanations now: you'll have to hear with the rest of the Council," and with that, he flung open the inner door and marched into the Council Chamber, leaving his two fellows-a golden-haired giant and darkling pygmy-to trail along in his wake.

At the appearance of the King, the Council leapt to their feet, their scraping chairs shattering the somnolence of the chamber. "Good morning!" said Valerius, moving briskly to the head of the table, and motioning for them to resume their seats. "I believe most of you know King Koltar here," he started, then interrupted himself to call for a herald. "Here," he said, "fetch a box, or a stool, or something for His Majesty that he may sit in dignity with the rest." Most of the men did indeed know Koltar, having helped liberate his land in the Hidden Valley, but several of the newcomers stared agape as the tiny figure, so childlike and yet so obviously mature, climbed up onto the offered stool.

"As most of you probably know," Valerius continued, "I was intending, with the arrival of His

Majesty here, to announce the final dispositions for our next move. Our fleet is in the harbor, manned and ready, your men are trained, their rations cooked-we've even seen to extra tent pegs! But instead of that, Koltar here has brought news of a situation in the south that raises new questions we need to discuss. I'll let him fill you in. King Koltar?"

From his perch, Koltar addressed the Council in a voice that was surprisingly deep and resonant for one so small. "Thank you, Your Majesty, and good morning. I see many familiar faces here-Grumwald, Daemon, Gainor, Zimlait, and the rest-my greetings to you all. And you, sir," he added, nodding to a rough, red-bearded chieftain beside Thorngere on the King's left, "We have not met, but I do believe you must be Ragnar. A special good morning to you. Your deeds have long been sung in Kantar, thanks to your friend Thorngere, here." Ragnar beamed at this, though it was apparent that he, too, was suffering the effects of the previous night's wine. He bowed in return as Koltar continued.

"As King Valerius mentioned, we have a situation in the south. Many of you, I know, are familiar with the Iblis and their resettlement in the Fortunate Isles-Indeed, it was you, Grumwald, and you Zimlait, and I believe Daemon, who took them there. For those of you who do not know, understand that the Iblis are a very crude, even bestial race, which have been the scourge of my people for generations. Several years ago, with the help of King Valerius and the noble Thorngere here, we were finally able to defeat them. Victory, however, brought its own problems, as we had to keep these people under virtual lock and key-and support them-simply to keep them under control. So we were delighted last year when Thorngere's discovery of the Fortunate Isles and the subsequent victory over Glaucon gave us an opportunity to get these people out of our Valley, and them a chance-we hoped-to build new and more productive lives.

"And for most of the past year, that is exactly what seemed to be happening. In fact, things seemed to be improving all around. After years of isolation, valuable trade links have sprung up between Kantar, Dulcai, and the Fortunate Isles-and of course, with you here in Zagorbia. In Kantar, for example, we have made significant improvements in agricultural output, and have been shipping large quantities of grain. The Iblis were herding cattle and sheep, and clearing land to grow taro and sugar. This freed Dulcai to focus all its energies on mining ore, and King Reuters is now shipping it to Kantar where we are smelting it, using charcoal made from Iblian timber. Most of the ingots are coming here, as I am sure you know, but our own smiths have also been making some exquisite weapons.

"So we have been delighted with this progress and growing commerce. For myself, it has been wonderful. For many generations my people were locked away in our Hidden Valley, and I never in this life thought that I would make such voyages as I have recently made, or see such sights as this fine harbor." And here, Koltar swept his arm wide, indicating the glorious panorama beyond the veranda.

"Now, relations with the Iblis during this process have not exactly been cordial, but up until about a month ago, I was confident they would improve with time. I thought that even the Iblis could see the benefits of peace and the value of trade. But I guess old habits die hard. Just about a month and a half ago, a trading scow from Dulcai pulled into the Fortunate Isles and saw one of our ships up on the beach. At first, they thought she had simply sprung a leak and had been careened for repairs, but when they sent a boat ashore, there was no sign of the crew and they found that the ship had been burned. The Iblis were terrified and wouldn't come near them, so they investigated further and found a clearing in the forest about a half-mile from the beach. There was a huge fire pit in the center, and off to one side, a pile of charred bones and sixteen skulls. Our men had all been killed and eaten."

Silence filled the chamber as Koltar finished speaking. Even the breeze that drifted in from the sea seemed suddenly chill, and the sun on the waters of the harbor not nearly so bright. For the men who had been in Kantar this news was not unprecedented-they had all heard the history of the Iblis, and how they had perpetrated such abominations on Koltar's people for generations-but that they had begun the practice again was still a shock. The Iblis had always claimed it was the lack of beef in the Hidden Valley that forced them into cannibalism and when Valerius brought in cattle, they vowed they would no longer savage the meat of their fellow men. Obviously, this was not the case.

"Where is Haradin?" asked Grumwald, a rangy, gray-bearded leader with a vicious scar down the side of his face and but half his teeth. It was he who had commanded the fleet that transported the Iblis to their new home, and he had dealings with their leader, Haradin, before.

Koltar shook his head. "Gone. He fled into the hills with a large number of the young men."

"Did the Dulcaians go after him?" This was asked of Koltar, but Grumwald looked across the table at Rondo, the Ambassador from Dulcai.

"No," said Rondo defensively. "Our men were too few and feared attack themselves. Nor had we sufficient force in Dulcai-our army being here with you. When he received the report, King Reuters sent me to King Koltar in Kantar, and thence here. The Iblis are small people, but Haradin has several thousand fighters if he chooses to resist, and he knows his terrain much better than we."

Grumwald grunted, apparently satisfied with this, but from the end of the table, another man rose who also knew the Iblis. This was Gainor, a swarthy warrior from the deserts east of Bangorum, who had left the sand of his homeland for the sea and become one of Valerius' most skilled captains. "Any sign of a connection with our friend Fantar?"

"None that we know of," said Koltar. "There have been several galley sightings in the waters between Kantar and Dulcai, but as far we know, none has landed in the Fortunate Isles. But perhaps Lord Thorngere will have better information on that from his contacts."

At the mention of his name, Thorngere started, as if his mind had been elsewhere. But he answered readily enough. "No, I haven't, and unless it's been very recent, I think I would have heard. Fantar has sent several ships down from his home fleet in Valeria-where I have very good contacts-but none of the crews have reported any strange islands... They're still trying to figure out what happened to the rest of Glaucon!" There was general laughter at this. Glaucon had been the only one of Fantar's leaders ever to find the Hidden Valley. But only his head made it home to report the discovery-preserved in a cask of brandy.

"Well," said Grumwald, "that tells me we don't have much of a problem. They don't have any ships, so if Fantar doesn't know where they are, they surely can't go find him. I say we just leave the dirty little buggers to rot there until we've finished our business, then deal with them."

"But they do have a ship," said Valerius, taking part in the discussion for the first time. "Was the Kantaran vessel burned beyond repair, Rondo?"

"Not for good shipwrights, Your Majesty, no."

"But they know nothing of ships!" growled Grumwald. "Neither of building nor sailing. Think you they could repair that ship, Valerius? You know them better than any. How could they rig her and man her? And where would they go? They would not know an enemy galley from one of our own, and besides, they'd be as likely to sail off the edge of the sea as back towards the coast... They don't even know where they are!"

"Odds are you're right, Grumwald," said Valerius. He was sitting pensively in his chair at the head of the table, pulling at his beard. "But I have an uneasy feeling about this. Haradin is not to be underestimated, as you said, Rondo. If any Iblis can repair and man a ship, it is he... Didn't he have the run of your ship for most of the voyage out, Grumwald? Not to mention the fine example of your seamanship? And what talk of Fantar and the issues of the outer world has he picked up? Besides, the very fact that he would risk open enmity troubles me. Haradin is too crafty and too much of a coward to go so far on his own. No, this whole thing gives me a queer feeling between my shoulder blades. I would rather not move forward with this at our backs."

The Council considered this in silence for some moments, then Grumwald slapped his hand down on the table. "If you want this bugger handled, Your Majesty, I can be underway by this afternoon!"

Chapter 3
PARTINGS

Of course, Grumwald did not leave that afternoon, or the next, or the next after that. No army in those days could simply pick up and go; not on the kind of expedition required to reach the Fortunate Isles. Given fair winds and weather, it was five days at least to reach the Hidden Valley of Kantar, all of it along a coast so rugged and rock-bound that landing ashore for even a single night was impossible. That meant sea rations for some five thousand men had to be prepared for at least seven days. And after resupply in Kantar, it was another day's sail south and then a full day's sail due west-straight out to sea and beyond even the sight of land-to reach the Fortunate Isles.

So it was not a journey to be taken lightly, and Grumwald's men had their work cut out for them, especially so as Valerius insisted on sending a force more than adequate to deal with the situation. His rationale was simple: though the Iblis were a small people (about half again as large as Koltar's folk) and no match for the burly northerners in open combat, Haradin had a big island to hide on and Grumwald would have a lot of bases to cover. Not only would he have to search several areas at once with sufficient force to deal with however large a band they encountered, he would also have to leave sufficient force in reserve to protect his ships and keep the main body of Iblis under control in his rear. And that was assuming there was no link with

40

Fantar and that there would be none of his forces to contend with as well.

Adding these things up, and given the need for speed, Valerius decided on a force at least four times as large as would have been necessary to deal with Haradin alone, and it was nearly a week before they were packed, victualed, assembled, and loaded aboard their galleys.

For Valerius it was a very busy week. Not only did he oversee every detail of Grumwald's operation-he had learned the art of command from the bottom up and was as fastidious about the welfare of his men as any nursemaid is about her babe-but he took the opportunity to reorganize the rest of his army as well. Zagorbia was not a large town and volunteers had been coming in at such a rate over the past few months that they had filled every available space within the walls, and had so filled the limited solid ground with their tents outside that there was not sufficient space left to drill and train. Valerius sought to remedy this by bringing the newer troops in as Grumwald's veterans rowed out to their ships.

And of course, he had to entertain King Koltar whose insatiable curiosity about everyone and everything "outland" made him a very demanding, though always delightful guest. New to the throne himself, Koltar had spent most of his thirty-odd years as a kind of jack-of-all-trades architect, engineer, inventor, naturalist, historian, archivist, and mythologist for his late aunt Salonis, the former queen. Blessed with a brilliant mind, Koltar was fascinated with how things worked and over the years had invented or improved upon any number of useful devices, including a functional ball valve, a fore-and-aft sailing rig for a galley, and an entirely new type of boat-which he called a 'catumaran'-which fairly flew across the water. He was also fascinated by all things 'outland', and as he toured the hot, bustling city with Valerius, he wanted to know about everything: how the brilliant white-wash was made that covered all the walls and houses; how great blocks of stone were raised up and placed in the battlements; how the paving stones were set; what the sanitation facilities were like in the city; how the piles were driven that supported the city docks; what kinds of fish were in the harbor and how they were caught; what the rest of the Zagorbian diet consisted of; how they supported themselves; what kind of tree was this; what kind of plant was that; and on and on until Valerius burst out laughing.

"By the Gods, Koltar," he said, "you are more inquisitive than a five year old!" The two were walking back uphill towards the palace along a street that skirted the tent-filled central square, attended by a loose file of guards.

"Oh, I beg your pardon, Majesty," he replied, his eyes alight at the perceived compliment, and except for his royal robe and long beard, looking every bit the five year old, "but I have dreamed of Zagorbia and other Outland towns all my life, and now to finally be here... Well, I guess I have too many questions."

"Not at all, my friend, not at all. I am actually quite surprised I can answer so many of them!" They stepped aside as a file of carts, heavily laden with sacks of grain, lumbered down towards the waiting ships. The drivers, surprised at seeing royalty, did not know whether to jump up and salute or to keep hold of their squealing brakes. Fortunately, they opted for the brakes.

"You will return to the Valley with Grumwald's fleet?"

"Aye," Koltar nodded. "There is still much to do before we can join you. And I find that things don't get done nearly so quickly when I'm not there."

"Ha! I know the feeling. Every cart needs its driver. But we should speak more closely before you leave... There are some other matters we need to discuss."

They met-Valerius, Koltar, Thorngere, and Grumwald-in Valerius' map room, high in the palace adjoining the council chamber. It was late in the afternoon, the day before Grumwald was to leave, and a sun as red as molten steel set sky and sea ablaze beyond the busy harbor and filled the chamber with a soft yellow glow. From the distant kitchens drifted the sounds of preparation for a great feast that was to fill the bellies of Grumwald's staff and senior officers one last time before they were reduced to skimpy sea-rations. Grumwald was in high spirits and elated to be starting such an exalted command. He had been a captain of men since Valerius' youth, and after Fantar had taken

Zagorbia, he had carried on as a corsair, ravaging these same waters until he was seduced by an offer of amnesty and promptly chained to a galley bench. Valerius and Thorngere had rescued him during a sea battle, and he had since proven himself as a dogged and mercurial commander. But this was the largest command of his life.

Valerius went through all the details of the plan one more time. His map consisted of a large three-dimensional, clay model of the Inland Sea and nearby coasts of the Outer Ocean, including all the known cities and villages as far south as Dulcai and north to Thuringia, Thorngere's home. Koltar himself had built the model for Valerius while they were in Kantar, based on Kantaran archives and others' descriptions of coastlines, harbors, and topography. The thing sat on several trestle tables and was so arranged that viewers could walk the seas and visit the various cities. Thanks to his recent training regimen, Valerius was having less difficulty negotiating the narrow gate between the Inland Sea and Outer Ocean. Grumwald was not so fit and, true to his mission, stood by the small side table that held the Fortunate Isles. Koltar stood on a stool to the north, overlooking Thuringia like a small god, while Thorngere slumped in a nearby chair.

"The key is speed," Valerius concluded, his eye following the rugged coast from his position by the heights of Zagorbia. "That's why you have such a force-so you can nab Haradin in one sweep and get back here for the rest of the festivities."

The others perked up expectantly at this, and even Thorngere left his chair. Until now, Valerius had let slip only the barest hints about his plans.

"For as soon as you get back-and hopefully, Koltar, you will bring your Kantaran cavalry along as well-I intend to strike immediately at the very heart of Fantar's empire... that's right, we attack Valeria. I intend to land here," he said, stepping lightly across the Inland Sea, "at Balac-you know the place, Thorngere. It's a good two days march from the city. Its harbor is large enough to accommodate our fleet, and the land thereabouts is very open, so we'll be able to get ashore and deploy quickly before we have to deal with any serious opposition. And we've an excellent resistance organization there run by one of my father's old commanders, Gamlarch. If we're lucky and can get word to him in time, Gamlarch's men may well be able to nab any messengers sent to warn Fantar, and we could actually surprise the bastard in his lair. But I don't count on that. In fact, it would even be better if we can lure him outside the walls, as he did my father, and crush him in one blow. Then, once the snake's head is off, killing the rest should be easy."

Grumwald wandered up from the Fortunate Isles and stood waste deep in the Outer Ocean, studying the tiny, crenellated walls of Valeria. "How many men can he field?"

"Thorngere?" Valerius deferred. "You've got the most recent reports."

"Word is, seven to eight thousand prime warriors in the city with another two to three thousand within a day's march."

Grumwald grunted. "Enough to hold us at bay if he keeps to his walls, then."

"Aye," said Thorngere. "But if he gets as much as a couple weeks warning to call up his reserves, he can field forty thousand."

Grumwald whistled softly. "That would put us in a tidy pinch."

"Not necessarily," said Valerius. "Reinforcements won't all come at once, and if we can stay between them and the city, we can likely beat them in detail without even letting Fantar out of the bag. As for a siege, I don't think we need be overly concerned. I have a couple tricks up my sleeve, and there are a couple other things King Koltar has been working on as well."

Koltar raised an eyebrow at this, but said nothing.

"So, you know a way in?" asked Grumwald, but Valerius only smiled.

"What about this Gamlarch?" asked Koltar. "How many men can he field?"

"That's a good question," said Thorngere. "According to Gamlarch, he can muster several thousand faithful, given adequate notice. However- and he said this to me again on my last visit, though neither of us knew what was in the offing-if the situation were such that we appeared in force with a good likelihood of success, most of the countryside would flock to our banners, and probably half of

Fantar's own reserve troops would desert with them."

"Is that credible?"

"I wouldn't be surprised. Things have not been going well for some time. Taxes are so bad the people are literally starving, and the only reason many young men join the army is for food: a lot of them horde their rations and smuggle them home to their families."

"How can this be?" Koltar wanted to know. "Is Fantar so pressed by enemies?"

"You have never lived in such a realm," said Valerius, "so you cannot understand. In the Empire, Fantar himself is the enemy."

Koltar cocked an eyebrow as Valerius sought the words to explain. "Look," he said, "in Kantar, your people and the Iblis fought for generations. Both of your economies-your whole way of living, in fact-was based on the war. Indeed, as you yourself know, there was a question whether your people could even survive without the war. But that's not the way it is in Valeria and the rest of the Empire. You fought with the will of the people: it was a terrible situation, but you all knew you could not survive otherwise. So you endured the sacrifice. Fantar conquered his Empire and rules by force. He does not have the will of the people: indeed, he represses the people in order to stay in power."

Koltar's brows furled as he processed this reasoning. Valerius went on. "Here's a practical example: when I was a boy, there were maybe thirty thousand people in Valeria and the immediate vicinity. Yet my father only maintained an Imperial Guard of a thousand or so men. For defense-though it was hardly required until Fantar came along-we relied on a citizen army. Because of this, taxes were kept very low: farmers could keep or sell most of their grain; merchants could invest their gold. But Fantar must maintain an army of many thousands, just to keep men like Gamlarch-and us, of course-from rising against him. That costs, especially so as his upper echelons are horribly corrupt and rake off huge sums for themselves. The result is that the people suffer under a terrible burden..."

"And because there are so many men in the army," Koltar nodded, his thoughts racing ahead with the idea, "there are fewer available to work the farms and to produce usable goods."

"Exactly."

"Interesting. But what about yourself, Majesty? I've noticed one or two soldiers around here at least."

"We, too, are a burden on those same people, but one they suffer willingly for the time being. Ever since we took Zagorbia last year, word has been spreading that a King of the Eye lives and is rising against Fantar. I don't know whether people believe I'm real, or whether they're just desperate enough to try anything, but with the help of Thorngere here, and survivors from the old order like Gamlarch and others from all around the Inland Sea, a huge resistance network has formed which smuggles in men and supplies by sea and overland from the east. And that's the real reason we need to settle this Iblis situation as fast as possible: this whole movement is like a wave. It's building now and gaining momentum, but if we don't achieve something soon, it will falter and die away. People cannot sacrifice that much. Supplies will stop coming, men will drift away, and hope will fade."

"Why hasn't Fantar attacked you here? He surely knows where you are, and it's not like he didn't have enough ships."

"I don't really know. I've been expecting an attack ever since we got here, of course, and can only speculate as to his reasons, but there are a couple things that may have forestalled him. One is the resistance itself. They've been igniting little brush fires all over the place, raids on outposts, forces that concentrate and threaten some town only to fade away into the hills, and of course the ships and small caravans that have been supplying us. Fantar has been scrambling to deal with all these things, not knowing whether I remain in Zagorbia or am planning to pop up somewhere else. The other thing is that Zagorbia is a tough nut to crack. It's nearly impregnable by land and easily defended from the sea: Fantar may fear that if he strikes and fails-as he did in Kantar-it will only fuel the flames of resistance further. He may feel time is his best ally and that if he can just keep things under control, our movement will die of its own weight. But I really don't know. He may be launching an attack even as we speak."

"Well, if it's speed you want," said Grumwald, plainly bored with all the talk of high strategy, "you won't get it with us jawing here. Besides, something is starting to smell awfully good. Permission to leave you, Majesty?"

"Yes, go ahead, Grumwald. We'll join you shortly." The old warrior bowed and turned to leave, but Valerius stopped him at the door. "And Grumwald..." he said. "What you heard here today?"

"On my life, Your Majesty. You know you can trust me there."

Valerius smiled. "That's why I told you, my friend."

"What if," said Thorngere as soon as the door was closed, "Fantar somehow gets wind of our plans?"

"We four are the only ones who know these plans," said Valerius.

"OK, but Fantar knows we must move in some direction very soon, most probably before the rainy season." Thorngere had now taken up station in the Outer Ocean and was intently studying the area around Valeria and the northern coastline of the Inland Sea. That coast, as he well knew, was rocky and formidable, and while it was dotted with small coves and inlets, in the nine-hundred mile stretch between the Outer Ocean and Palmeria, there were only two bays sufficient to harbor a fleet: Valeria and Balac. "What if he decides to concentrate his troops-say somewhere near the sea-to be ready for that eventuality? Since he already has sufficient force to hold Valeria, wouldn't it make sense for him to concentrate near Balac?"

50

"But you have had no reports of any concentrations."

"True, but my newest reports are two weeks old. And the season is young yet. He might not even be planning a move for another month or so."

"All right," said Valerius, irritated at the logic in Thorngere's observations and the threat it implied. "What do you suggest?"

"Only that we raise as many troops as possible. I have no doubt that Gamlarch can raise a goodly force, and I certainly do hope half of Fantar's army deserts, but I would still feel safer with better numbers."

"And you would get them?"

"From Thuringia," said Thorngere, pointing to his own homeland in the mountains north of Valeria. "If I could raise the northern Chieftains and sweep down to join you and Gamlarch, we could deal with whatever Fantar has to offer."

Valerius and Koltar, too, now studied the map intently, as if they could see in the vague clay lumps of mountains the hundreds of stony villages that dotted Thorngere's homeland and the thousands of wild northern warriors swarming down from the very passes Fantar himself had used when he first took Valeria nearly a generation before. "Will they fight?" Valerius wanted to know.

"Well, this whole notion has only just occurred to me," said Thorngere, "but I would not be surprised. The northern chieftains-my step-father especially-have never wanted to take on Fantar, but they know what's happened to the rest of the Empire and they know-or they will soon-that they'll stand alone if you fail. Besides, there are a lot of young bloods in those mountains who'd fight just for the joy of it."

"How do we make it happen?"

"All I have to do is convince my father to call a Weapons Take. Any chieftain has that right and any warrior can join him. If I leave tonight, we can join you in two months' time."

"And you can convince your father?"

"I can try." The three men stood silent for several long moments, then Valerius made his decision.

"I like it. Take my greetings to your father and his people. I know your step-father had some difficulties with mine-you being the chief result," he said with a wry smile. "But tell your father it is our intention to renew the bonds of friendship which have let us live in peace for so many generations, and that with you now recognized as our brother in flesh as well as in spirit, it is our wish that those bonds grow ever closer. In return for his help, we will grant whatever wish is in our power... Or some such stuff as that. You have my full authority to negotiate the best terms you can. When can you leave?"

"Well, Elusive is always ready, but I agree with Grumwald: something is starting to smell awfully good!"

"Ha! Tomorrow, then, after you are feasted. In fact, you can sail with Grumwald's fleet, then break off north. Now, anything else before we eat?"

"Yes, one thing," said Koltar. "What are these 'tricks' I'm supposed to be working on to help take Valeria?"

Valerius laughed again. "I thought you could make a machine that would fly over the walls of Valeria the way your catumaran flies over water! But do you mean to tell me you're not working on something in your shop?"

"Well, there may be a thing or two."

"I thought so."

On a brazier in the main hall, surrounded by his chiefs and Grumwald's officers, Valerius burnt the thigh pieces of a young ox wrapped in fat, and prayed to the Gods for the success of their mission. Then the men fell to, gorging themselves in a great feast; the men of rank in the palace, the rest around their fires, crowded along the shore. When they could eat and drink no more, they slept where they lay, and it was late the following morning when the galley crews rowed out and brought their already laden ships alongside the docks for the troops to board. All day the procession continued, those already manned resting at light anchor while the rest crawled in under oars and gorged their fill of men. Full fifty ships there were, including several fast transports, and it was not until late in the afternoon that Grumwald dipped his pennant to the palace and nosed his flagship towards the sea.

Koltar waited till the last, standing on the dock like a child beside Valerius and Ragnar, while Thorngere took his leave and was rowed out to Elusive. "He still pines, doesn't he?" said Koltar, watching as the distant Thorngere clambered up his ship's side, his golden mane flashing in the sun.

"Well, we don't speak of it, he and I, but I believe he does," said Valerius.

"I had hoped to see him restored to his old spirits, but your sister Princess Vahla casts a strong spell."

"Aye, she does that. And my good brother Thorngere took a hard fall. But here, sir, you had best be off yourself. Grumwald will be half-way to Kantar before you've set sail at this rate!"

Koltar smiled up into the dark face of Valerius. "I'll pass him within the hour, Your Majesty!"

"Well, see that you do. And hurry back with your cavalry. We will have need of them on the plains around Valeria."

Valerius took another tour of the city to make sure all was settled and secure after the commotion, then retired to his private chambers for a quiet evening with the pregnant Eomer. But he was not quiet in his mind. While there was nothing specific he could put his finger on, he had a vague sense of unease, like he had forgotten or overlooked something. Eomer noticed as they sat out on their veranda under the rising light of the full moon.

"You seem unsettled tonight, my Lord," she said, taking his massive right hand between two of her own.

"Ah," Valerius shrugged and then smiled down at her, "just too many cares, I guess. Shepherds get anxious when their flocks are abroad at night."

"Is that all?"

"I guess so. Grumwald is more than up to the task, but I still worry. And I worry about Thorngere."

"About him going north?"

"Well, not that exactly. Just about him. Even Koltar noticed. He mentioned it just before he left. I'm afraid he'll do something stupid."

"Like what?"

"Well I don't know." Valerius got up and began pacing. "It's just like there's something gone out of him, something not there. Like yesterday in conference: here he comes up with this great plan, but all the while he's talking, it's like he's reading from a scroll, like he doesn't really care about anything. You know, it's been over a year."

"Some wounds take longer to heal. Look at you, my love. Sometimes I can feel you stiffen in your sleep at night and I know you are dreaming again of the fires that burned Valeria."

Valerius stopped and looked at her sharply. "How would you know that?"

"Sometimes you cry out in your sleep. Oh, I know you big strong warrior types don't like to admit such things, but if such a wound can gall you after all these years, why cannot Thorngere's wound gall him? After all, both are born of love."

Valerius resumed his seat and took Eomer's delicate hand between his two massive paws. "This warrior type has no problem admitting his love for you... Both of you," he added, sliding a hand over the mound of her belly. "Did I ever tell you you're lovely in moonlight?"

Eomer gave him a kittenish smile and curled up under his outstretched arm. "I just think Thorngere is more sensitive than you realize."

"Well, I think Vahla was right to go off with Volkmir. Sister or no, the woman's a witch."

Under the same moon, some leagues to the north in the Outer Ocean, Thorngere stood at the rail by Elusive's helm and watched the inky water slide beneath her counter. He was thinking of Thuringia, his mountain-ringed home; of his mother, and of the man, Thornalon, who even though he knew Thorngere had been whelped by the High King, had accepted him and raised him as a son. It had been more than three years since Thorngere had been home, despite the fact that during much of that time he had been sailing all over the Inland Sea and back and forth to the Hidden Valley of Kantar. He could easily have arranged a visit, his conscience told him now. But the truth was, he had never been comfortable with Thornalon. For one thing, the physical difference between them-Thornalon was short and gnarled like a mountain goat while Thorngere was tall and fair and nearly as massive as Valerius himself-made his adoption apparent to all (though, in conscience, he could not say that Thornalon had ever loved him less for it). Nor was it that he had assumed his mother's shame, for in truth, she felt none. She had been a wild, untamed beauty who loved to roam the high places, and had come to Thornalon already with child, and had been fiercely proud to claim the High King's seed. No, the discomfort came from

Thorngere himself, from his innate sense of otherness. For all his youth he had dreamed himself a creature of Valeria, and when that city fell-he was but thirteen at the time-it had seemed like some higher part of him had fallen as well, and he had spent many of the years since in search of it.

So it was with mixed feelings that he watched the moon shimmer over the silken sea as Elusive bore him homeward, for he was also eager to see those faces he loved, and to roam again in the high places he loved as much as his mother. But he also knew that her keen gray eyes would look into his and that she would see this leaden thing that hung from his soul like a millstone. And she would know.

And to the east, as that brilliant moon set into the gray mists of early dawn, an army bestirred itself and marched westward across the sands to ascend the ridges below the towering walls of Zagorbia. And in his bed, with his beautiful queen curled by his side, Valerius was awakened by shouts of alarm.

Chapter 4
BESIEGED

The walls of Zagorbia followed the line of the ridge as it descended the base of the peninsula and curved westward to where it sank into swampy lowland south of the city. From here the wall went straight west over a short half-mile of open ground, then curved north again along a swampy stream bed until it emptied into the harbor just east of the stubby, thumb-like headland that protected the harbor from the prevailing west winds. Inside the walls, the town nestled comfortably in the hollow of the surrounding rocks, its streets and buildings rising like the seats in an amphitheater to the southeastern corner where the palace complex stood alone, surrounded by its own high wall.

It was, as Valerius had said, a very defensible position, and as he stood with Ragnar atop the high, northeast bastion and surveyed the land around him, he was struck again by just how strong it was. But would it be strong enough? From the east, along the shore, marched a long, serpentine line of armed men, their tail not yet visible in the shimmering distance, their head, still a half mile away and approaching the verge of forest where the hilly peninsula met the swampy mainland. They came silently, with neither drum nor horn, and whatever banners they had were kept furled and out of sight.

"Perhaps they're friendly," said Ragnar. "They look to be nice fellows."

Valerius grunted, but did not reply, and along with several thousand other defenders who lined the walls, continued to study the approaching host. Below them, the ridge dropped off precipitously and fell in a steep scatter of rock, brush and twisted trees, to the forest floor some eighty feet below. It was scalable, by a nimble man with both hands free, but when he got to the top, there was no place else to go except for a narrow path that stretched along the base of the wall. There was no room to mass troops there, no room even to rest a siege ladder at an angle sufficient to climb, and no way in except through a few very stout and well barred posterns. Most important from the defenders' point of view, there was no place to hide. If an army tried to scale the ridge, a single rock, casually tossed from the wall, could take out an entire file of men.

But Valerius doubted they would try that. What they would do instead is what a river does when it meets an obstruction: flow around it. They would move to the south, try to mass their men on the narrow stretch of level ground where lately Valerius' own men had camped, and try an assault from there: that and try to work around the harbor edge and gain entrance that way. But even there the task would be daunting. Everywhere the walls were high-fifteen feet at their lowest point along the ridge, twenty along the low ground-and thick-made of parallel rows of dressed and mortared stone, filled in with rubble and paved over on top with a sturdy battlement. And they were in good repair. Just within the month Valerius had the entire outer surface re-mortared with a mixture of sand, lime and water that had so impressed King Koltar. There was not a finger hold to be had along its entire length. Nor was there a safe spot to stand between wall and swamp: the whole was within easy bowshot, and bows there were aplenty among the defenders crowding the walls.

"Where do you suppose they're from?"

Valerius shrugged. "The lookout said he could see a fleet hauled up on the beach, so they could be from anywhere."

"If they've got a fleet, why not attack the harbor?"

"I don't know. They may have thought we're too strong there, or they may still be planning on it and are waiting until we're fully engaged on the walls." The head of the line was well into the woods now and Valerius could see fleeting shapes though the foliage. It was difficult to estimate numbers, but the tail end was now in sight a couple miles down the beach. Several thousand, at least. And as he suspected, once they reached the ridge, they began moving around to their left.

"They don't seem to have much in the way of siege equipment," said Ragnar.

"I noticed that. I see a few ladders here and there, but that's all. They probably couldn't haul it along the beach. I suspect they'll wait till their lines are established, then bring it up by ship."

"They won't get anywhere without it: I was four years out there looking up at these walls."

"Well, if I have anything to say about it, they won't get anywhere with it either."

"You want to sally out? Catch them off guard?"

"Would you be off guard?"

"No."

"Neither is he."

Valerius' father had done that when Fantar first attacked Valeria: ignored the advice of his generals to stay behind the city's thirty-foot ramparts and summon his allies. Instead, he had marched out in full regalia, banners flying, trumpets blaring, drums beating cadence for the gaudy citizen army: Fantar's wave caught them like toys on a beach and smashed them against the very walls that should have protected them. Valerius had been just fifteen at the time, too young to fight officially, but he had switched places with an older boy-a burly fellow, like himself, named Balazar-and had marched out with the van. Brought down early by a blow to the head, he awoke to find the city aflame and himself an orphan. He had born the name Balazar for fifteen years and had seen many another king repeat his father's mistake as Fantar conquered the Empire.

"What then?" Ragnar wanted to know.

"They are our guests, Ragnar. We should await their pleasure. In the meantime, how about some breakfast?"

Ragnar bowed, his scarred face twisted in a crooked grin. "Your Majesty is ever gracious."

Food was brought to the two leaders and the men on the walls were rotated down to arrange their own messes. Others were sent out to put the fleet in readiness while the serpentine trail of men slithered into the forest and coiled about the walls of the city. Finally, there was a flurry of activity along the edge of the southern woods. A small party emerged into the open, unfurled several banners-among them Fantar's Wild Boar-and with a flourish of trumpets, marched up to within fifty paces of the wall. Valerius and Ragnar made their way to a point opposite just as a gaudily armed fellow with a huge purple plume on his helm, stepped forward and bellowed in a clear, parade ground voice.

"I am Markus Vincipius, Imperial Viceroy of Falkan, Cartho and Zagorbia. I seek the renegade who styles himself Valerius!"

"I know him from Cartho," said Ragnar, sotto voce. "He was a pick-pocket in the old days."

Valerius smiled grimly and nodded. "Answer him."

"What would you if you find him?" Ragnar yelled.

"His life is forfeit! I am to return him-or his head-to my Lord Fantar in Valeria to answer for crimes against the Empire. I call on you all to lay down your arms and open your gates!"

Laughter rippled along the walls at this, then quieted as Valerius himself stepped forward and mounted the battlement. He, too, was resplendent, with gold and silver inlay on his helm and breastplate, a long purple cloak swirling about his form, and the great red gemstone of Kings flashing red in the bright morning sun-though at his side was still strapped his old, war-worn falchion in its plain leather scabbard. It was the weapon of a man at arms and had once belonged to that self-same Balazar.

"Markus Vincipius!" he called out, his huge voice echoing clear in the still morning air. "You have found him who you seek! I am Valerius Everreigning, Rightful High King of Valeria and all the Inland Sea. Hear me! I defy you, and I repudiate your Empire. Your lord is a murderer and a usurper! Fall on your knees now and acknowledge me as the King of the Eye or your blood will stain the earth on which you stand!"

"Expect no mercy, then!" Vincipius yelled into the silence that followed Valerius' words. These preliminaries complete, Markus marched back to his lines, and immediately a flight of arrows erupted from the wood line. Then, with a tumultuous shout, several thousand armed men rushed to the assault.

The din carried several miles to the south where Vahla and Chad were picking their way down from the mountains along a stony, twisted path. They were mounted-she swaying atop a white palfrey, and he on an aging mule with another trailing behind, loaded with baggage-and had been traveling for several days. They stopped at the noise.

"Do you think we're too late?" Vahla asked.

"Sound like men yelling," said Chad, "but hard to tell. No clang of sword. Come, Chad know a high place." He lead them north through the trees and up a rocky slope to the base of a bald outcropping. They tethered their beasts here, and clambered to the top. In the distance, shimmering in the morning haze, they could see the walls of Zagorbia, solid and linear against the rocky bulk of the peninsula beyond. Vague, colored shapes of men lined the walls, but there was no other action to be detected. Nor could they hear any noise just now.

Suddenly, a swarm of other colors surged about the walls, and the shapes atop blurred in motion. In a few minutes, the sound of shouts reached them again, and in the distance, they could see numbers of shapes rising up the walls, apparently mounting ladders. But these were thrown back, the shapes dropping among their fellows, and in a few minutes more, the swarm receded, leaving here and there, a few tiny splotches of color, lying still before the walls.

"Not get through today," said Chad. "Army there."

"Aren't you the master of understatement," Vahla muttered. Then aloud, "Well, what do we do now?"

Chad looked at her blankly, the idea of choice seemingly quite foreign to him.

"What's that way?" she asked, pointing east.

"East."

"Yes, but what's there?"

"Sand. Forest end. Desert start. Very hot."

"Does anyone live there?"

"Some. Live in tents and smell. Some villages along sea, though, then Cartho."

"Where the Oracle is? How far is that?"

"Oracle live in cave. Cartho a city. Chad been there. He know the way."

"How far?"

Chad looked east and screwed up his pointed face as if he could see the distant metropolis. "Four days. Maybe five."

Vahla considered. She had not really thought of anything beyond getting to Zagorbia. But with an army encircling the place, it was plain she could not get through-and for a young, attractive woman riding essentially alone (and Vahla was more than passingly attractive) it would be foolish to even try. Volkmir had said her heart would guide her, but her heart told her nothing. She was tired and sore from five straight days of riding and walking, and wanted nothing more than a hot bath. But she would have to do something. A siege could go on for months. Besides, Volkmir had mentioned a new power in the east. Maybe she could get help. Or at least a bath.

"We go east then," she said. "To Cartho."

Despite his apparent limitations, Chad was an extremely resourceful guide. Through the rest of the day and into the night, he led Vahla along a circuitous path right through the heart of the swamps surrounding Zagorbia and right around Vincipius' besieging army. It was a thick, dank place with huge Cyprus trees rearing up from the slimy waters on either hand, vines and creepers sweeping across the path, and who knew what creatures slithering among the muck and mire. Vahla quickly lost all sense of direction and simply trusted that Chad knew where he was going. Several times, at least, she gave herself up for lost as the narrow, not-quite-path ahead disappeared into green water. But always, around the next tree or bush, it wound on and on. How it was possible, she did not know, but though she traveled for miles that day through thick, utterly cloying jungle, she and her horse remained dry-shod.

They camped that night on a tiny island, their only fire the soft glow of several pieces of punk wood Chad had fired under the cover of brush to keep the swarms of bugs at bay. They ate a cold paste of coarse flour and swamp water and spoke in whispers. To one side of them-and not all that distant either-were the fires of Vincipius' reserve troops. Vahla could hear the distant murmur of their voices, and envied the vague shadows of them, cooking meat on spits. Wrapped tightly in her cloak, she fell into a cheerless sleep.

In the morning, the ground seemed to rise as they went on, and the dense jungle thinned so that here and there, patches of sun shone through. From her left, Vahla could begin to smell the salt air of the Inland Sea and in the open spots, occasionally feel a hint of breeze. But at the same time, she felt more threatened. Though the dank waters still swirled along both sides of their path, they were being drawn ever closer to Vincipius' host. She could sense an increased tenseness in Chad as he led them along, walking now and leading their mounts. At a halt they held a whispered conference.

"Swamp end soon," Said Chad. "Path take us to river ford. Very close to ships, but only way out."

Stealthily, they crept along a brush-lined path, the ground growing hard and rocky underfoot.

Suddenly, the path dipped, swept around an outcropping of rock, and disappeared under the broad, flowing waters of a river. For some minutes they stood in the shadow of the rock, scarcely breathing as they watched and listened for signs of activity on the further bank. It was quiet. Moving to the water's edge, they looked upstream and down. All was clear. Across the river, the ground was dry and firm, the path rising to disappear in a pleasant looking wood of oak and elm. To Vahla, the river seemed like a boundary of sorts-certainly the end of that dismal swamp, but also something more-and she felt sudden longing to cross it. At Chad's nod, she mounted her palfrey and followed him into the water.

She held her breath as the river swirled around her horse's withers, wetting her to the knees. But his step never faltered, and in moments only, he emerged on the other side and stumped up the path into the woods. Vahla felt a flood of relief and spurred her horse ahead when a squad of armed men stepped out from the trees directly in her path.

"Good morning, my lady," said the foremost one, a swaggering, bandy-legged veteran with a leering face and very few teeth. "What brings such a lovely thing as yourself out here this morning?"

Vahla thought fast. In a previous career she had been a dancer, and had dealt with fellows like this before. "I have come to seek commander Hagman," she said in her haughtiest voice, picking a name at random. "But it seems we've taken a wrong path. And you are?"

"Sergeant Whitman 'o the fourth, ma'am," said the fellow with a mock bow, his features softening only a little.

"Excellent, sergeant. Then perhaps you can direct me."

"I'm not familiar with your gentleman, my lady." This with just the hint of a sneer. "But if you'll accompany me back to camp, I'm certain we can find him out."

Camp was a ramshackle stone hut in a nearby clearing, around which Whitman's company had dug their fire pits. "The records is in here, ma'am," he said leading her to the door. "If you'll just step in, we can look him up. Your man can wait out here."

The hut contained but a single room and had not been occupied in many years. The roof over one corner had partially collapsed. Sunlight streamed through a number of other holes, and debris of various kinds littered the floor. Whitman's troopers had piled some of their gear along one wall, but there was no indication of any records. The place smelled strongly of mold and animal dung. Vahla turned to see Whitman with his back against the door, the leer now open on his face.

"Well!" she demanded, "where are these records?" But a note of fear undercut her bravado.

Fumbling with the tie at his waist, the sergeant dropped his leather breeches and exposed an already erect member. "I think there's a little something we should look at first," he sneered, wagging the thing. Then he advanced on her.

Moving quickly, Vahla snatched something from the pouch at her waist and threw it. A bright green flash exploded around the man's groin, the force knocking him back against the wall. As the smoke drifted lazily up through the roof, Whitman stood, looking down at himself in utter astonishment. All the hair on his stomach, groin and upper thighs had been burned away. The skin was a bright pink, and his erection wilting quickly. Striding forward, Vahla grabbed the man's testicles, jerked him away from the wall and pressed the point of a jewel-hilted dagger to his throat.

"Now, Sergeant," she hissed, "you will see us properly on our way to Cartho, or I'll cast a spell to fry these little eggs entirely. Do you understand?"

Eyes wide with terror, Whitman nodded dumbly.

"Well," laughed Vahla as she and Chad trotted along the open shore, some miles beyond Vincipius' last outpost, "I don't know if your late master was the fraud he claimed, but he certainly knew some interesting tricks!"

Chapter 5
THE ORACLE AT CARTHO

East of Zagorbia, the land leveled out and became a desert. The mountains, which lined the outer coast and ended at the Zagorbian promontory, fell away to the south leaving a huge, arid basin of dust and sand that extended for more than three hundred miles until they swept north again, bringing with them the moisture and vegetation needed to support human habitation. Here, nestled in the foothills surrounding a quiet harbor, and ringed by a patchwork of carefully tended fields, was the city of Cartho. Not as large as Zagorbia, and unfortified by tradition, it existed to serve the Oracle which, over the past thousand years or so, had grown to become an institution of influence and power.

Man has ever been a superstitious creature, overly obsessed with his fate and eager to grasp any means to better his odds. And in every civilization, those who can credibly claim to offer such an advantage are rewarded with power and munificence. This was especially true in the ancient Valerian Empire, and nowhere more so than at Cartho where the labyrinth of caves in the mountains south of the city provided a natural setting. From early days, soothsayers and fortunetellers of all stripes had set up shop in these precincts and hawked their services. Eventually, a guild of sorts had formed, which over the centuries had evolved into a powerful organization with a substantial hierarchy.

People came from all over the Inland Sea to seek their fortunes. Indeed, in times of peace and prosperity, regular junkets were run from all the leading cities, ferrying pilgrims into Cartho's welcoming harbor. Here they were met by well-practiced attendants, housed and fed according to their means, and according to their needs, provided access to a wide variety of divination services. People sought answers for everything, from the whereabouts of lost pillows, or the fate of missing loved ones, to the success of various ventures, and even to the fate of entire nations. And for the right price, there were answers for all. Starting in the back streets of the town itself, and spreading up through the layers of caves, was a virtual carnival of fortunetellers, culminating-for those with matters of sufficient moment (and sufficient means)-with the Oracle herself.

But these were not times of peace and prosperity. Fantar's ravages had not touched the town itself, but by pillaging the rest of the Inland Sea, they had effectively gutted the trade. Few now were the ships that entered the harbor and of those that did, most carried military types who asked little and paid less. Gone were the hosts of merchants whose greedy obsessions with their shifting patterns of deals and arrangements provided the bulk of the fortune trade. Gone, too, were the legions of regional aristocracy who, because they had too much of means and time, also had questions. All that was left were the truly devout who would sacrifice any means to seek wisdom and prophecy, and there were fewer and fewer of these. Indeed, the major question these days was survival.

Vahla, too, had questions in plenty, but after five more days of wind, sand and saddle sores, all she wanted was that bath. They had met no trouble after leaving Vincipius' army-indeed, the only disquieting thing they had seen at all was a huge pile of skulls in the desert west of Cartho, a monument to Fantar's earlier ravages-and still early on the sixth day, she rode confidently into the town and made her way to a modestly priced inn, a respectable distance from the taverns along the waterfront. She took their best room and registered under the name of her mother, Vauhna. The place had its own bathhouse and she immediately set Chad to hauling water. Soon, she settled into a hot, sudsy tub with a deep sigh of contentment.

She had not thought much during the journey-sitting on a horse day after day tends to numb the mind as well as the butt-but once the grit and grime were scrubbed away and she settled back into the steamy water to relax, her thoughts began to flow, and the questions began. Where was she going? What was she going to do? She had set out with only the vaguest plan to reach Zagorbia and warn Valerius, but she'd been too late for that. So what now? Volkmir had said follow the advice of her own heart, but what did that mean? Aside from the one thing she would not think of, her heart told her to help Valerius. But what could a single female and a half-witted servant do to stop an army? Well, she was not just a single female; she was sister-well, half-sister-to the Rightful King of Valeria. That made her royalty, didn't it? She was a princess. Ought that not count for something? Yes, if word got out it would count towards her death. But she was also an apprentice mage, wasn't she, almost a sorceress in her own right? She hadn't exactly been idle during her year with Volkmir, and hadn't his tricks already proven useful? Useful, yes, but she also knew they were only tricks, and that she had, indeed, mastered precious few.

So, what? Volkmir had also mentioned a power rising in the east: the name Asperides floated in her mind like the sponge in her bath. She still had her dancer's skills, and her looks: perhaps with a little guile, some connections and one or two of Volkmir's tricks she could meet this fellow and convince him to help Valerius. It was an absurd thought, akin in magnitude to her changing the course of a river, but hey, wasn't it almost as absurd to think of her killing Fantar? And she had almost done that. She still had his dagger to prove it (which, if she were caught, would convict her). So why not try to sweet-talk this Asperides? She was a princess, wasn't she? And what else did she have to do?

Stay ahead of the game, Volkmir had told her. That was the trick to all sorcery. It wasn't a question of power, but of leverage. If you were clear-sighted enough, and if you were open to the will of the gods, you could anticipate events. You could place yourself at the vortex, at that one place and one time when some act or word-something insignificant even-could change the course of events. But how did one do that? Ah, the old pedant had lectured, that is the easy part. The difficulty is in seeing just how easy it is, and being patient enough to let it happen. Or not. That is the hard part. "The cup holds wine," he said, "but it does not fill itself. The trick is to be nearest the servant's hand when the master calls for drink."

That's what I need to do, she thought as she stood up and reached for her towel, place myself near the hand of the servant. But at that moment, the door was kicked open and Chad walked in, his hands each hung with a bucket of hot water. The two stood there, frozen for an instant, and Vahla watched his eyes sweep her body. Defiant and proud, she endured the gaze. "You very beautiful, Lady," he said, a strange sound in his voice. Then, setting down his buckets, he handed her the towel.

Vahla spent the afternoon wandering the markets of Cartho, reveling in the sights and smells of civilization. She had been over a year in Volkmir's mountain lair, and while she certainly did not lack for creature comforts, she had missed the hurly-burly of city life more than she realized. At first she went about cloaked and cowled-feeling a need to be inconspicuous-but as she quickly realized she was far from the only lady out for an afternoon's shopping and, as the day was bright and warm, she soon shook her raven hair loose, tossed her cloak to Chad, and proceeded on her rounds like a girl let off from school. Nor was that all he had to carry, for soon those few necessary items she sought began to pile up in Chad's arms and he seemed to walk a bit closer to the ground.

Well satisfied with her outing, she decided to eat that evening at a small tavern near the hotel. It was a pleasant place with an open veranda and a screened off section for more discriminating patrons such as herself. The waiter recommended the local wine, which was excellent, and she ordered a baked fish seasoned with herbs. There had been no fresh fish in the mountains and she found this one so good she had to stop herself from gorging on it like a barracks soldier.

The setting sun suffused her little corner of the veranda with a soft glow, and with her meal cleared away, she leaned back against the latticework screen and sipped slowly from a second glass of wine. On the morrow there would be many things she'd have to attend to-arranging passage east, hiring a maid servant, outfitting herself more appropriately for the role she intended to play-but for right now all she wanted to do was relax.

Yet without intending it, she found herself listening in on a conversation at a table on the other side of the screen, in the public section. Had they been speaking in normal voices, she would probably not have paid any attention. But that they were obviously trying not to be overheard aroused her curiosity in an idle sort of way, and as the best opportunity for listening required that she stay precisely where she was, she listened. From the tone of the voices, one man was giving a report to another. And when the name Fantar entered the conversation, Vahla began to listen intently.

Fantar, it seemed, had sent an ambassador, and he had landed that day. His name was Owen-a name which evoked a familiar grunt from the second voice-and he had not only come with a large entourage, but reportedly with a large amount of gold as well. Moreover, the speaker knew someone on the crew of Owen's ship who said that this was not just a state visit, but that Owen was here on Fantar's behalf to hear the Oracle.

"To hear the Oracle? Fantar, who violently denies the existence of any power or god outside himself? What would he want with an Oracle?" the second voice wanted to know.

Well, said the first, apparently Owen had got rather deep into his cups with the captain one evening and was overheard going on about how Fantar was growing increasingly paranoid. He was suffering from recurring nightmares, imagining assassins lurking around every corner, and generally showing signs of an incipient madness. He raved on and on about facing threats from all sides, even about seeing the ghost of Valerius himself. He knew he was doomed and didn't care about that, the drunken Owen had said. But he was being driven mad by the sheer number of possibilities. So he had sent Owen to the Oracle, the first voice concluded, to discover the true manner of his end.

"Being driven mad by the possibilities? Oh, that's great!" said the second, his deep voice rumbling with laughter. "What a reward for service to the Empire!" Then, after a pause, "Well, I don't know what we can do about this, but it's certainly something our friend Thorngere should know about."

At the sound of that name, Vahla gasped involuntarily and there was a sudden silence at the other table. In moments, two figures approached in the gathering twilight and seated themselves at her table. One was a short, swarthy fellow who looked like he could be a dockworker, but the other was tall and well-groomed with long hair framing deep-set eyes and a bemused expression.

"So," this one said, leaning conspiratorially close and studying her intently, "you know Thorngere, do you?"

She shot back a look as intent as his own. "I may," she said. "But what concern is that of yours?"

"Thorngere's business concerns us very deeply, ma'am."

"Is that so?" said Vahla, her eyes searching his.

"It is indeed," said the fellow, his eyes searching hers in return. Then, after a long moment, his face opened into a grin. "I am Bokmar, ma'am, at your service."

"And I am Vahla."

"Vahla. I know that name. There was a woman by such a name at Kantar. She stood on the cliffs with the old Mage, then helped tend the wounded-especially Thorngere. Would you be that Vahla?"

"I might," said Vahla, smiling now as well. "You were at Kantar?"

"I was, lady. With Thorngere. And let me ask you something else: we heard rumors, not long since, of a sorceress visiting one of Vincipius' outposts near Zagorbia: appeared in the shape of a demon, she did, and fried some fellow where he stood. You wouldn't know anything of that, would you?"

Vahla thought of a cup, and of a hand, reaching. "Tell me, Bokmar," she said, "how would you like to send this Owen back to his master with a very special message?"

"I would indeed, lady. I would indeed."

That night, as she lay in her bed, Vahla tried very hard not to think of Thorngere. But he kept materializing in her mind like some persistent ghost: no sooner would she banish one image than another would pop up. There was Thorngere the peddler, as she had first seen him when she fled from Valeria after trying to kill Fantar; Thorngere that next morning, emerging naked and godlike from the river, a fish flopping on the end of his spear; Thorngere the fearsome warrior revealed in the fight at Gamlarch's house (you are no peddler, she had said then, and knew in that instant that she loved him).

But no, she tossed to her other side, she would not think that way. She would not. But here he was again, Thorngere the captain and lover as they took ship to Kantar; Thorngere the king's companion; Thorngere the ambassador; Thorngere her man... Again she thrust the image away only to have it return, insistent and intrusive: Thorngere walking in the hills with her, singing a song from his youth; Thorngere smiling and radiant after a feast; Thorngere as he awoke in the morning, sitting in a pool of sunlight on the side of their bed, his eyes puffy and hair all tousled; Thorngere wounded and bloody, sprawled like a corpse on the field at Kantar; and then, worst of all, Thorngere's face at that moment when they discovered they were more than lovers; that they were siblings.

Vahla buried her face in her pillow and tried to stifle the wracking sobs, but that last face of his would not leave. It haunted. That and the empty thing he had become after. How could she have caused him so much pain? It didn't matter that she knew nothing of his relationship with Valerius; she should have known, should have seen. She knew of her own relationship. She should have said. But how could she? Valerius didn't even know. No one knew but her mother and her nurse-and Volkmir. And who would have believed? She could not have said. But how could she not? How could there be so much pain?

Thorngere's face swirled with the pain in her mind and would not go away. Not until the tears came, until she had sobbed and choked and soaked her pillow; and not until the cramps in her stomach began to subside and her breath returned in long ragged gasps; not until then did it fade, when sleep stole about her like a velvet cloud and she began to sink into soft oblivion.

But then, at that last corner between wake and sleep, in that last little spark of semiconscious thought, Vahla's mind also replayed the incident in the bath with Chad: the way he had looked at her. She had often wondered, during her time with Volkmir, about the manhood of such a creature, about whether the seemingly empty part of his mind affected that as well. During that whole year and more there had not been the slightest glimpse of anything in Chad other than the deferential, incredibly resourceful servant. Then there was that look. But it was not quite a lustful look. It was different somehow. Softer, like light. It was like his thick, clouded face had opened for an instant and she had glimpsed something bright. And with that thought, sleep took her.

Chapter 6
THE PROPHECY

The Oracle of Cartho sat at her worktable, busily writing out lines of verse, and as busily, scratching them out again. She was a tall woman, well into her middle years, with a long face, short-cropped auburn hair, and a fragile, fading beauty that had required increasing support these past few years. Reed thin by temperament and abstemious by habit, she sat ramrod straight at her desk and wrote with a quick, disciplined hand. Normally, she would not be the one to actually write a prophecy-indeed, more and more these days she did not even appear in costume herself, leaving the details of the business to her underlings, while acting herself more as a chief executive-but it was not often one had the opportunity (the onus?) to foretell for the Emperor himself, and she felt that this task was best left to her own hand.

But it was not coming easily. A score of unsatisfactory attempts littered her desk and one part of her brain was castigating the other for allowing herself to get so out of practice, even while that other part was feverishly working up new ideas. It was not as though she had no direction. Fantar was certainly well enough known, and as usual, the Oracle's agents had been busily pumping this Owen for information from the moment his destination was known. But what did one say about such a creature as Fantar? And how to say it with just that precise amount of ambiguity that would at once assure the broadest interpretation and the largest gift?

Oracle making at Cartho was not a hit or miss proposition-the business had not survived for nearly a thousand years by accident-and if divine inspiration was involved, it was an inspiration well codified and documented. Had she so desired, the Oracle could have had access to any of a hundred dusty volumes of prophecy. Indeed, she had composed nearly a volume herself during her tenure, and was a thorough mistress of her craft. But the records, she felt, would be of little use on this occasion, for whatever prophecy she delivered would be repeated throughout the empire and be parsed by a thousand minds. These few words would be her legacy, she thought, and that, she knew, was her chief difficulty.

She was interrupted from her labors by an acolyte, scratching at her door to ask if she would like to interview an applicant to the order. The Oracle snapped in irritation and almost slammed the door, but a quick glance at the applicant stopped her: here was not the normal fourteen-year-old, in tow by a mother unable to arrange a suitable marriage. Here was a full-blown woman, and one of rare beauty at that. As one who appreciated the power of feminine beauty, here also, she thought, might be something worthy of consideration. Besides, a brief respite from her labors could provide just the inspiration she needed. Smiling in her stiff, formal way, she invited the woman in.

In the brighter light of her study, the Oracle saw she had not been mistaken. The woman was indeed beautiful, with long raven-colored hair cascading about her shoulders; a round, bright face with prominent lips and large, almond-shaped eyes that seemed to smolder beneath dark lashes; breasts so plump and full they seemed to float in the air before her; and hips that would stir the loins of any man-and many a woman. Beneath the thin muslin of her blouse, a pair of pert nipples made the Oracle's fingers twitch. Taking the woman by the arm, she led her to a small couch.

They sat, facing each other. The woman was very shy and diffident and it was with some difficulty that the Oracle got her story. Her name was Mira, it seemed. She was from Falkan, a town along the coast to the east, and had only arrived the day before. She had come, she insisted, to serve the Oracle, but when asked why, she demurred. She felt the call, she said, had always yearned to serve, would do anything.

"Come, come, Mira, my dear," said the Oracle, her arm stretched along the back of the couch and her head inclined in what she hoped was a kindly and sympathetic manner, "I'm sure you are very sincere in what you say, but you must admit, you are not our usual type of applicant. What did you do in Falkan? Did you live with your parents?"

No, Mira shook her head and would not look up, but the Oracle could see a blush begin to rise in her cheeks.

"You have... you have not left your husband, have you?

Mira looked up sharply, her eyes wide and imploring. "Oh, please!" she cried. "Please don't send me back," and she clutched the Oracle's hand.

"There, there, my dear," said the Oracle, patting the girl's hands and stroking her forearm. "You mustn't be frightened. Tell me now, did he beat you?"

"No," said Mira, looking down again. "It wasn't that... May I?" she asked, looking towards the sideboard.

"Certainly, my dear. Forgive me. I should have offered."

Mira poured them each a cup of wine and returned to the couch, sitting closer now, her hand automatically resting on the Oracle's. "You're so kind," she murmured. "I knew you'd be kind."

"We only have your interests at heart, my dear," said the Oracle and took a deep drink to steady herself. "But you must be completely honest with me. So, tell me now, you've left your husband..."

"Yes, but it wasn't because he beat me," said Mira, her eyes pleading belief. "That would almost have been better..."

"What was it then?"

"It was... It was the sex."

The Oracle's heart started to pound. "You didn't like it?"

"It's not that I don't like sex. It's just... " Again Mira demurred and looked down at her lap.

84

Nervously, her fingers traced a line along the Oracle's inner forearm. "I do like sex," she said, looking up again.

The Oracle took another drink, and then Mira's story came out. She had been married only two years, and while her husband was not a bad fellow-she loved him in a way, really- it seemed he preferred boys. That was not so bad in itself-she could even understand how someone could enjoy that-but there was only one way he could satisfy himself with her, and that she couldn't stand. It was just so filthy and horrid, she shuddered, and so painful! But to leave him for that would be a public humiliation, and she couldn't bear that. So that's when she thought of serving the Oracle: it was the only way.

The girl was near tears now, and the Oracle set her empty cup aside and drew her close. She patted her back and made soothing sounds. Mira snuggled in. She rested her head on the Oracle's bony shoulder and felt the woman's cheek and honeyed breath against her forehead. The Oracle held her quietly and the two sat very still. Gradually the patting motion slowed down, then stopped. Mira felt the Oracle's head rest more heavily, her breathing deepen. Slowly, the girl disengaged herself and eyed the Oracle closely. Then she got up and strode quickly to open the door.

"Out cold," she said as Bokmar and another man entered.

"Excellent," said he, verifying that the Oracle was, indeed, sleeping quite peacefully. "Everything else is secure as well. Good timing, too: we just got word that Owen is on his way."

"Good," said Vahla. "By the time she wakes up, we'll be long gone and she'll be none the wiser."

"And you're sure she won't talk?"

"She's the Oracle of Cartho," said Vahla. "How could she admit such a thing?"

Owen of Rodale was a career diplomat whose skills had served him well through turbulent times. A minor clerk in the tax assessor's office when Fantar's army overran Valeria, he had escaped death by turning state's evidence, as it were, and providing his new master with valuable information about the wealth of various leading citizens-wealth which was subsequently transferred to the new royal coffers, a small piece yielding to Owen in the process. And in the years since, his knowledge of accounting and his uncanny instinct for assessing true value-not to mention ferreting out secret hiding places-had been a significant financial boon to Fantar's enterprises for which he was rewarded with ever more influence. Some people felt this made Owen a traitor, but he did not choose to view it that way. Rather, he thought of himself as actually helping save those Fantar plundered (even though quite a number did not survive the saving) since resistance would obviously mean death. And if his talents had leant themselves to this purpose and had helped him in the process, well, so much the better.

So Owen was an eminently practical man (some would say piratical), always setting his sails for the wind that blew, and not much given to speculation on higher matters. He was especially not given to speculation on matters such as the one which presently occupied him, as he made his way out of the city at the head of his small entourage and wound his way up the well-trodden path towards the highest cave on the hill, that of the Oracle. Religion had always been something he secretly sneered at as fodder for fools, and the thought that someone would actually pay hard-earned (or even unearned) money for such things as divination and prophecy was... well, it spoke volumes in Owen's mind.

However, being a practical man, and knowing his master's proclivities in this regard, he dutifully set his face into a mien of high seriousness as he strode the dusty path. It was a pudgy face-indeed, all of Owen of Rodale was rather pudgy and short-capped by an equally pudgy nose (growing a bit purple and veined at the tip) and a pair of small, very quick eyes. But what Owen may have lacked in stature, he made up for in hair: rich, lustrous hair that had grown nearly down to his waist. Particularly vain of this asset, he had it groomed and braided daily by a pair of servants, and kept it neatly tied at the back of his head. So particular was he that he would not wear hat or hood, and when he was forced to be out in inclement weather, had those same two servants walk beside him, supporting a small canopy on poles.

But there was no need for a canopy on this fine morning, and Owen's hair was plaited and ribboned in splendor to match his robes, which were cloth of gold with rich red embroidering. He felt it incumbent on his office that his person match the magnificence of the gifts he brought to please the Oracle, for if he doubted the power of divinity, he was sure of the power of munificence.

He was also a bit nervous despite his skepticism, for the Oracle of Cartho was reputed to be a difficult creature, as given to cursing and humiliating pilgrims as to offering divine wisdom. He was also unsure of proper protocol for such an encounter, and as a diplomat, he liked to be prepared for any contingency. Yet, strangely, he was unable to find anyone to enlighten him. It seemed part of the mystique of the place that while the words of the Oracle remained burned in the minds of those who heard them, the more rudimentary details of the meetings seemed to dissolve: no one could actually remember how they were escorted into the Oracle's presence, what transactions were involved regarding the gifts, how they made their questions known, etc. This was unsettling for one such as Owen who preferred to work from a position of empirical knowns.

He was relieved, then, to be royally welcomed at the cave's mouth by a delegation of servants and escorted, with all due honors, into a lavishly furnished side chamber where his party was served refreshments and bade to take their ease while the Oracle prepared herself. Ensconced at a private table, Owen availed himself of some delicious spice cakes and calmed his nerves with two large goblets of honeyed wine before a servant approached and, bowing deeply, motioned for him to follow.

Bearing a single torch, the servant led the way along a steep, winding tunnel that delved deep into the side of the mountain. They went for some distance, the air growing colder by the minute, the tunnel narrow and cramped in one spot, open and cavernous the next. Side tunnels led off in every direction, vast chimneys opened overhead, seemingly bottomless pits gaped in the middle of the path, and water cascaded down the walls and in places ran in streams along the path. Owen did not like the place and as they went, became more and more unsettled. It was a maze, a frightening, dangerous maze, and he kept close on the heels of the servant as they tramped along. At one point, the way grew so narrow and torturous that he had to squeeze through sideways, the cold, wet rock pressing against him, snagging his robes. The servant, sliding on ahead, rounded a corner and suddenly, everything went black.

"What!" Owen yelped into the echoing darkness. "What's happened? Where are you? Strike a light there!"

But there was no response. All Owen could hear was the trickle of water along the floor and a hushed, hissing sound of cold air in dank space.

"Hello!" He yelled again. "What's happened there? Why don't you answer?"

"Owen of Rodale," came a sudden, ominous voice, echoing in the darkness. Whether it was that of the servant or another, he could not tell.

"What is this? Strike a light there this instant, I tell you!"

"If you seek the light, Owen of Rodale, you must seek the Oracle."

Owen sputtered and yelled but no amount of fuss on his part could elicit either light or further response. Instead, the darkness seemed to deepen and between yelps, the silence grew more ominous. Obviously, this was part of the ritual, he told himself: a bit of theatrics staged to impress supplicants with the awesome power of the Oracle. But he liked it none the more for the rationalization, and was no more able to quell the sudden churning in his bowels. The thing he must do, he told himself, was go forward. There was no going back. Even if he could find the way and did not drop into a pit-both of which were highly improbable-what would he then say to Fantar? That he could not find the Oracle because he got lost in the dark?

Fear is not an ideal substitute for courage, but it can be an effective one. Stretching his hand along the slimy wall, Owen inched forward, tapping along the floor with his foot and sliding sideways. Reaching the corner around which the servant had disappeared, his hand momentarily flailed in empty air, but then, sweeping left, encountered hard rock again. The tunnel widened and he was able to face forward, advancing with a hand on each wall. The path rose beneath his feet and the walls became drier. Sliding a foot forward, he encountered a step, then another. His right hand found a railing, and at the top of a small landing, his left hand touched a heavy curtain. Thrusting it aside, he stepped forward into a huge, vaulted chamber, lit by a dozen torches.

The Oracle stood between two lighted braziers on a shelf of rock in the center of the chamber. She wore a ceremonial mask of the taloned god, framed by her rich black hair, and below, was dressed in a sheer, wispy gown that in the firelight silhouetted the shape of her body. It was a lithe, young body, and as Owen drew closer, he could see that she wore very little else other than the gown: the dark nipples on her breasts were plainly evident.

"Owen of Rodale," she said, her voice sibilant and musical but with an edge of authority. "Why do you seek the Oracle of Cartho?"

Owen bowed his best diplomatic bow. Now that it had come to words, and now that he had seen this Oracle, he felt he was on firmer ground. "I am come, Madam Oracle," he said smoothly, "to seek the wisdom of the gods on behalf of our master, the Emperor Fantar of Valeria."

"And why would Fantar send you, Owen of Rodale?" Her voice had a lilting sound that reminded Owen of silver bells. "Is he too great to seek the gods himself?"

"Far, far from it, Madam Oracle. In fact, his highness bade me specifically to beg your forgiveness that he was unable to attend you himself. But matters of state are so pressing, he hopes the gods-and you-will understand." Owen drew even closer and allowed his eyes to roam the woman's frame: nipples were not all the flimsy silk revealed, and despite himself, Owen's pulse began to quicken.

"Then what would your master, who is too busy to attend the gods?" The voice had a bit of an edge now and Owen acknowledged the rebuke with a nod of his head.

"My master would hear his destiny."

"His destiny?"

"Yes, my Lady. He bade me say this unto you: 'Oracle of Cartho, know that I am Fantar, Conqueror and Emperor of Valeria and all the Inland Sea. By my sword has an ancient, enfeebled realm been swept away and a new, powerful state been built in its place. Everywhere my armies are victorious; the people call my name. In every city around the Inland Sea, my magistrates deal justice; my strong arm protects the people. This I have done, Oracle, and am assured of my greatness. But still I am beset on all sides. The more I conquer, the more my enemies multiply; the more I build, the more hands seek to tear me down; the greater my justice, the more heinous the plots against me. Oracle, I do not expect gratitude. I know I am but a man, and that I must someday die. I accept that. But I would ask of you this: that I may know the manner of my fate so I may better prepare to meet it.'"

"So, your master would know the manner of his end that he 'may be better prepared to meet it?'" There was just the slightest trace of scorn in the Oracle's voice. Owen could not help but smile himself.

"Yes, my Lady."

"Is he not aware that knowledge seals fate?"

"He has been told, my Lady."

"Then let us see, Owen of Rodale, what the gods will say to this master of yours who is too busy to attend them."

Of what happened next, Owen was able to retain no clear memory. He had a clear recollection of the Oracle stepping back between the braziers on the stage, spreading her arms wide and beginning a chant, but of what she chanted, or to whom, or even in what language, he was never sure. Every time he called it up, the memory seemed to slip away. He recalled feeling somewhat dizzy and wondered if the wine had been drugged. His hearing and vision, too, seemed distorted for from somewhere, strange music began and filled the chamber with an eerie, pulsing sensation that swirled like a wind. And the chamber seemed to swell, like a water bladder filled with air, only he was on the inside and the ceiling and walls began to pulse out all the while the Oracle was chanting. His memory did not want to accept this-for Owen was a very practical man-but that is what his senses recorded.

Nor was this the strangest thing his senses recorded, for as she chanted, standing between fire and fire, arms and legs spread wide, head thrown back and white, warbling throat exposed, the Oracle seemed to grow. Owen squeezed his eyes and shook his head, then looked around wildly for something solid he could hold on to. But his feet were rooted to the floor, while before him, the Oracle-that lovely, enticing vixen of a few moments before-was swelling into something entirely different, something entirely horrible. From her shoulders now, Owen saw huge dark green wings, and on her arms, sinewy muscle stretched and swelled. Her hands became claws and on her face, the mask became the very face of the taloned god. This God leapt forward then, to the very edge of the platform, towering over Owen of Rodale, and Owen dropped to his knees, shuddering with fear. Nor was he the only one, for behind a pillar near the back of the chamber, Bokmar, too, watched in awe, his knees growing weak beneath him.

"Owen of Rodale," hissed this creature, its voice as hot as fire, its eyes, red as live coals, boring into him, pinning him to the ground with terror. "Say thus to your master:

"Though you look north, south, east, and west,
Oh, killer of kings, you will have no rest.
You fear what your dark eye sees in the night,
Yet by he whom you half see will you die in the light."

The next thing Owen remembered, he was stumbling back down the tunnel, well lighted now by torches set in brackets along the walls. His head ached, his vision swam, his stomach still churned, and -he was horrified to discover- he had at some point during the prophecy lost control of both his bowels and bladder. Stumbling back into the room where the rest of his party waited, they shrank from the sight of him. What did you see, they wanted to know? But Owen only stared at them, thinking, '*it was the God I saw: the God himself.*'

As Owen fled the Oracle's chamber, Bokmar came out from behind his pillar, his eyes still wild with fear. Taking a deep breath, he looked about the room, then down at his own hands. That they were the same hands seemed to reassure him and when he looked back up, the chamber was as it had been before, but the girl was slumped on the dais. He started for her, but her servant, Chad, was there already and helped her to her feet. Bokmar was just as glad: he was not sure how close he dared come to this creature. But when she removed the mask, it was just Vahla.

"I'm sorry," she said. "I got dizzy there for a minute."

"How...?" said Bokmar. "How did you...?"

"Lady learn many tricks in mountains with Mage," said Chad, guiding his mistress to a small antechamber and handing her a cup of wine.

"Well, I must say," said Bokmar, pouring himself a cup with shaky hand and tossing it off gratefully, "you have become quite the sorceress indeed."

"I prefer the term Enchantress," said Vahla, her composure recovered now.

"Then Enchantress it is, my Lady," said Bokmar, bowing deeply. And as she and Chad left the Oracle's cave, all of Bokmar's other people bowed before her as well.

"What happened?" Vahla asked Chad.

"You make pretty good Oracle," said Chad

"What did I say?" And when Chad repeated the prophecy, "Oh," she said, "I was going to say something about Valerius."

A visibly changed Owen of Rodale took ship the next day to bring word from the Oracle to his master. And within two days, word had spread throughout the community at Cartho of a powerful Enchantress who had taken the shape of the Oracle to appear before Owen, then conjured the God himself to appear. When Vahla walked through the streets now, crowds parted before her and heads bowed. And when she sought passage east to Palmeria, she found herself treated royally indeed.

As for the real Oracle, she was spitting mad. But when she saw the pile of gold and treasure Owen had left, and when she heard the words of the Oracle itself, she pursed her lips, nodded a grudging approval and went on with her business. As the saying went, one need not look a gift horse in the mouth.

Chapter 7
WEAPONS TAKE

Elusive rode easily to a single anchor, close inshore at the mouth of the river Elbe, awaiting either wind or tide to turn in her favor. They had arrived with the tide the evening before, but the late breeze had turned offshore, and with darkness falling, a good night's sleep had seemed preferable to a long pull upstream with the sweeps. Now with the bright morning sun warming the land and the last of the ebb swirling beneath his counter, Thorngere stood at the rail absorbing the sights and smells of his homeland.

It was green, this land of Thuringia, and tall, the ground sweeping upwards in a series of verdant, forested curves from the rocky shoreline to merge with the majestic peaks that etched the sky. And the smell was fresh and clean, a mixture of pine, and granite, and humid earth. To the south, in the lands surrounding the Inland Sea, browns tended to predominate, and warm, fecund smells. It was not that vegetation was lacking, but the climate was more arid and the grounds cover spotty. Here it was all green, from long, lush grasses, to thick bush and hardy branch. Too steep and rocky to farm in most places, heavily forested in others, and with human habitations scattered amongst hidden dells and streams, the vistas of Thuringia were as wild and natural as when the gods first set men among them.

Elusive stirred to the first of the flood tide and Thorngere ordered the anchor up. Under main alone and with a light sea breeze, Elusive gradually gathered way and began pushing her bluff bows upstream. Thorngere remembered the first time he had sailed out of this river. Valeria was newly fallen and one of the local chieftains had called for a Weapons Take to help the cities of the south. Not many men responded-Thuringia had never been an official part of the Empire, and its affairs were considered none of theirs-but Thorngere was barely fifteen at the time and mad for adventure. He lied about his age and, without even telling his parents, had sailed off in a war galley to join the fight. It had been five years before he was able to return-on a recruiting mission of his own that time-and twenty years since that first trip, but he was still able to recall that magical sensation when the ship first lifted to the ocean swell and the horizon spread vast and empty before them. How filled with possibilities that empty sea had seemed! And how fast things change, he thought ruefully, and turned his attention to the business at hand.

The river was fairly wide at its mouth, like an estuary, but narrowed a few miles inland as the banks steepened, and began to wind through hill country. After the first bend or two, they lost the wind, and shortly after, the current overcame the tide and they had no choice but to man the sweeps. Thorngere took the helm and steered wide of the strongest currents near the bends, but it was still a hot and tired crew that, some six hours later, secured Elusive to a rickety jetty in the small fishing village of Gan, a scant three hour climb from his home. Thorngere was surprised to see the village elder, an ancient named Corloc who had been elder in Thorngere's youth, waiting at the dock, and he vaulted the rail to greet him.

"Welcome Lord Thorngere, Atheling of Thule," said Corloc formally, tilting his rickety frame in his best attempt at a bow. "The gods must have been kind indeed for the messengers to have reached you so soon."

"Messengers?" said Thorngere. Corloc had not remained Elder of Gan for over thirty years from a lack of perception. Seeing Thorngere's blank expression, he quickly changed his tone.

"Aye, lad, messengers. About Thornalon."

"What about him?" asked Thorngere, his ambivalence about returning home suddenly replaced by anxiety.

"Well, I'm sorry to be the one to break the news, my boy, but your father has taken ill, very ill. In fact, they don't expect him to live from what I hear. They say he's been calling for you..."

Whatever else Corloc might have said was lost on Thorngere. Leaving Elusive under the care of his captain, Boltar, he set out immediately for his village, taking only a small squad of men as an escort.

Thorngere's village lay in a broad upland valley at the head of a small lake. Surrounded by arable fields, timber built, and supporting a population of several thousand souls, Thorndale was the largest village in the region of Thule, serving for what passed as a capital by default, and lending to its leader, Thornalon, the status of Chieftain. But as Thorngere topped the rise at the valley's head, it already looked like a village in mourning. Although several hours of daylight remained, workers had already come in from the fields, and the streets were empty of children. Doorways in the plank houses were open and dark. In the marketplace, groups of men conferred in clusters, turning to acknowledge Thorngere as he passed, but making no move to come forward and greet him. He felt, as he passed through the town and mounted the rise towards the palisaded compound where he grew up, like he was moving through a painting, or through a full-scale version of Valerius' map, where everything around him was imitation, a still life, and he the only thing real.

This notion shattered abruptly when he saw the face of his mother, Panella, waiting for him at the doorway. It was a drawn face with hollow cheeks and haunted eyes. She looked frail of a sudden, this mother who had always been to him the image of vivacity. There were broad streaks of gray in her hair now and an incipient grief hung about her like a heavy cloak. She stepped back from the door as he entered; her eyes drinking in the powerful mass of him as he filled the frame, then came to him. "My prayers have been answered," she said.

He held her delicately, as one would a small bird. "Does he live?"

"Aye, he lives. He has been asking for you. Come." The public rooms of the Great House were filled with the leading men of the region. They rose and bowed in respectful silence as Thorngere and Panella passed through to the private quarters in the back. Here, too, were more intimate acquaintances and members of the Elders' Council, filling the small sitting room and standing in the hall by the entrance to Thornalon's private chamber. They pressed against the walls as Thorngere passed and he could hear the sibilant hiss of their whispers behind him.

The heavy wooden shutters in Thornalon's room had been fastened shut and the room was lit by a cluster of candles on either side of the bed. Thorngere's sister and her husband sat at the foot and an empty chair-presumably his mother's-sat by the head. Thornalon lay like a corpse with his hands neatly folded on the cover and his long wispy beard splayed across his chest. Thorngere was shocked at the sight of him. The image he carried of Thornalon was of a tough, vigorous little man, gnarled and gray, but with energy enough to outdistance many a younger man and a temper that could snap like a turtle. But that image was nothing like the sallow, shrunken thing he saw before him. How could he have gotten so small? He was like a bag of bones under the sheet. His forearms were sticks, and his hands like old, worn leather gloves. The skin on his cheeks and on the sunken lids of his eyes was like wax, shiny and translucent.

Moving quickly to the bedside, Thorngere's sword got between him and the chair and he realized, suddenly, that he had not even removed his helm and shield. He did so quickly, but at the soft rattle of arms, the old man stirred, and as Thorngere took the chair, he opened his eyes and reached out a hand.

"Thorngere," he said, his voice no more than a whisper, but his eyes lighting up. "My son."

Thorngere's heart wrenched. He took the wrinkled hand and held it, returning Thornalon's gaze. The eyes, at least, were still his father's. "I am here, my father. How are you?"

"Better now that my eyes behold you, lad. They all seem to think they're about to be rid of me," he said and his eyes flickered, indicating the world at large, "but I'm too ornery to die."

Thorngere tried to speak but a lump obstructed his throat. He smiled at his father and tried to swallow it down. "Shall we organize a hunting party then?" he said at last, but the words sounded stilted and lame.

"Well, maybe not hunting quite yet," Thornalon whispered, the ghost of a smile playing about his face. "But I wouldn't mind a mug of ale!"

"Ha! I'm sure you wouldn't. But you'd have to sit up to hold an ale mug, and I'm not sure you're quite up to that yet."

"Give me a few days," said the old man, his attention already beginning to slip.

"All right," said Thorngere, blinking back moisture. "A few days then." And he patted the old man's hand as he drifted off to sleep.

Along with his family, Thorngere sat by Thornalon's side through the evening and long into the night, leaving only for brief intervals to greet old friends and deal with the necessities of nature. They spoke softly of homely things while the old man slept peacefully. He had been failing for some time, Panella said-after all, he was nearing eighty- but then a few weeks ago he had come down with a summer cold. It was just the sniffles at first, but it had gone to his chest, and a week ago or so they had decided to send the messenger. She was amazed he had gotten there so quickly.

Thorngere felt a sudden pang of guilt and embarrassment that the messenger had not reached him, that his coming, in fact, had nothing to do with his father. He murmured it was luck alone that brought him, that he was on the king's business.

"The king?" said his mother. "What king?"

"King Valerius," he said, surprised at the question.

"Oh, yes," his mother nodded as if recalling something from distant memory. "We heard something about a fellow setting himself up as Valerius. I didn't know you were involved."

"Yes, mother," he said, looking at her directly. "I am involved, and he is Valerius."

Now it was his mother's turn to look surprised. "He really is...?"

"Yes, mother, the real Valerius. My brother."

"Oh," she said simply. Then after a time. "So, you won't be staying?"

"I can stay for a time, mother. I have some time."

True to his prediction, Thornalon's fever broke the next morning, and he woke up hungry. By noon he was sitting up, feeding himself with a spoon, and hollering for ale. The would-be mourners cracked wise about what a tough old buzzard Thornalon was, how he was too ornery to die, and so on, and dispersed to their homes. Workers returned to the fields and the noise of children again filled the streets. Feeling he was able to get on with his own business, Thorngere left him that afternoon and took a long walk through town and along the lake, greeting old friends, commiserating with the loved ones of those gone, and being introduced to a whole new generation of children. Everywhere he went he felt he was treated with a new respect. It was not that he had ever been treated disrespectfully-even without being the chieftain's son, he was still a prime warrior and probably the largest man in the village-but now, as he spoke with elder after elder about convening a council for that evening, he sensed a greater deference. Yet it was not until the meeting itself that he realized why.

The Elders' Council consisted of about thirty men. They met in the Chieftain's Great Hall, sitting on benches along the walls. A large fire burned on a raised stone hearth in the center of the hall, at least some of the smoke escaping through a hole in the thatch above. Ale and honey cakes were served and while the men were settling, Thorngere paced nervously about the fire, gathering his thoughts. He hated speaking in public. Clearing his throat and raising his hands for silence, he was about to begin when the doors at the back of the hall-those leading into the private section of the house-were thrown open and Thornalon himself hobbled in, assisted by two attendants, and followed by a third carrying a large chair. A flurry of excited conversation broke out, followed by a ripple of applause as the old man took his seat by the fire. He was frail but held his head high and eyed the room like a game old cock.

"Father!" said Thorngere. "I am delighted you could make it."

"And why wouldn't I make it?" The old man snapped. "I'm still above ground, ain't I? You think I'm going to lay back there like a sack while you're out here scheming about succession?"

"Succession?"

"Aye, succession!" Thornalon sputtered. "You think I don't know what you've got planned? Well, I'm not dead yet and you'll not be talking about taking my place, or holding Council meetings without me for a good while!"

Along with the rest of the room, Thorngere was shocked into silence. Then he broke into a broad grin and bowed low before his father. "My father," he said, "and members of the Council, I most humbly ask your pardon for not making myself plain. It was not to discuss succession that I called this meeting. And I most certainly hope there will be no occasion to have a Council meeting without you, father, for a good long while."

There was another round of applause at this and the old man looked mollified but still petulant. "So, you wasn't going to talk about succession, eh?"

"No, father," Thorngere assured him. "Believe me, that's the last thing I want to do."

"Is that so. Well, who the hell do you think is going to succeed me? Answer me that, any of you!"

"Why," Thorngere stammered in the sudden silence of the room. "I never thought about it. I guess I always assumed my sister's husband..."

"That bandy-legged, fart-sniffing toady? Why, there's not a man in this room would follow him to a festival. No, the man who succeeds me has got to have brains, and balls enough to stand up for the interests of Thule. Who is that man going to be, that's what I ask?"

For a long moment, Thornalon glared about the room, the only sound the loud snapping of a log in the fire which sent a small shower of sparks onto the floor. Then he continued, "I say that man is you, Thorngere, and I defy any man in this room to tell me different!"

Far from defying, the men in the room began to applaud and cheer. Thorngere held up his hands for silence. "Father, I am honored that you have such confidence in me, but..."

"Good!" the old man interrupted. "It's settled, then."

Again, the room broke into cheers, and laughter, seeing the old man's design. Again, Thorngere held up his hands for silence, but someone began to chant, "Thorngere! Thorngere!" and they all took it up, and Thorngere stood there, his hands raised like a choir director, and looked around at all the faces in the room. They were faces he had known from his earliest days, faces that were old now but had once been young and strong. And

106

he thought of these faces as young boys, of himself as a young boy, chasing about the streets. He thought of the boys he had seen that day, in the same streets, and how they would one day become men. He thought of the lake, and the men in the fields, and the tall mountains circling the sky. And in a flash he thought of all the places he had wandered over the past twenty years, of all his longing and searching. And when his pleading hands were finally answered and the chanting died away, he looked for a long moment into the shadows that hovered above the rafters, and then into the crafty eyes of old Thornalon.

"All right," he said, "I accept. But," he continued, forestalling further applause, "you must understand that I am also oath-sworn to another and that if you accept me, you must also accept him."

This sobered the crowd immediately. It had been known for years, of course, that Thorngere was off fighting Fantar. It was also known that these fighters had coalesced around a claimant to the Everreigning line, and that they had recently scored some success with the conquest of Zagorbia. But even though it had also been rumored for years that Thorngere himself was a bastard of the old High King, his level of involvement with the resistance and the nature of any relationship he might have with this Valerian pretender were unknown. Suddenly, however, it appeared that these distant things might have a direct and immediate impact on their own fortunes and they listened carefully as Thorngere continued.

"But let me go back and tell you why I called this council," he said, "and let me start with a little history lesson. You all know something of Fantar's conquest of the old Valerian Empire, so I won't bore you by going over the details. But what I do want to stress is this one key fact: Fantar could have been stopped many times during his circuit of the Inland Sea, if-and I emphasize that word-IF the cities in his path had acted together. Now it is also true that he gained strength and momentum as he went, and perhaps there was a point where he became unstoppable, but what I say is still true: if cities like Palmeria and Bangorum and Durumkai had joined together and sent a combined army into the field against Fantar, he would be but an unpleasant memory today. But they did not. They were bickering at the time, these three great city-states, arguing over trade rights and tariffs. And Fantar-not being a fool-further poisoned the waters between them by sending operatives in to make false promises to the leaders, and to spread hateful rumors among the people. The result, of course, was that Bangorum sent only token force to support Palmeria, Durumkai refused utterly to support Bangorum, and all three fell separately. The cities were razed, the kings and leaders put to the sword, and their heads piled high outside the gates. Their skulls are still there today if any of you care to go look.

"But their story is not unique: it was repeated again, and again, and again until the entire Inland Sea became Fantar's private lake. You all know this.

And you also know that Thuringia is guilty of the same behavior, and that of all those original states, Thuringia is the only one Fantar has not crushed. Why this is, I do not know: some of our people may have been nice to him when he was a brigand in the hills after old Valerius banished him; or maybe he just hasn't gotten around to Thuringia yet-maybe our little escapades in the south have been keeping him too occupied. I don't know. But I do know-and you know, too-what peril you are in. Those mountains are not so high they cannot be crossed, and Thuringians can only hope they do not give Fantar a reason to cross them.

"But I do not want to belabor this, or try to frighten you. If you're not frightened already there is no help for you!" This drew a laugh from the council and some nervous shifting of seats. "What I want you to consider is why-why did the cities not join together? Why could they not put their differences aside? They were not at war with each other. Quite the contrary: there had been peace around the Inland Sea for generations. Nor were they so foolish as to believe Fantar's promises, nor so blind as to not see his intentions-especially after he had pulled the same stunt four or five times. So why?

"I believe I know why. I was in many of those cities and fought before their walls. Some of you here also came south to taste a battle or two, if I recall. There was an increasingly large band of us-refugees and survivors-that fell back before Fantar and fought him again and again. I was surely not privy to the high councils of these cities, but I know what our leaders counseled them, and I know what happened time and again. Those cities wanted help from their brethren, they asked for it, tried to negotiate terms. But the simple, stupid fact is they could never agree. Self-interest got in the way of the common good and there was nobody with sufficient authority to bring them to their senses.

"You see, Fantar was really smart in attacking Valeria first. The Empire had always been a loose federation of independent states, but Valeria and the person of the High King had always provided a centralizing authority. Just as Thornalon here always settles disputes among you, so disputes between the city-states of the Inland Sea were always settled by the High King. Without him, the whole thing fell apart. So now, the Inland Sea lives under the thumb of an incredibly cruel and corrupt tyrant, and Thuringia peeks over the mountains, hoping Fantar won't notice us."

Thorngere paused here and poured himself a mug of ale while the Council muttered among themselves. What Thorngere said was too true to argue, but his last remark had stung. Thornalon sat with his chin on his chest, apparently asleep.

"So what's to be done?" Thorngere resumed, his clear voice startling them back to attention. "As I see it, there are only three possibilities. One, you can do nothing. The Inland Sea will continue to suffer, and you can live in fear. Two, some other power can emerge and conquer Fantar, and who knows what will result? Thuringia may or may not be on his list, you may or may not be better off, or you will continue to live in fear. Three, you can rise up with the people, and free the Inland Sea. You can help rebuild the old Empire of independent states, retain your own freedom, and with a powerful ally to the south, live without fear.

"That's what thousands of men are doing in the south right now: rising up of their own free will, and throwing off the bonds of the tyrant. And how are they able to do it now when they could not before? Because the one ingredient that was missing then-the one thing that would have allowed Palmeria and Bangorum and Durumkai to act together-is back. The High King. Valerius Everreigning, High King of Valeria and all the Inland Sea.

"I know you have all heard talk of this Valerius, and many of you probably think he is just an imposter, some adventurer out to grab some glory. But he is real as sure as I stand before you. On that you have my oath and my life. I have fought beside this man and been his friend for twenty years. It was I who helped rescue him from the Hidden Valley of Kantar; I who helped him reclaim his name and the ancient power stone of the High King, The Eye of Valeria. Fantar pulled that stone from the headless corpse of the old Valerius and when he tried to use it, it burned out his eye because he is not the rightful High King. Yet Valerius uses it, and with his vision we defeated Fantar's naval forces and freed Dulcai, we defeated Fantar's army under Glaucon and liberated Kantar, we have taken Zagorbia. Believe me, Elders of Thule, Valerius is real. The High King has returned!

"And now, that word is spreading around the Inland Sea like fire. Daily, men and ships join us from all over the Inland sea-so many men we can no longer fit them inside the walls! And soon, very soon, this vast army will move against Fantar. And when it moves, it will be like an avalanche in the high mountains, picking up mass and speed and power as it goes, blasting asunder all who stand against it. We will be a force greater than Fantar ever dreamed, even at his height. And why? Because we are free men! We fight for our homes, our futures and ourselves.

"That is why I called this Council today, Thornalon," and at the sound of his name, the old one perked up. "I am oath sworn to Valerius, High King of Valeria. I am also a blood Chieftain of Thuringia, Atheling-and now if you will, High Chieftain-of Thule. As such, I call on the men of Thule, of all Thuringia, to take weapons and rise up with me, rise up with King Valerius Everreigning, King of the Eye, High King of Valeria and all the Inland Sea: Take Weapons and crush Fantar; rise up and be free!

Chapter 8
NORTH AND EAST

Men were moved by Thorngere's speech. Moved that night, and other nights as he tramped from village to village, region to region throughout Thuringia. And everywhere, men came forward, knelt to kiss the hilt of his sword, and swore their oath to Take Weapons and muster with him at Thorndale on the full of the next moon. But it was exhausting work: up at dawn for a full day's march-usually over a mountain-a late afternoon and early evening spent politicking with local leaders, the rousing bonfire speech at night, then the inevitable rounds of toasts and glad-handing which often lasted into the wee hours, only to be off with the next dawn to begin the process again. Only twice in the three weeks that followed, did Thorngere pass back through Thorndale to check on an increasingly vigorous Thornalon and to catch a few extra hours rest for himself.

But he was very encouraged with the response. More men came forward at night than would actually come to Thorndale on the day, of course, but even taking that into consideration, he felt he would easily muster four to five thousand, a larger force than had been gathered in Thuringia in memory. Apparently, his message struck home. Many, many men told him they had been watching events in the south with increasing concern, but had seen no opportunity to effect change. Now with the return of the King of the Eye-and with leaders like him, they flattered-they saw a real chance, and swore, at least, that they would be there in the fore to take advantage of it. How many men would still be "in the fore" when he reached Valeria was an open question (nor did he give any indication that Valeria was their destination) but for now, he was able to send messengers ahead to Gamlarch with a very optimistic report: he would join forces with him a week after the next new moon in the foothills of Dunlor, two days march northwest of Balac and an equal distance northeast of Valeria itself.

His recruiting tour completed with several days to spare, Thorngere returned home to tackle some of the more mundane chores of his new Chieftainship that Thornalon had been unable to attend to during his illness. It was also clear that Thornalon had no intention of resuming full duties, whatever the state of his health, and Thorngere needed to find an able steward who could act in his absence. It was under the pretext of arranging an interview with such a man that his mother began to ply her oar in the waters of his fate.

Panella had invited Baneluc and his wife for dinner, she announced to him in passing one afternoon. Baneluc was an old family friend-Thorngere remembered him as a gangly, acne-faced teenager when he was a boy-and his mother allowed that he might make a suitable candidate. Thorngere would have preferred a more business-like approach to such an interview, but dinner had to be eaten in any event, and if this man did turn out to be a suitable candidate, a strong personal tie with his family would be an added plus.

As it turned out, it would have been hard to find a less suitable candidate than Baneluc. Still gangly, though now well into his middle years and with a long, horsy face deeply pocked and scarred from that ancient travail, he was as simpering and silly a man as Thorngere had ever met. And his wife, a pudgy thing with cheeks as round and red as apples and teeth bucked out like she had just eaten them, was just as bad. They brought their daughter with them-which Thorngere also thought strange for an occasion that was ostensibly business related-and spent the entire dinner bragging about the list of suitors she had acquired and the vast extent of their own wealth. The man had never considered seeking a place on the Elders' Council, knew virtually nothing of the affairs of Thorndale or Thule, aside from those that directly concerned his own pocket, and had the physical presence of a whipped dog. It had been Thorngere's initial intention to take the man aside after dinner to discuss the Stewardship in more detail, but he discarded that notion before the main course was served, and excused himself before the cordials, pleading a prior engagement.

That engagement involved a couple mugs of strong ale at the tavern in town with his captain, Boltar, and lasted until he was sure Baneluc and his boring brood were gone. But his mother was waiting up for him in the sitting room when he returned and plainly wanted to talk.

"So," she said, motioning him to a seat next to hers, "what did you think?"

"I'm sorry, mother, but I do not believe he could command the respect of the Council and without that..."

"I don't mean that simpering wattle," she said. "I mean about the girl, Sasha."

"Sasha?" Thorngere gave his mother an uncomprehending look, and then slowly, the light dawned. "Oh, mother," he smiled, patting her hand, "from what I heard, she has suitors enough without me. Besides, she's just a child."

"She's the same age I was when I married Thornalon. And you're already older than he was then."

"Really? Well, I appreciate the thought-really-but..."

"Baneluc is very wealthy."

"Yes, I recall hearing something about that. But really, mother, she's just not my type."

"What is your type?"

"My type?" Suddenly it seemed very warm in the room and Thorngere wanted out. "Oh, I don't know," he dissembled. "I guess I'll know her when I meet her." It sounded lame.

"Thorngere," his mother said, gripping his hand, "look at me. I am your mother. I nursed you when you were a babe. I know you. I know that your heart is sad. I can see the pain in you. There was a woman, wasn't there?"

"Yes, mother, there was."

"Did she die?"

Thorngere drew in a deep breath and exhaled sharply, knocking the candle flame out of kilter and shattering the room's soft light with dancing shadows. "She might as well have."

"Another man?"

Pain lanced through him as keen as a blade and he could see it reflected in his mother's eyes. "Not as you think."

She waited, gripping his hand, watching him. The pain swelled up inside him, filled his chest like an air bladder and constricted his throat so that for a moment he could neither breathe nor talk. Tears filled his eyes and his limbs trembled. For an instant he almost succumbed, like that little boy whose tears his mother used to soothe. But as quickly, a vast anger flared up in him like a battle rage. He leapt from the chair needing to strike, and reared back his arm to smash at the wall. But he held his fist, trembling, and spun on his mother, his face contorted, his eyes burning with accusation.

"No, not as you think, mother," he hissed. "Not as you think. It's worse than that. Much worse. She's Valerius' sister!"

Now it was Panella's turn to reel from an emotional blow. As if physically struck, her body hurled itself back in the chair, her arms, which had reached out, following Thorngere as he leapt across the room, now fell lifeless in her lap. Her eyes stared wide and her mouth fell open. But no words came out, only a stunned silence.

"That's right, mother," he hissed again, "my sister!" And he spun on his heel and stalked out of the house.

It was near midnight when the rage quieted and he stopped climbing. He was high in the hills south of the town, and was surprised to find himself on the shoulder of a high meadow where he often used to play as a boy. From the verge, he could look out over the entire valley with the lake and the town nestled far below. He used to squint his eyes and imagine the bristly town as a caterpillar curled around a dewdrop lake, and he sat on the same rock now, recalling those distant days. But another face kept thrusting itself into his thoughts, and beside it those days, and the lake, and the town, and the valley itself seemed hollow and bare.

More than a thousand miles to the south and east, the harbor at Palmeria opened like a huge basket into which, over the centuries, had dropped the lion's share of Inland Sea trade. Protected by an island just offshore to the west, and a rocky headland to the south, the harbor offered a sheltered basin some two miles long and nearly a mile wide. Along the shore, stone jetties had spread over the years until nearly the entire length bristled with finger piers. Hundreds of ships could dock at a time in Palmeria, and in good times, many more were building on the ways that dotted the shore. This kept its many warehouses and market squares overflowing with goods and its merchant princes awash in gold. If Valeria bore the crown of the

Empire, Palmeria bore the crown of commerce. It had been this way since the beginning.

But the harbor that opened before Vahla was very unlike the harbor of old, and the city, which towered above it very unlike those gilded towers of legend. Like Valeria, Fantar had sacked and burned Palmeria in the second year of his reign. Unlike Valeria, he had expended little effort to rebuild anything but its essential shipyards. Resentful of wealth more than power, he had slaughtered its chief merchant families, sanctioned all trade, and tried to starve the city out of existence. For years its blackened timbers and crumbled walls had stood out above an empty harbor like ancient ruins.

But cities are like infections. They take root in places and grow, often without direction or control. They are a natural confluence of the human tide and will erupt so long as there are men. Those forces of trade and habitation that originally shaped Palmeria were still active. A merchant from the south with a cargo of grain had to land someplace, and Palmeria was still the safest harbor. A shepherd from the north who sought to sell his wool had to take it someplace, and Palmeria was still the best market. And someone had to unload that grain, and factor the wool, and feed the workers, and house the cooks, and so over the years, as Fantar's power grew and his attention drifted, and as those he placed in charge of quelling the city sought to make it just a bit more comfortable for themselves, and as those who helped them sought further and further afield for goods, the city began again to grow.

In recent years, with the succession of a new viceroy, and the need for ships to control the empire, all remaining restraint had been cast aside, and the city Vahla saw as her ship entered the crowded harbor and pulled towards one of the piers was like a huge construction site, swarming with activity both in the many shipyards along the shore and in the city itself. Young Asperides had different notions than his master, Fantar, about what constituted glory for the empire-and for himself-and having inherited wealth measured in tons from his father (it was ostensibly Fantar's Treasury), he had set about making a place for his name.

Vahla's ship docked at a pier near the southern edge of town and with the captain's sincere good wishes (he had been very solicitous during the voyage) her small entourage disembarked and made its way through the bustling streets to a house which had been pre-arranged for her by Bokmar. He had been helpful in other ways, too, finding her a handmaiden who could be trusted should she overhear something she shouldn't, augmenting the modest store of coins she had brought from Volkmir's lair with a portion-a commission, he called it-from Owen's gift to the Oracle, and providing her with the names of several people in Palmeria who might be useful should the need arise. The numerous trunks and now rather extensive wardrobe, Vahla had arranged for herself.

Bokmar had also filled her in on what little was known about Asperides, and helped her work through her plan. Asperides, he said, was ambitious-

a fact that was plainly obvious to anyone visiting the city-and not unconditionally loyal to Fantar. He ruled in Fantar's name, of course, and paid due public homage, but it was believed he saw himself more as Fantar's successor than as his servant. The son of Armagon, one of Fantar's most successful generals, and the first member of the second generation of Fantar's elite to take power, it was known that he was highly favored at Valeria-else Fantar would not look the other way while Palmeria was being rebuilt-and it was believed he was being given his head to see what he could do. Fantar himself was without offspring and it was rumored that the idea of adopting Asperides had been discussed. But it was also rumored that Asperides might find this route too slow, that he abhorred the cruelty and brutality of Fantar's rule, and sympathized with the ideals of the old order.

In sum, said Bokmar, the man was an enigma: highly capable and intriguingly disaffected, yet as dangerous as an adder.

Thus, worried that the name 'Vahla' might still be associated with the attempted murder of Fantar, they decided she would travel under the name of Vauhna. For those who might ask, she was a sorceress-which allowed her to travel with relative impunity-who had come to Palmeria to visit an ancient shrine in the mountains east of the city. Her only real concern now was how to arrange an audience with Asperides and, assuming that could be done, how she could sound him out about Valerius without losing her own head. But she was not at the house more than an hour before the first of those problems was solved by the appearance of a messenger with an invitation from the Viceroy-Asperides himself-for later that afternoon.

If Asperides had spent freely to rejuvenate the city, he had been positively lavish in the restoration of the ancient palace, and Vahla was impressed not only with the extent of the construction and quality of the work, but also with the evident taste with which Asperides had decorated: no ostentation reigned here, but a simple elegance. Rather than gaudy bouquets in the antechamber to which she was shown, a single flower graced a table, resting in a slim, long-necked vase. And rather that an entire pallet of colors jarring the walls, simple whites and blues predominated, with here and there, murals on quiet, pastoral themes. It was, Vahla had to admit, regal. And that was strange, considering its creator was but the scion of a brigand.

It was also, Vahla noted, in keeping with her own appearance. She wanted to look stern but alluring, and after consultation with her maid and Chad (who, curiously, had definite opinions on the subject) she had chosen a white silk gown with a light blue sash, finished by a stunning, but elegantly simple blue robe. For jewelry, she chose an embroidered gold necklace inset with a single opal, and matching earrings. Her hair was worn up, piled regally on her head and held in place with golden combs set like a crown.

And despite the fact that her palms were sweaty and her stomach all-aflutter, when she was shown into Asperides' presence, she could see from his eyes that she had chosen well. He arose as she curtsied and bowed in return. "They did not exaggerate when they said an Enchantress had come to grace our city," he said, taking her hand and bringing it lightly to his lips. "I am charmed."

He was a well-favored young man of middle height, with honey blond hair that curled about his ears, and watery blue eyes that gave his expression a distant, impersonal look. Perhaps five years Vahla's senior, he had the easy assurance of one who is seldom contradicted, and a quick, ready smile which he flashed broadly as Vahla replied, "They did not waste any time bringing you the news, your Highness."

"I have many sources of information. Besides, news that the Oracle of Fantar had arrived would not be delayed in any case-not by any who value their skins."

"You overrate me, your Highness, I am not the 'Oracle of Fantar.'"

"Indeed?" he said, raising an eyebrow. "But come," and he led her to a shady, inner courtyard where several cushioned chairs and a small couch surrounded a low table. He motioned for Vahla to sit in one of the chairs and sat on the couch next to it. Waving away the servant, he poured wine for them both with his own hand. "So, I have been misinformed, then: it was not you who pronounced doom upon our revered Emperor?"

"It was the Oracle, your Highness. I was but the vessel."

"I see. And a lovely vessel you are," he said, toasting her with his glass. "But tell me-you are not an initiate of the Oracle, am I correct? How did you manage to insinuate yourself as 'the vessel'?"

Vahla's heart began to hammer in her chest, but she met his gaze steadily. "Do you doubt the veracity of the Oracle?"

"No, indeed I do not! And I salute you: from what I heard, yours was the most genuine Oracle to come from Cartho in some time. I can't wait to hear what the old bugger makes of it."

Now Vahla smiled demurely and touched her glass to his. They sipped and probed each other's eyes over the rims. Asperides wore a slight smirk, as if he knew the punch line of a joke and was just waiting to ruin the teller's moment. "But I also hear that oracle making is not the least of your talents."

"Is that so, my lord?" Vahla was coy in return.

"Yes. I heard that a woman meeting your description-a sorceress of some repute, I am told-appeared in the shape of the horned god and reaped considerable havoc on one wing of Vincipius' army outside Zagorbia. Can I assume that was you, too?" Asperides gaze was level and steady now, but the light blue of his eyes was like a mist, hiding his intent.

"I may have passed that way, your Highness. But you know how rumors are."

"So, not an entire wing of the army?"

"Hardly, my lord."

"And the shape of the horned god?"

"Your Highness, sometimes it is better not to question what the gods give others to see."

"Indeed?" said Asperides, raising his brow. "I will bear that in mind. But you are a sorceress."

"I prefer the term Enchantress."

"There we are in perfect agreement! But tell me now-Vauhna, is it? If this question is not too presumptuous, to what do we owe the honor of your visit to Palmeria?"

"I am come to visit the Shrine at Darlung, my lord."

"The Shrine?"

"At Darlung. Your Highness is not familiar with it?"

"You must forgive me: I was not raised in the old beliefs."

"Of course. I'm sorry. It was at Darlung that the old Empire was established. You have not heard the story?"

"No, indeed. But please, go on."

"The plains of Darlung are at the base of an ancient volcano, and according to legend, this is the site where ancient Valeria and Palmeria struck the deal to forge the Empire. Palmeria had the Valerian army surrounded when the original Valerius came forward and said there would be no battle between the two cities, that their interests were too alike for them to fight: Palmeria had the wealth and trade, Valeria the favor of the Gods. Thus, they should form a partnership and rule the Inland Sea: Valerius would be High King, providing power and vision, while Palmeria would provide for the needs of this world with trade and commerce. 'Ha,' said the Palmerians. 'What power do you have? You are surrounded. And why should we make you High King when we clearly have the upper hand here? Valeria is nothing compared to Palmeria.'

'Why?' Valerius repeated? 'Because I know what will be,' and he showed them the great Eye of Valeria on his chest. But they would not believe, so Valerius said, 'Look up at yonder mountain. Before the sun sets today the Gods will show you a sign,' whereupon, he went back to his tent. The Palmerians did not dare attack that day, and sure enough, just as the sun was about to dip below the horizon, at the last possible second, the mountain erupted in fire and thunder. Twin streams of fiery lava poured down the mountain, encircling both armies, and in the morning, the Palmerians knelt before Valerius as High King."

"A very charming story, Vauhna the Enchantress. But the gods must surely have changed their minds since: why else would Valeria have fallen?"

"Why else indeed? Perhaps the High Kings needed to be reminded of their duty."

"Or, perhaps it's time for a new order."

"Fantar's?"

"Or another."

"There already is another."

"The Pretender Valerius?"

"He does not pretend, your Highness. And he has already reclaimed the Eye."

126

"Then am I to assume you are allied with this Valerius?"

"People in my business who ally themselves with temporal powers tend not to survive very long."

"Then why is it that you go to the Plains of Darlung?"

"I am a vessel, your Highness," said Vahla. "I go to place myself at the hands of the master."

Asperides raised an inquisitive eyebrow and sipped his wine. "Meaning?"

"All the signs portend great changes, your Highness. I did not make up Fantar's Oracle: I merely delivered it. His time is drawing short. Valerius is rising, but he is besieged in Zagorbia. I go to seek the gods will."

"And if the gods have something else in mind altogether?"

"That would be most interesting, indeed, your Highness," said Vahla archly, and held out her glass for more wine.

"I see," Asperides replied, pouring. "Well, if it is the gods' will you seek, I suppose the least we can do is help."

Chapter 9
THE ROAD SOUTH

Within the week, the valley of Thorndale began to fill with all manner of tents and shelters as the promised musters started to roll in, and Thorngere was soon buried in the chaos of organizing an army and planning a campaign. Turnout was even better than he had hoped, and soon even the hillsides were flowering with habitation. And problems, for men simply trooped in and set up camp, giving no thought to their fellows, or to fuel supplies, or even to basic sanitation. Thorngere appointed marshals to try and keep lanes between the groups (and to keep the Gordevians from defecating beside the Tortulians' campfires and the Burgundians from tramping through the Palomians' cooking area on their way to fetch water) but the men were little inclined to take instruction from any but their own leaders, and it often required Thorngere's personal presence to settle petty disputes. This problem went all the way up the chain of command as well, for each group commander considered himself Thorngere's personal choice for second in command, and there were many ruffled feelings before an effective command structure was finally hammered into place. Then there were the feuds and disputes between groups, some of which had been going on for generations. The Lambarians, for example, inadvertently set up camp directly beside their archenemies the Colophians one afternoon while the latter were off drilling. Serious fighting erupted when the two discovered each other, and Thorngere even suffered a slight cut on his arm while trying to separate them.

But these were minor difficulties compared to the problems of logistics. Inconceivable as it seemed, entire villages of men, under supposedly seasoned leaders, marched off for a campaign of unknown duration, without having packed anything more than a lunch! Sensible men would take more provision on an afternoon's hunt than some of these brought to march off to war. Some even arrived hungry. And they had to be fed, of course-fed regularly, and in increasingly enormous quantities. Most were armed after a fashion, fortunately-for given the time and resources available, there was no way Thorngere was going to come up with swords or spears in any quantity-and most did have sufficient clothing and camp gear, but food and the cartage to haul it south remained a difficulty.

Time for training was another problem that could not be solved. There was simply no time to teach these men how to fight as a unit. Those who had any kind of experience at all (and there were several hundred who had spent time fighting in the south) were given rank of some kind and told to begin drilling the troops in their units, but overall, the army grew like a mob and moved like a herd. And trying to command them, someone quipped, was like raking water.

But time was also a blessing in a way: because there was no time, they could not eat up food they didn't have; because there was no time, petty squabbles could not fester into serious disputes; and because there was no time, the army had to march, ready or not, and the knowledge of that seemed somehow to seep through the ranks and imbued all with a spirit, if not of cooperation, at least of adventure.

But as time moved inexorably on, Thorngere felt increasingly less adventurous and more harried. He had been in senior positions any number of times, but this was the first time he had sole command of a significant enterprise, and he quickly began to realize the truth behind all the old cliches about the 'burden of command' and the 'loneliness at the top.' It was not the magnitude of the decisions he had to make that got to him-after all, the weight of nations did not depend on whether the Burgundians drew water from the upper stream or the lower-but the sheer volume of them. As a command advisor, he had ventured opinions on various topics whenever he felt inclined or qualified to do so. As commander, he was required to have not just opinions, but rulings on all manner of things whether he knew anything about them or not. And while it was all well and good to "take counsel" in matters where he knew nothing at all, there were simply too many matters and not enough of either good counsel or time to take it. Decisions had to be made. The ones he made right were accepted as a matter of course and instantly forgotten, while the ones he made wrong-and there were one or two-rankled and abraded on the common consciousness like boils. He was, for example, rated a total idiot and command disaster by the Palomians for siding with the Burgundians, who, now that they had been ordered by Thorngere himself to draw water from the lower stream, felt they had an absolute duty to tramp through their neighbor's cooking area.

But again, time was an ally in limiting absolutely the number of possible decisions-good or bad-he could make, even though his growing horde did everything they could to extend the time he had to spend making them. In short, he was getting very little sleep, and when he did get the chance, a thousand details plagued his dreams. It was all well and good to delegate, but he quickly learned that if he did not question every detail, it would be lost. Besides, the notion of delegation had always conveyed to him a sense of emptying out, a relieving of responsibility; now he saw it as a filling up, an attempt to stem a flood tide, and it carried with it a sense of drowning.

But the valley did fill up with men, the storage bins did fill up with grain, the men were kept more or less filled with food, and the baggage park filled with all manner of carts and oxen. Leaders were chosen, and men assembled near them, a functional command structure appeared to evolve, and in a very little amount of time, really, since the first small contingent came marching in, Thorngere had an army-an army of nearly 8,000, if you counted camp followers and hangers on, and an army that was ready to march (or at least as ready to march as they were to remain, locust-like, in the valley of Thorndale!) a full day ahead of schedule.

That's when Thorngere got word that Thornalon had dropped dead.

He had been doing so well, people forgot he had been sick. In fact, he was getting ready to join Thorngere on the first part of his march that morning. But, Panella said, when he stood up from tying his sandals, he put his hand to his chest and said, "that's funny," and fell over dead. Just like that.

There was no question of marching that day, of course. Such a death was too ominous. But neither was there time for the normal three days of waking. Instead, Thorngere hoped the quantity of mourners would make up for the quality of the wake, and had Thornalon set on his pyre late that same afternoon before the entire assembled host. He himself felt very little reaction. Harried from all the frenzy of organizing, bleary from a lack of sleep, and wracked with anxiety over the enormity of his undertaking, the shock of Thornalon's death just refused to register. When an overloaded wagon bed is already resting on its axles, throwing something else aboard will have no effect on the springs. Thorngere felt so flattened, and his father's death was just one more thing he had to deal with. But he knew he would react later.

And that was probably just as well under the circumstances, for he was able to deliver a highly acceptable, perfectly public eulogy without batting an eye. Had circumstances been otherwise, he would have agonized over the words, not knowing what to say, and not done nearly so good a job at it.

As it was, Thornalon had his praises sung in a most clear and articulate battlefield voice, and had his life commemorated in the largest and most spectacular funeral ever held in all Thuringia. If these things matter at all to the spirit, Thornalon's rose happy as the heat from the flames bore it off to the heavens.

That evening, Thorngere had a quiet supper with his mother and sister's family. It was a somber affair. No one had much appetite, and for once even his sister Brendel's kids were quiet and well behaved. Panella looked like a waxen figure, sitting through the meal without touching her plate. Brendel and her husband sat across from her, staring down at their plates and only picking at their food. Thorngere sat at the head of the table and felt awkward. He was the acknowledged master of the house now, but still a foreign presence in it. And he was now the official High Chieftain of Thule, but would be leaving before he even commenced his duties. Daneloc, Brendel's husband, made several attempts at conversation-asking Thorngere questions about the army and the campaign-but it was plain he cared little about the answers, and his questions only highlighted the fact that he was not coming along. Thorngere's terse responses were each followed by an embarrassed silence, and when Brendel excused herself to put the children to bed, Daneloc scurried off with her, seeming quite relieved.

The servants cleared the table and poured Thorngere and Panella more wine. As they left, a silence as sentient as light filled the room.

Thorngere had barely spoken to his mother since the night he had blown up at her. He was quite sorry-it was, after all, hardly fair to blame her for his unfortunate romantic entanglements-but the subject was still too painful for him to want it brought up again, so he had avoided her. Now he didn't know what to say and felt incapable of consoling her.

Nevertheless, he cleared his throat, determined to try. But she forestalled him and laid her hand on his arm. "Thorngere," she said, her face suddenly coming alive, "there is something we must speak of."

"Now?" The urgency in her voice startled him.

"Yes, it's something you must know. I never thought so-in fact, I thought I was doing you a kindness-but I know now I was wrong. You are your own man and would have achieved greatness in any event, without my lies."

"Lies? Mother, what are you talking about?"

"I loved your father, Thorngere-Thornalon, I mean-and honored him his life long. He knew I was with child when he married me, but he accepted me and raised you as his own, and never one word of reproach did I ever hear from him."

"Well, of course, you were bearing the High King's child. How could anyone...?" But again she forestalled him with a raised palm.

"No, let me finish. That's just the point, you see. That was just a convenient excuse, a cover. But now you need to know. Thorngere, you need fear no sin with this woman: King Valerius was not your father."

"Not my father?"

"No, it was not the High King at all. He had the reputation as a ladies man-that's what made it so easy-but he never cast a glance at me. So, you see, you may pursue this lady as you will. There is no barrier, no taboo!"

Thorngere was too stunned to react. Or, his emotions were so conflicted there was no net result. Either way, he sat stupefied. His mother had lied to him for his whole life? He was not of royal birth? Valerius was not his brother? Vahla not his sister? It was too much to absorb.

"Who then?" he managed at last. "Who is my father? Who am I, mother?"

Panella seemed to gain composure from Thorngere's distress. She felt relieved of her great burden for the first time in years and knew that once the impact had settled in her son's mind, he would be happier for it. He did not need to be born royal: he was royal. Now, he would be free to pursue the great love of his life: love she had been denied. Smiling softly, she shook her head as the distant memory of a young man rose before her.

"He was just a nobody, a troubadour attached to the King's court. But he was so handsome, Thorngere! You favor him so it catches in my throat to look at you sometimes. But I was just young and foolish. I thought he would take me away with him, take me back to Valeria to live at court. I thought I would be a great lady," and here her voice began to break and she wrung her hands. "But then the King was gone, and all his entourage with him, and I was alone. I don't know that I was ever anything at all to him, just a passing fancy. And then, when Thornalon began to take an interest and I found I was with child... well it just seemed so easy to blame the High King."

"Did you know his name, mother?" Thorngere asked gently.

"Yes," she whispered, rocking back and forth softly now, seeking comfort. "His name was Bartholm-'Bartholm, the Bard.' He had such a voice, Thorngere," she said, looking up, her eyes swimming with tears. "You should have heard how he could sing!"

The next day, as a warm summer sun rose over the mountains, the first ever army of Thuringia took up the march and headed for the high southern passes to Valeria. At its head rode a massive warrior, resplendent in silver and burnished steel, and wearing the rich, russet cloak of the High Chieftain of Thule. He carried his helm with its red plume in the crook of his left arm, and let his long golden hair float free in the bright light of the new day. Thorngere was as happy as he could ever remember, and the mountains that soared around him soared no higher than his heart and not nearly so high as his hopes. For Vahla was not his sister.

But they were not five miles out when the messenger he had sent to Gamlarch returned with the news that Valerius was besieged and under heavy attack in Zagorbia.

Chapter 10
AT THE BATTLEMENTS

The same sun found Valerius on his battlements, looking out over the previous day's carnage and awaiting a fresh attack. In place of Thuringia's fresh mountain air, the atmosphere around Zagorbia was thick with the cloying scent of blood and excrement-which would soon putrefy-and in the narrow fields outside the walls, he could read the tale of the previous day's assault as if it were a scroll. It had been a near thing. Vincipius was proving to be a stubborn, resourceful enemy and Valerius was an increasingly angry and frustrated man.

It was Vincipius' first full scale assault and he had taken the time to prepare well for it. For weeks he had kept up a series of light, probing attacks designed to test the city's defenses and lull Valerius and company into a false sense of security. He had employed some catapults to try and batter the walls (and to hurl decomposing bodies into the city to break down morale); had set a series of fires along the wall to drive the defenders away while he attacked with siege ladders; had tried a series of night attacks; and had even sent a token naval force around to try the harbor's defenses. All these were unsuccessful, but while Valerius sensed they were not total efforts, he was not able to determine the size of the force against him. When he had sortied, for example, instead of the enemy reinforcing its position or flanking him, they had been too quickly driven off. And the galleys that tested the harbor did not even seriously engage. That had been such an obvious feint that Valerius had reinforced his walls instead of the waterfront, sure that a landward assault would be coordinated with it.

But Vincipius was making his preparations. While he employed five catapults, he was preparing fifty. And while he knew that a few large stones or fires would hardly break down the walls or cow the defenders of Zagorbia, he conceived that a concentrated barrage using all of these tactics might do the trick. So while he kept Valerius occupied with one hand, he was busy in the background with the other.

Deep in the swamps, out of sight even from the highest sections of Zagorbia's walls, he was erecting not one, but three wheeled towers. These were massive things with several fighting platforms, heavily planked on three sides, and with long drawbridges that could drop down onto Zagorbia's walls even as archers above rained death down onto the defenders. And to get them to the city, he built a wide, corduroy road. From dawn till past dark, thousands of men carried rock and baskets of dirt to fill in a path through the swamp. Others felled trees and built twin log embankments to keep their work from washing away. Others smoothed and graded, while others still-working long grueling shifts-used heavy logs with flattened ends to tamp down and harden the surface so it could carry its intended load.

As the work neared the city it was noticed by the defenders, of course. But they thought it was just part of his general excavation plan, for at the same time, Vincipius was working under archery fire from the walls to fill in several swampy areas so he could have more room to form his troops for an assault. "Industrious fellow," Ragnar had commented one afternoon, as he and Valerius watched dual lines of warriors-one carrying a large shield and the other a basket of dirt-file in and fill, "if he doesn't have a battlefield, he makes one."

That they were doing more than making ground became apparent early on the morning of the assault when specially designed barges, loaded with catapults and rocks, were poled through the swamps and neatly docked at prearranged spots. Mounted on skids, the catapults were quickly slid ashore and started firing, while the barges went back to the quarries inland for more ammunition. Valerius sortied quickly, hoping to destroy the catapults before Vincipius could bring up support troops. He also thought to use Vincipius' newly made solid ground against him, reasoning that if it was good enough to form a massive attack, it could equally well support a massive defense, and that by taking the best ground, he would have Vincipius at a disadvantage.

This was the first part of the tale Valerius was able to read by the position of the dead as he overlooked the field. It had been a good idea, but from this perspective on the morning after, it was clear why it had failed: in terms of fluid mechanics, it came down to flow rates. Valerius had three sally ports and a small gate along the southern walls. The ports would allow men to exit in single file, while the gate was wide enough for a file of four men abreast. If it took each man a second to pass through, Valerius could thus put men in the field at a rate of seven per second. But with the addition of the new road, and by ferrying men in by barge as well, Vincipius-who had clearly thought this through beforehand-was able to field men at twice that rate. Not only did Valerius fail to destroy the catapults, he was quickly overwhelmed and driven back behind his walls with considerable loss.

It also became quickly apparent that this assault was not another feint, and that with all his men amassed at last, Vincipius clearly outnumbered the defenders. But he did not attack immediately. He let the massed catapults shower the defenders with rocks, while regular archers wafted in flight after flight of arrows. Then, when the barges returned with fresh ammunition, short logs that had been smeared with pitch were set alight and lofted into the city. This attack went on for over an hour, while from deep in the swamp, hundreds of men toiled away on long ropes, hauling up the siege towers.

There was one unexpected calamity: the weight of the first two towers weakened one section of the road and when the third passed over, the road gave way and the tower toppled into the swamp. But this only made more men available to haul the other two, and when the defenders saw them lurching into view, they knew they would either have to bring

140

them down, or die, for if Vincipius breached their walls, there would be no quarter and no mercy.

Valerius was not without machinery of his own, and he employed it now as these towers lumbered into position. With rocks falling on the city like hailstones, there was no shortage of ammunition for his catapults and Valerius soon had them all concentrate on these stalking monoliths, a man on the walls acting as a spotter for each. Soon a hail of boulders was falling on them, but while quite a number of haulers were smashed and maimed-Valerius could see their squashed remains along the rutted wheel tracks of the towers even now-those few boulders that struck the towers were not sufficient to topple or seriously damage them. On they came, skirting the periphery of the field, then turning and advancing straight on the city itself.

This was the signal for the main assault as well. The main battle lines formed around the towers, the men in front forming shield walls two-high, and the men behind holding their shields above their heads. Still, as they neared, archers on the walls were able to do considerable slaughter, while Valerius' catapults were also able to score with increasing frequency, often smashing through the protective planking. One hit was nearly successful early on. A rock the size of a man's head smashed into some poor fellow right in front of the left hand tower, driving his mangled corpse and itself in under the front, left hand wheel. The tower drove up onto this obstruction and tilted alarmingly before it shuddered and dropped back, dead in its tracks. At that moment, too-perhaps as a result of the added strain-one of the hauling lines parted, sending an entire file of men sprawling and knocking the protective shield wall awry. An instant shower of arrows dealt much death before they were able to re-form, and many who fell never rose. Still, the interruption in the tower's progress was temporary. In moments the rope was retied, the rock and remains scooped out from under the wheel, and the thing lurched onwards.

Valerius tried two other things while the towers advanced, and the remains of these efforts he could also detect among the slain. The left-hand tower he tried to set afire with flaming arrows, while against the right-the one nearest the gate-he personally led a sortie of strong men with battle axes, hoping to topple it.

The fire arrows were futile. Vincipius had foreseen that response, obviously, and having no shortage of water near at hand, had stationed men with buckets high in each tower and detailed other's to keep them supplied. Those arrows that stuck were quickly doused, and soon the entire front of the structure was so soaked it would not light anyway.

Valerius had somewhat better luck, but it cost him several friends and nearly cost him his head. Burmac was an old friend from his soldiering days, from before he was able to reclaim the Eye Stone and his name. He was a burly fellow, nearly Valerius' height but even broader in the shoulders and hips. Burmac was the only one who could out-wrestle Valerius-'Balazar' in those days-and in battle he was a sheer terror. But when Balazar, Thorngere, Grumwald and the rest took to the sea after being routed from Zagorbia the first time, Burmac had quietly returned to his home and farm near Balac and hid his sword in the loft. When he heard from Gamlarch that Valerius had returned and that he was none other than his old friend, Balazar, he pulled his sword down, gathered a few friends as hardy as himself, and made his way back to Zagorbia. It was this group who approached Valerius, axes in hand, and suggested a sortie against the tower. And because it was Burmac, Valerius insisted on leading them himself.

As the gates were yanked open, a file of archers cleared an initial path, then this group, with Valerius and Burmac in the lead, charged headlong. There were only about twenty of them, but with Burmac wielding a huge double-bladed axe, and Valerius his great butcher's falchion, the enemy leapt from their path as if they had been scalded. Only the general press of opposing troops forced any contact at all and the group soon hewed through these and was among the haulers at the tower. Quickly, they formed around Burmac and another man as they began chopping away at the front axle.

But Vincipius' troops were not to be pushed aside so lightly, and once they had recovered from their initial surprise, they pressed heavily on the small group, while archers began picking them off from above. Valerius even had an arrow glance directly off his helm before another man stepped in behind him and covered them both with his shield.

Then the man chopping with Burmac was brought down by a spear thrown from the stairwell above and Valerius realized they would not have time to cut the axle before they themselves were cut down. Grabbing the fallen man's axe, he leapt to the outside of the wheel and quickly chopped away the wooden retaining pin. Then with a great heave, he and Burmac yanked the wheel loose and the corner of the tower smashed to the earth with a huge crash and grinding of timber.

Everyone leapt away, trying to get out from under the tower, then froze for a few seconds, waiting for it to collapse. But it didn't. It just sat there. And when Vincipius' men realized it was not going to fall, their anger flared and they attacked Valerius' disheartened group with sudden fury.

Valerius and Burmac's dwindling crew formed into a tight circle and began hacking their way back towards the gate, but the press around them was very great. One after another, they began to fall. Only another sortie from the gate opened a path and saved them. Valerius and Burmac were the last ones back inside but even then, as the gates were being pushed together and just as Burmac turned his back, a spear hurled from outside flashed between the two portals and buried its head into the back of his neck. His spinal cord severed, Burmac collapsed in a heap, dead before his head hit the ground. And within twenty minutes, Vincipius' men had jacked up the tower, remounted the wheel and re-launched their assault.

The final attack was horrific. Just as the towers were about to lower their long drawbridges, the catapults on the periphery began launching large bundles of burning sticks into the city. The smoke from these hung over the walls, choking men and stinging their eyes. Then, when the press about the closing towers was greatest, several hundred men broke from the woods carrying siege ladders. These went up as the tower bridges crashed down, and in instants, attacker and defender fought hand to hand all along the wall.

It was a near thing. As fast as the men on the walls pushed the ladders over, the men on the ground put them back up. And when the men on top tried to pull them up, those on the ground held them back. Then Vincipius brought archers up. They were able to drive the defenders back from the ladders just long enough for the attackers to mount, and soon little pockets of enemy fighters established themselves on the very walls.

Around the towers fighting was even fiercer with the press so tight around the bridges that men could not even raise their weapons. They just shoved, or even bit, while those behind them reached over their heads and prodded with swords and spears. And the noise was like the tortured screaming of some great beast; not single sounds but a huge moaning like the roar of a gale at sea.

Valerius had a few moments of sober reflection after his escapade at the tower. Not one, but several of his leaders lost their tempers at his narrow escape and told him-in very strongly worded language-that

145

that was not the kind of thing he should be doing; that if he died, they would all surely follow. Ragnar was especially furious and in the midst of a heated exchange, actually fell to his knees and begged forgiveness when he suddenly realized he had called his High King a "stupid bastard"-not the kind of thing one should call the heir to a thousand-year line.

So Valerius stayed clear of the heaviest fighting, climbing instead to a higher part of the wall and directing the defense from there. And it was this that finally saved the day, for seeing how desperate the battle along the walls and around the towers was getting, he finally called in his last reserves. All along, he had been expecting Vincipius to attack from the sea as well and had stationed a strong contingent along the waterfront to meet this expected move. But with the walls fully enveloped and no enemy galleys in sight, he released these troops who clambered up the ramparts and smashed into the attackers in a fresh wave. The pockets forming around the ladders were hurled bodily off the walls and their ladders smashed by rocks from above. Long lines were hurled around the tower uprights, and one after the other were pulled over and toppled into piles of broken timber.

When the last one fell, Vincipius signaled a retreat and his host backed off, bloodied and temporarily bowed, but in good order and in no way beaten. While his men were still leaving the field, his barges pulled up, reloaded their catapults and poled away. All that was left on the field were the dead. Able to relax at last, the defenders were surprised to see that the light was quickly fading: they had fought all day.

Now Valerius stood at the same spot on the wall, looking out over those same dead as they began to swell under the rising sun, and wondered what trick Vincipius would play next. And if he would be able to counter it. Clearly, the man knew what he was about, and had enough troops to affect his will. In his mind, Valerius reviewed the terrain around Zagorbia one more time, but could see no way to launch an effective counterattack. The very things that made the place so good for defense also made it nearly impossible for offense. There was no place he could put sufficient troops in the field or gain any room for maneuver without being immediately faced with overwhelming numbers. It was as if he was at the narrow end of a funnel, and while he could effectively block the exit-or hoped he could-there was no way he could push back the other way: at least, not until Grumwald returned and he could send an amphibious sweep around the outside. But there had been no word from Grumwald for the past month.

A movement from the edge of the field interrupted his thoughts and he watched as an official contingent picked their way forward under a flag of truce. Ragnar joined him and they went to the lower wall to parley. "Has your master sent you to surrender?" the latter yelled out, but the laughter along the walls at this wisecrack was not as loud as before. The previous day's fight had shaken everyone.

The emissary ignored the barb in any event. He had come, he said, neither to offer surrender nor to seek it. What His Excellency, Vincipius did request was a simple truce, that each side might recover and duly honor their dead. Yes, Valerius thought, and to clear the field for your next assault. But he nodded a terse acceptance and walked away.

He went to the palace and took the narrow outside steps up to the roof and looked out over the harbor and western sea. It was peaceful there, and the air seemed clearer, but the sea to the west and south was empty of ships. Once again Valerius lifted the large red gem on his chest and held it to his eye, scanning the horizon in hope of visions from beyond. But other than the light playing through the stone, and a sense of shadow as he passed the dark headland, he saw nothing. Shaking his head, he retraced his steps and went down the stairs and into his chambers.

Eomer was sitting in the light from the far window, working at her distaff, the large mound of her belly serving as a shelf for unwound wool. She smiled as he entered and returned his kiss with that bemused, preoccupied air pregnant women have. It hurt him to look at her, she was so beautiful. He flopped down in a large chair opposite.

"Good morning, my Lord," she said, taking up her spindle and attaching a thread. "All quiet on the walls?"

"There's a truce to bury the dead."

Eomer worked quietly for a while, her left hand pulling the flaxen threads from the distaff and deftly twisting them, while her right held tension with the spindle and wound up her work. It was unusual for Valerius to return at this hour of the day, and she cast covert glances at him. He had not removed his helm or war gear, so it was plain he did not intend to stay, but he made no move to address her either. Instead, he stared out the window with his chin on his fist.

"Is everything all right, my Lord?"

"As right as can be expected under the circumstances, I suppose. I just hate seeing a battlefield the day after. There's no choice when the fight comes and every man takes his chances. But afterwards, you see so many who have lost their chance. It's such a waste."

"You're still troubled about Burmac, aren't you?"

"Burmac and the others. He has a wife and two young sons in Balac, you know. His eyes lit up like candles when he spoke of them. Now they'll never see their father again, never know the man he was..."

"Somehow, I think they'll hear his story. You won't let his memory die."

"Not his memory, no. But he's gone. Oh, I'm sorry to be so gloomy, my dear, and I don't mean to burden you with my troubles-Gods know you have enough on your mind already-but it just gets to me sometimes, that's all."

"You are a kind man, how could it not? But you must try to look beyond it to the future."

"Aye, you're right, I know. But sometimes it's hard to see any future from here. The trouble is, it just seems there's never any choice about all this, and I don't know if I'll be able to offer young Valerian there any choice-even any life at this point. You are young, Eomer, and the young are naturally optimistic. But I am no longer young. My beard is flecked with gray and yet, I have been at war since before I could grow a beard, since before you were born. Never with any choice. My father did not want war, but he didn't have any choice: it was just there one morning, clamoring before his gates. And I have been trying ever since to end it. Will I be able to offer young Valerian any better life than mine? I hope so, but I just don't know."

"I know," said Eomer, lowering her spindle and smiling deep into her husband's eyes. "I know what kind of man you are, and I know how the men look up to you and respect you. I also see how the movement has grown over the past year since Kantar, and how hope is spreading all around the Inland Sea. I know that young Valerian here will grow up in a free Valeria, and that his gray-bearded father will be a revered High King."

Valerius smiled in return, warmed by his wife's confidence. "Thank you, my dear. I get too caught up in things sometimes, I know. Burmac really got to me. But you have made me feel better. Now, you must excuse me. I have to assemble my council and see how we can make these dreams of yours come true."

The Council Chamber was as serene as ever with its vista of pure blue sky and veranda overlooking the deeper blue sea. No visions of war had yet penetrated here, but the faces in the room were lined with them. Until the day before, they had all felt securely impregnable behind Zagorbia's massive walls. Now that security had been shaken. They were not yet in imminent danger, and being thorough professionals, they were willing to accept risk, but they also knew they faced a foe as resourceful as themselves, and one with superior numbers. They were a long way from beaten, but for the first time they had to acknowledge the possibility.

The key was Grumwald: if he returned soon, he could sweep around, take the enemy's ships and attack his rear. If he was too late and Vincipius had time to launch another major assault, well, it would be a near thing.

"But what can we do to slow him down in the mean time?" was what Valerius wanted to know. They argued about it for hours without coming closer to a solution.

"How about we sail around and attack his ships?" suggested one.

"Too risky," was the reply. "Outnumbered as we are, we dare not split our forces any further."

"How about another sortie, but in greater force?"

"I fear the results will be the same as yesterday. He can bring more men to bear at any point, faster than we can. We have no room to maneuver: he does."

"What about a night attack?"

"You'd all end up in the swamp! By now he knows the terrain out there better than we do."

"He doesn't know it better than me." This was from Ragnar and the room turned to listen. "I say let me take a small party around by sea to the mouth of the West River to the south and set up my resistance operation again."

"What good will that do?" Valerius asked. "Vincipius has scouted the whole area and will surely catch you."

"Listen, Your Majesty," said Ragnar, "we spent five years in those swamps with Tarpon having nothing to do but find us, and he never did. I grew up in those swamps. I know paths the badgers don't know. Vincipius will never find us."

"Even so, what good can you do?"

"We can harass them," said Ragnar, looking pugnacious. "We can sneak into their camps at night and slit a few of their throats! At the very least it will help distract them from you. Plus, we can keep an eye out for Grumwald. You don't want him sailing back here in broad daylight. That will take away the element of surprise. We'll stop him by the river and send to you for instructions."

"Well," said Valerius, still dubious, but at that moment a herald entered to say Vincipius was on the field and wished to speak with the King.

All the dead had been cleared away when Valerius and his Council mounted the walls. Vincipius and his entourage were ensconced in some state in the middle of the field. Vincipius rose when he saw Valerius, and struck an orator's pose.

"I have come to see if you have reconsidered surrender," he said, his voice ringing theatrically over the field.

"Not I," Valerius replied, his own voice deeper, bell-like. "Have you?"

"Let us not play cat and mouse here Valerius. You are a valiant fighter, I warrant you that. You have all earned due honor. But you know it is just a matter of time. There is no need for you all to die. Here are my terms: you Valerius, will renounce any claims to kingship, put down your arms and open your gates. We will allow you all to depart to your homes without harm. Only you, Valerius, will have to face Fantar's justice."

"Vincipius," said Valerius, "you are here under a flag of truce, and I will honor that. But enough of such talk or I will loose my archers on you."

"It's useless to talk so, Valerius. We'll only whittle you away. How many of your men went down to death yesterday? How long can you defend this place?"

Suddenly, Valerius was struck with an inspiration. Leaping up on the battlement, he held the Eye stone up by its chain and let the sunlight flash through it. "Know you not what this is, Vincipius?" he yelled. "Know you not what power it represents? It is you who are in trouble here, not I!

By the power of this stone, I am Valerius Everreigning, Rightful High King of Valeria and all the Inland Sea. By the power of this stone, I command the living and I command the souls of those dead. Hear me, Vincipius, and hear the curse I place upon you! Sleep no longer, for from this night on the dead will enter your tents at night and murder you in your beds. And the longer you stay here to fight the living, the greater will be this host of the dead. Now begone or I will loose my archers on you!"

At this-indeed, ever since Valerius held up the stone and the red beams flashed among their ranks-the soldiers around Vincipius started shielding their faces and shrinking away. And when Valerius said he would command the souls of the dead to attack them at night, they were clearly frightened and began edging back towards the woods. But Vincipius scoffed it off.

"Think you to frighten me with children's stories?" he yelled. "We will see who frightens first!" And he stalked off.

"Yes!" shouted Ragnar as Valerius hopped back down onto the parapet. "We'll give him children's stories that will wake the dead!"

Chapter 11
THE FORTUNATE ISLES

What bothered Grumwald most were the bugs. They swarmed around his head wherever he went, and whenever he swatted one, several more took its place. And they bit. He and his men were covered with tiny red welts that itched like the furies. Some had swollen up like tomatoes and sickened. Several had even died. Then, there was the heat and incessant rain; the thick cloying maze of jungle; the fact that at any moment, wherever you were on this god-forsaken island, an Iblis spear might find your throat; and of course, the fact that after nearly a month of exasperating effort, they were no closer to nabbing that bastard Haradin.

In fact, Grumwald was furious: furious at the bugs, at the island, at Haradin, at his own commanders who were even less able to cope with the situation than he, at the Iblis who skulked through the bush like wraiths; furious at everything. Never in his life had he been more thoroughly furious, not even when he was chained to a galley bench and forced to row till he dropped. That was simple compared to this. There he had the option of an honorable death. Here he seemed to have no options at all. It just made him want to scream.

Grumwald swatted at the swarm of buzzing critters and looked up and down his line: thirty veteran warriors, sweating and stinking in heavy war gear, slogging along in single file down a narrow, twisting jungle path that clawed and

155

whipped them at every step. They were escorting prisoners-a sickly group of five women, two children, and an emaciated old man, all as naked as the day they were born-and kept their weapons at the ready, fearing an ambush at every turn. They were headed towards the stockade he had built at the far end of Iblis Town (as his men had come to call the place). This was the only place he could keep the Iblis under control, and catching them all seemed to be the only way of eventually catching Haradin.

The Iblis were not a pleasant people. Squat and heavy browed, they were slow of thought and speech, sullen and quick to anger. The women, Grumwald-and thankfully the vast majority of his men-found especially repulsive. Two years before, he had led a fleet from Kantar carrying the entire Iblian population and had settled them here in the Fortunate Isles. They had helped ferry all their belongings ashore, had helped them build temporary shelters along a lovely stream at the head of the bay, had even given them herds of cattle and sheep, a gift from King Valerius in exchange for their promise to give up their cannibalistic ways. Then he had left them to start new lives in their island paradise.

And new lives they had, though they were unlike anything Grumwald, Valerius or any of the rest of them could have imagined. The Iblis had, as far as Grumwald could tell, gone completely wild.

When his fleet dropped anchor in the lovely, sheltering bay, the entire population fled inland and he found the village empty and derelict. They had still been living there, but had done nothing to improve or even maintain the place since Grumwald had left. Palm fronds used for thatching had long since rotted away, ridge poles had fallen, entire huts had toppled and no one, it appeared, had made the slightest effort to repair them. They had simply continued living there in increasing squalor, getting wet when it rained, piling their refuse, and watching their belongings rot. But that was not all. The fields they cleared had gone fallow, and the remains of the cattle and sheep herds, which were to be their mainstay, wandered untended through the jungle. It appeared the Iblis were subsisting entirely off the land, and when Grumwald's men began to catch a few, they found them filthy, emaciated, and almost entirely naked.

Suddenly, the column halted and the men crouched down and drew together, raising their shields and intently scanning the bushes around them. No one was quite sure what had triggered the alarm, but all knew an attack could come without warning from any direction. One thing the Iblis had mastered was their jungle surroundings. They moved like wraiths, hardly bothering with trails at all. They climbed trees like monkeys, and could disguise themselves so well with foliage you could not see one if you were standing next to him: until, that is, you felt his knife in your throat.

The alarm passed without incident and the column moved on. The frustrating thing was that the Iblis wouldn't stand and fight. Not that Grumwald could blame them: they knew as well as he that they were no match for the burly northerners and that if they did stand and fight they would be easily crushed. So what they did instead was skulk and kill, and disappear again into the thick forest. Half a hundred men had been lost already-some even dragged off and eaten-and Grumwald had been forced to change his tactics in response.

He had first thought to simply make a sweep of the island, herding the population and rebels into some convenient corner where they could deal with them. But the jungle made that impossible. His men could hold no line of battle; in fact, were forced more often to move like he was now, in small columns along jungle trails, often in single file. The Iblis, somehow, were not so constrained, and not only were they able to slip through his 'screen' at will, they were able to attack it with impunity.

His next move was to try and beat them at their own game. Instead of trying to force his army through the jungle, he sent out small, thirty to forty man units to search out and engage Iblis fighters. But the Iblis chose not to engage. Some success was had when his men staked out various spots-the intersection of trails, water holes, and such-and lay in hiding themselves until parties of the enemy happened along, but it was clear that unless they got very lucky, this approach would take months to succeed: months they didn't have.

So his latest scheme was to try and reestablish his battle line, but in a manner that suited the terrain. Rather than have his line move through the jungle, he had begun establishing a series of enveloping rings, beginning with a solid perimeter around the town itself. Half his men would move out along the trails for a quarter mile or so from one perimeter ring, then hack and slash their way through the jungle until they had established contact with units on either side. Once the second ring was firmly established, smaller parties would work their way through the intervening jungle a section at a time, flushing out everything that lived. This approach was bagging a lot of Iblis, but not a lot of warriors. And now that the ring system had moved some miles inland, resistance was again springing up in their rear so that parties transporting prisoners, like the one Grumwald was leading now, were coming under more frequent attack.

A sudden flash of movement in the bush to his right caught Grumwald's eye. He spun and raised his shield just in time to deflect a thrown spear. Up and down the line there was a sudden flurry of tumult as the attack rippled along its length. Men yelled and leapt into defensive pairs as they had drilled, standing back to back as other missiles were hurled from both sides of the trail.

Grumwald stood with his back firmly pressed against his partner's, his nostrils flaring as he glared into the bush from where, seconds before, near death had come. He saw nothing. Up and down the line, motion ceased as others did likewise; standing at the ready, staring after an enemy who was no longer there. Then Grumwald felt the man behind him slide slowly down, then topple suddenly. He turned to find the man at his feet, gripping the shaft of a spear protruding from his stomach. The man gritted his teeth and looked up a Grumwald in mute apology for failing to maintain his cover.

Grumwald knelt to check the wound. It was in the man's right side and shallow-the spearhead had only partially penetrated his leather corselet. A survivable wound, with luck. With a quick jerk, he yanked the shaft free, and then tore a section off his own cloak for the man to staunch the blood.

Two others had not been so fortunate, however, and during the commotion, the prisoners had fled, disappearing into the dark forest like fleeting shadows. Crude litters were fashioned for the dead from Iblis spears and battle cloaks, and the line moved on only to discover, as they rounded the very next bend, that they had been attacked within a hundred paces of their own main defensive perimeter around Iblis Town.

Leaving the unit to its sergeant, Grumwald made his way to the stream and waterfall that emptied into the bay beside the town. Tossing aside his sweaty helm and heavy breastplate, he plunged into the water, waded up under the overhanging rock, and fought his way into the cascading falls. Gasping and sputtering, he staggered as the cold water ricocheted off his head and beefy shoulders and the torrent surged around his waist. Surrendering to it at last, he flopped onto his back and let the current drive him out into the quiet pool downstream. Here he floated, momentarily cool, and tried to sort out his options.

He could leave; that would be the most gratifying thing. He was already behind time and would much rather spend a year fighting real battles around Valeria than spend another day in this wretched jungle. Besides, there was no way these Iblis were in league with Fantar. They could just leave them here to rot and come back in their own sweet time. Hell, they never needed to come back for that matter. There was no way these Iblis would ever even get off this island. He really was wasting his time here: precious time.

Or, he could stay and try to complete his mission. But he couldn't do that the way things were going; that was too slow and too costly. Besides, he didn't know how much longer he could keep his men under control. To keep enduring provocations like today without being able to fight back was too much for any man. Even this morning, he had to personally stop several men from killing the prisoners; and that was before the ambush. They would be even less happy now that the prisoners had fled and two of their own had died instead. And this went on day after day. No, they would break soon if he did not do something.

What he ought to do, he thought savagely, was haul ten prisoners out of the stockade, gut nine of them in front of the lines and send the tenth into the jungle with a message for the rest: from now on, five Iblis would die for every one of Grumwald's. Plus, another would die for every day Haradin stayed loose. That would be something they could understand.

But if he started playing rough, Valerius would not like it. He had expressly ordered that they fight only rebels-Haradin's warriors-not the Iblian people. But Valerius was not here, and had not foreseen this situation when he gave those orders. Who were 'rebels' now? Since all the Iblis ran off, didn't that make 'em all rebels? There were no 'people' left. Who was it that was killing his men, anyway: some band of feather-wearing warriors, or any bloody piss-ant Iblis who could hide in the bush and heft a spear?

A distant commotion caught his attention and when he lifted his head, he found the current had swept him right out of the stream and into the bay. On the shore, one of his adjutants was waving his arms and yelling. Grumwald waved back and swam to shore.

"My Lord," cried the man as Grumwald waded ashore, dripping, "a messenger from Zagorbia!" Grumwald spun in the direction the man was pointing, and there, sure enough, was a new ship, just setting her anchor among his fleet. The Valerian banner hung limply at the masthead and, even as he looked, a boat was dropped over the side and figures began climbing down into it.

"Well, don't just stand there, man!" Grumwald snapped. "Fetch me my clothes."

His toga was soggy and rank as he pulled it on, and his armor heavy and hot, but as best he could, he made himself look the successful commander and hurried off to his command tent to receive the messenger. The man, when he entered, looked as if

162

he had just stepped from the parade ground: clean and freshly shaven, wearing a burnished breastplate and brilliant red cloak, his polished helm and plume tucked beneath his left arm. And beneath his armor he wore a crisp white toga that made Grumwald feel like a brick maker. The man snapped to attention and slapped his chest in salute.

"My Lord, may I present the compliments of His Majesty Valerius Everreigning, Rightful High King of Valeria and all the Inland Sea to Lord Grumwald..."

"Yes, yes, yes," Grumwald interrupted, "get on with it. What's the message?"

"My lord!" said the man, snapping to and saluting once more. "I am instructed to inform you that Zagorbia is under siege. The King has been attacked by land by an army under one Markus Vincipius."

The irritation in Grumwald's face was replaced by a sudden keen interest. Here might be the answer he was looking for. "Vincipius, eh?" he said. "I knew him of old. A sodding engineer is what he is. And what does the King instruct?"

"Sir. I am instructed to tell you that the King does not believe he is in immediate danger but that he would be most happy to see you."

The scowl returned to Grumwald's face and he grunted. But before he could reply further, another messenger burst in, this one presenting an entirely different picture. He had come from inland and reeked like a bog. His armor was smeared and stained, his cloak torn, and he had neither shaved nor bathed in weeks. Yet he, too, snapped to attention and slapped his chest with every bit as much military precision as the other.

"Commander," he said without prelude. "We've got him! A whole mob of rebels cornered in a canyon."

Grumwald looked quickly from one to the other and made his decision. "Let's go," he said and snatching up his own battered helm, lead the way from the tent.

Chapter 12
THE GODS' WILL

Vahla surveyed herself in a polished bronze mirror while her maids fussed about, making tiny, last minute adjustments to her ensemble. Satisfied that her hair was piled high on her head just the way Asperides liked it, that her lips were rouged and moistened to just the right degree of sultriness, and that the deep V-neck of her gown revealed just enough of her swelling breasts, she hurried from the house and into the waiting palanquin. This was the first time she would see Asperides since her return from the desert, and she wanted to leave nothing to chance.

The palanquin swayed and jolted as the bearers jostled their way through the crowded streets, and between the swinging curtains she could see the guards pushing back the curious. One young urchin ducked under the guard's arm and actually managed to climb halfway inside with her-begging all the while in a high pitched, foreign staccato-before being grabbed by the scruff of his neck and tossed aside (but not before Vahla managed to press a small coin into his palm). It was strange, she thought, how any day of the week she could leave her house and walk the streets in relative anonymity: but let her climb into the Viceroy's sedan chair, with its muscular Nubian bearers and files of armed guards, and she suddenly became a parade. Same person, she thought, but a dramatically different presentation.

She hoped to make a similarly dramatic impression on Asperides. Lying back among the plush cushions, she reviewed her plan one more time. She had never really intended to go to Darlung. The whole thing was to be merely a ruse, an excuse for her being in Palmeria while she worked on Asperides. But he had been too helpful by far: within days of their last meeting, she had found herself atop a camel at the head of a caravan headed east, and for the next three weeks had endured the most miserable journey of her life. It was far worse than her desert excursion to Cartho, and nearly as uncomfortable as her wild flight from Valeria after trying to kill Fantar when she had nothing to eat for days and not even a pair of shoes to protect her feet. This had been better than that, but not by much.

Now that she was back, she hoped to make up for lost time by putting her trip to good use. Long and hard had she thought through this during her desert sojourn, devising and discarding at least a dozen stories before finally settling on one she believed would have the right balance of symbol, mysticism, and reality to be convincing. Still, convincing Asperides to help Valerius was not going to be an easy task. He was interested in her: that much was clear from the way his eyes had kept devouring her during their last meeting. But switching sides was serious business, and Vahla knew there was no way Asperides would risk everything in order to satisfy a simple lust. Was there the potential for more? She shook her head softly: he had too much ego to love anyone else. His rebellious sympathies? They were just that, she thought. He would mouth them, perhaps even feel them; but only until the instant they ran counter to his own personal interests. Then there was no contest.

No, what she had to do-and it was her only hope, really-was use all her wiles to convince him that not only would his interests and ambitions be best served by acting with her and Valerius, but that this path was ordained for him by the gods themselves. If she could do that-and while he was skeptical, she knew he was just superstitious enough to be vulnerable-there was a chance. If not... Well, 'if not' could be dealt with another time.

Asperides met her in the blue foyer of his private chambers and bowed low over her hand. "Madame Enchantress," he said with his customary smirk, "your beauty has bloomed even in the desert."

Vahla gave him a look of what she hoped was high seriousness. "What you see in me, your Highness, is the flowering of the Gods' will." It was always good, Volkmir had told her, to set the tone early.

"What I see," Asperides laughed, "is that our luncheon will not be filled with light banter and pleasantries! But come, let us eat and then you may tell me of your encounter with the desert spirits."

They ate in an inner chamber just off the courtyard where they had sat before. It was a light luncheon of fresh salads, fruit, and cold, marinated duck in a jellied sauce that was so tender it fell apart when she tried to cut it with her dagger. Despite his prediction, Asperides did keep up a light banter, chattering on about various affairs in the city, building projects he had in hand, ships that had come in from various parts, a festival he had held at the launch of a new trireme. He was trying to impress her, of course, though Vahla thought he did seem genuinely interested in the welfare of his city. But she also saw he was dissembling.

For her part, Vahla was silent and tried not to respond to his chatter. She kept a somber mien, suitable for her purpose, and watched him with a solemn expression she hoped would unnerve him. And it seemed to be working: his eyes kept darting away from hers, and his conversation grew more and more random as he tried to maintain a facade of sardonic ease. Still, she found it hard not to respond to his quips, and even laughed outright at one point when Asperides described how one of his servants spilled soup on one of the city's leading-and most pompous-merchants. Finally, when the table had been cleared, he dismissed the servants, poured more wine, and turned serious himself.

"To the desert," he said, raising his glass and meeting her gaze directly for the first time.

Vahla touched his glass and smiled in return. "To the Gods' will."

Asperides nodded. "It is never wise to speak of serious matters when there are servants about," he said. "But tell me now, how was your desert Shrine, for all I can see of 'the Gods' will,' is that it is lovely."

"You would not have thought so if you had seen me a while ago... it took several hours of soaking in a hot tub to remove the desert."

"I would like very much to have seen that!" Asperides said, archly.

Vahla flushed-more in anger at herself than embarrassment-and let the remark pass. She had not intended to provide such an obvious opening.

"I'm sorry," said Asperides, unrepentant. "That was impertinent. But, your trip was not a success then?"

"On the contrary," Vahla smiled, forgiving him. "I just marvel that the gods choose to inhabit such inhospitable places. A week and a half of travelling and when we get to Darlung, it is absolutely barren. The Shrine is nothing more than a pile of rocks on an empty plain between two spurs of the mountain. You couldn't feed a goat there. And when the wind kicks up, the sand will blast out your eyeballs. We had a storm one night and in the morning our tents were half buried."

"So what did you do? How does an Enchantress go about discerning the gods' will in a place like that?"

"Well, to tell the truth, I didn't know. People think that sorcerers invoke powers-and we do have our ways. We can do small things. But the powers are not ours. We do not really control them. We attract them and conduct them, but they are not of us. The gods act through us: and ultimately, they act as they choose.

"So I didn't know what would happen. We spent several days camped there, and I did all the invocation rites I know, but nothing seemed to happen: the wind and the sand still blew and that pile of rocks just sat there. And if there was still fire in that mountain, it gave no sign. So, I was ready to come back-was even wondering if 'no sign' was the sign, and what it might mean.

"Then, one morning as I left my tent, I looked up and saw a small cloud sitting on a shoulder of the mountain. It was as if some clouds had blown through during the night and this one bit had gotten snagged and stuck there, like a tuft of lamb's wool on a thorn. I expected it to drift away, but it didn't: it just hung there and finally I said, 'I'm going up there.'

"The climb took most of the day, but when I got there I saw that the cloud was actually steam coming out of a small glade: there was a pool in there with hot water trickling out of the rocks above. I thought, 'well, there must be fire in this mountain after all,' and turned to go when I saw a ram among the rocks on the other side of the glade. He was a beautiful ram with thick fleece and great curved horns. But he seemed to be struggling. I went over and saw he had a leash around his neck and the end was caught in the rocks. I knelt down to free it and heard a growl. There, behind another rock and no more than fifteen feet away, was a mountain lion, crouched and ready to spring."

"What did you do?" Asperides face reflecting shock.

"I didn't know what to do. I just froze for I don't know how long. It was probably just seconds, but it seemed like forever. Then, from up behind me, there came a shout, and a shepherd boy came leaping down the rocks like a young god, flinging stones. The lion took fright and ran off and the boy freed the ram. He didn't say anything to me, just smiled this incredibly beautiful smile that went right to my heart. Then he and the ram turned and walked off.

"I wasn't thinking much of anything at that point, the whole thing had been so sudden. But when the boy and the ram reached the edge of the glade, they stopped to look back at me and...well, they vanished. Just evaporated into thin air. And when I looked down, there on the rock was a sprig of laurel."

"And you think this was your sign?" Asperides was leaning back in his chair, watching her intently over the rim of his glass.

"I do. And I think you were that shepherd boy with the beautiful smile."

"You do? And what about the ram?"

"He was the rightful High King, Valerius Everreigning, besieged in Zagorbia."

"I see. Then the lion, of course, would be Fantar. But you know, shepherd boys sometimes get eaten by lions."

"Yes. And sometimes, they also marry princesses."

171

"Interesting choice." Asperides sat for some time in contemplation, then, as if he suddenly recalled something, excused himself and left the room. Closing the door behind him, he walked down a short hallway and entered an adjacent chamber. Here an older man turned from a peephole in the wall. He was a grizzled fellow, with close-cropped hair and beard, and wore the breastplate and tunic of Fantar's Valerian Guard. Asperides lead him away from the wall and spoke in a horse whisper.

"What do you think?"

"It's her, I'd swear. Vahla la Danceur, she called herself."

"She calls herself Vauhna now."

"Either way, she's the same I saw dance before the Emperor, the same as tried to slit his throat. I even recognize her dagger: it's Fantar's that she tried to stick him with. Shall I call the guards?"

"No, not just yet. She's not to be taken lightly, this Vahla. Besides, she may be useful."

"How so?"

"She wants me to help this upstart pretender, Valerius, that Vincipius has besieged in Zagorbia."

"Yes? Well, from what I hear, old Vincipius has a tiger by the tail there; word is his best assaults have failed and now this Valerius has raised the spirits of the dead against him. His men are being murdered in their beds."

"Aye, but what if this Vahla could help us get a force right into the city?"

"What if she finds out what you're planning?"

172

"Then, my dear Gorman, you will die a most uncomfortable death."

"I'm sorry," said Asperides, returning to the table. "I have too many things to remember. But let's say this shepherd of yours did agree to help Valerius; let's even say he was someone like me who could command a considerable force. How would he get into the city? Valerius would hardly let an ostensible enemy into Zagorbia."

"I could get you in," said Vahla, trying to keep control of her expression.

"Then you are in league with Valerius."

"Let's say he has reason to trust me."

"You know," said Asperides, filling their glasses and giving Vahla a sly look, "I also recall hearing a report that when Valerius defeated Glaucon in-Kantar, was it? -there was a young woman up on a cliff wielding his magic Eye Stone... You wouldn't know anything about that, would you?"

Vahla met his eye over the rim of her cup. "Let's just say he has good reason to trust me."

"I see. But you know, that report also indicated this woman bore some relation to Valerius: she was his sister or something. Would you know anything about that?"

Asperides could see Vahla's pupils widen and her cheeks flush, but still, she held her gaze steady. "Let's just say," she said again, "that he has very good reason to trust me."

"I see." Asperides looked into Vahla's dark eyes for a long moment, then raised his glass. "When you said a shepherd boy might marry princess, I assume were you being allegorical?"

"That, my lord," said Vahla, touching his glass with her own, "is a very interesting question indeed."

Chapter 13
THE BATTLE OF DUNLOR

They were late getting started, as usual, and
Thorngere was having trouble controlling his
temper. Why a group of grown men could not get
up, get their gear together and be ready to march in
under two hours was beyond him. He could
understand it the first couple days; they were still
new to the routine of an army on the march. But
after a week? How long did it take for someone to
figure out that when the drums beat in the morning,
and the sergeants yelled, you got your ass out of
your bedroll, grabbed a bowl of gruel, broke camp
and got ready to go? Forty-five minutes, an hour
tops, and they should be lined up, ready to march.
Yet here the sun was well up and he was still riding
up and down the line, haranguing and cajoling
recalcitrant units to get a move on. And getting
hotter by the minute.

Of course, it did no good to fly off the handle.
Only sergeants and petty officers had that luxury.
High commanders were supposed to maintain an
aura of regal authority. A commander shaking his
warriors by the scruffs of their necks would hardly
maintain their respect. It would be too common, and
besides, he might be tempted to shake too hard in
some cases. Like with the Burgundians whose cook
tent was still not broken down and whose captain, a
scrawny younger son of an elderly chieftain, was
standing around, joking and laughing with his men.

Then again, sometimes even regal high commanders could be pushed too far. In sudden fury, Thorngere leapt from his horse and advanced on the young fellow, thrusting his face within inches of the other's and screaming: "Where in the hell do you think you are, on a picnic?"

Thorngere was a good head taller than the young man, and nearly twice as broad in the shoulders: the sheer volume of all this personality pushed the man back. And as he backed, Thorngere's snarling face advanced. "Answer me, you pukey-faced little bastard! Didn't you hear the order to pack up and march?"

The man opened his mouth but Thorngere had no time for his reply. "You have just ten minutes to get in line, ready to march-the whole goddamn pack of you!" he yelled to the world at large, "or you go to the rear and march with the women. Do you hear me? And you, my friend," he said, poking the young man on the chest with a force that shook him, "will not be a commander. You'll be my personal groom!"

A crowd was gathering quickly, but as Thorngere remounted his horse, they scattered into a flurry of activity. Eager hands grabbed anything they could carry. Two men yanked the center pole out from under the cook tent even as others tore the stakes from the ground. All up and down the line, in fact, the pace quickened as a sudden sense of urgency spread like a stiffening breeze. Thorngere felt better than he had in days.

But as he turned to continue up the line, a messenger pounded to a halt before him. The man had been riding hard and had to draw breath before he could speak. Gamlarch held the valley of Dunlor with near five thousand foot, he gasped. But a force from Valeria had discovered them and was even now forming to attack.

"What size force?" Thorngere snapped.

"Unknown numbers, my lord. They just appeared on the verge of the forests to the south."

"Do you know what units? Could you see their standards?"

"They bore the standard of Fantar's Imperial Guard, my lord."

The day grew hot. They were out of the mountains proper now, descending into the lower hills that lined the northern basin of the Inland Sea, and descending into a vast pool of humid air that marked the southern latitudes. Sweat trickled into Thorngere's eyes and along the curve of his spine beneath his corselet. He was uncomfortable on the horse, driving it forward in his impatience, then holding it back and feeling all the while, though irrationally, that he could move faster on foot. He was used to marching, his body built and inured to it. Riding was a strange, novel thing, like this impending sense of peril that squeezed his intestines and sent little tingles along his skin.

They were moving along a rutted, two-wheeled track that wound through dense forest, the line of march by now strung out over several miles. Thorngere had no visibility; even on the hilltops he could only see as far as the next bend in the trail. They had been marching for hours now, pressing on as fast as he dared, and he was growing increasingly worried. Though he had sent scouts out ahead, he still had only the vaguest notion of Gamlarch's position, and no notion at all of where Fantar's troops might be. They might even be lying in wait beside this very trail, where a concerted attack could snap his extended line like a twig.

But what could he do? Any line of march would stretch in country like this. If he moved slowly enough to keep his line together, he increased the risk that Gamlarch would be overwhelmed before he arrived. Yet, if he moved too fast, he would arrive with insufficient force to help him. So he spurred his horse ahead, then pulled him back; rushed ahead, and held back. He felt like a dog on a leash.

Overhead, the sky was that rich, clear blue of high summer. Not a cloud marred its purity. Thorngere loved days like this at sea, aboard Elusive, when there was just enough wind to fill the sails and cool the decks and absolutely no reason or way to hurry anywhere. He would just loll about the deck on days like this, soaking up the sun, letting the breeze soothe his skin, maybe take a leap overboard every now and then if the winds were that light, the day that hot. You could totally relax on days like this at sea and let all the cares of this world drift away. Even if you were on a desperate mission, you could still just let it go. There was nothing else you could do. You had no choice.

He had no choice now either, unless you counted the option of failure. That was the irony. You always thought of the commander as the one who had choice: everyone else did as they were told and he was the one who did the telling. But as Thorngere saw now, this was a mere illusion of choice. The only real choice was that of initial objective. Everything else flowed from that like water in a streambed. All he as commander could do was direct, select the shortest, most efficient path. Or fail.

He thought of King Valerius, his commander. Did he have any choice, really? From the time they escaped from the Hidden Valley and he reclaimed the Eye, had he really any choice? The Mage Volkmir had once said there was a cycle in things, an ebb and flow. Valerius-if he yet lived-was as much impelled by that force as Thorngere was now. It was like steering Elusive before the wind in a blow: yes, he had the helm and could steer the ship, but he was not really in control. He could only respond, push and pull the tiller bar as the ship yawed and plunged in the following sea. One mistake and she would broach, fatally.

That's what he was doing now, trying to avoid a broach. He had heard nothing from or of Valerius since that first messenger told him he was besieged. But this little ship, this plan they had concocted, was running before the wind, and now he was at the helm. In his mind he tried to penetrate the thick forest ahead to read the situation around the plain of Dunlor much as he would gauge the waves at sea.

What would Fantar do? Would it even be Fantar? He doubted that: they had been trying to corner Gamlarch's band for too long for the Emperor himself to still be in the field. It would be one of his minions, then. But which? Gormlath headed the Imperial Guard at last report-though the posting did change frequently with its master's whim-and he was a ferocious bastard. If it were he, there would be no dance and maneuver: as soon as his troops were in place he would go straight for the throat... As would Fantar himself in this situation. Fantar was a great one for stratagems and deceits before troops took the field, but put an enemy in front of him and he attacked like a mad dog.

So Gamlarch would already be engaged, the issue, perhaps, already decided. Could he have held? Thorngere had no notion of the numbers involved, but raw troops against the Imperial Guard? Spurring his horse, he rode ahead to the top of a rise and stopped to listen: the din of battle could carry for miles. But he heard nothing. Could it be over then? The breeze was at his back, flowing down from the mountains. That would carry sound away. And besides, Gamlarch was no fool. He had been Commander and Chief of the Imperial armies under the old High King, Valerius' father. Maybe he had stood. Maybe he had beaten them off and both forces were regrouping. Maybe they had done their dissipation trick again, melting away even as the Guard launched their assault. Gods knew Gamlarch had played that trick often enough.

Or maybe Gamlarch was already dead. And if he was, what was Thorngere riding into? Was he hearing the silence of an impending ambush? Or did they even know he was here? Peering through the thick foliage and down the twisting track to where it slipped around a bend, Thorngere could see nothing. Behind, the head of his column of wild Thuringians tramped up the hill and pushed him forward like a following sea.

The sun was westering when he rode out of the trees to survey the wreckage of battle on the Plain of Dunlor. He was very much too late. Messengers had reached him in early afternoon when he was still some miles away, and he could read the truth of their reports on the field before him. They had run. Riding diagonally across the field from the northwest, he saw the unmistakable signs of flight. Armies that fought and lost left bodies: armies that fled left gear. Only as he approached the eastern verge-nearly a quarter mile from where their line had stood-did he begin to see the first bodies: bodies sprawled on their faces, speared from the back. They had broken and run before the lines even met.

Only here, where the ground swept up behind a line of trees at the edge of the plain, had there been any serious fighting. At least part of the line had turned and stood. Here were dead with honorable wounds, and mixed among them, a few bearing Imperial colors. But they had not stood long: the line of flight continued on up the slope, disappearing in the shade of the trees. According to his scouts, the Guard had hardly bothered to follow but had reformed and marched off to the southwest towards Valeria, jubilant in their easy victory and even leaving their own dead. Shaking his head sadly, Thorngere turned and rode slowly back towards his own troops, just now filing out onto the plain.

Several days later, victory fires burned high in the fabled city of Valeria, court of the Fantaran Empire, and for a thousand years before that, seat of Valerius Everreigning, High King of Valeria and all the Inland Sea. It was a walled town, with crenellated towers and tall spired roofs, set at the head of a broad harbor and surrounded to the north and east by a fertile plain. Late into the night the fires burned all along the walls and the raucous sounds of celebration drifted seaward with the smoke. Inside the palace, musicians were kept to their strings long after their fingers lost feeling, while at long tables in the audience chamber, Gormlath and his lieutenants were feted by the Emperor himself.

Fantar was a huge, bestial looking man with a wild, unkempt mane, a graying, greasy beard and the leather patch that had earned him the name, 'One-Eye.' A formidable fighter in his youth, his once powerful frame had dissipated into a slovenly hulk and he sprawled on his throne, the remains of his feasting spattered across his chest and belly. Crouching by his side, chained to his chair like a mastiff, and eating scraps that were tossed to him, was a tiny man, not half the size of his master. Naked but for a ragged loincloth and as filthy as the floor he squatted upon, he had nonetheless, an air of alertness and intelligence about him and watched the proceedings with a sharp eye.

At a sign from Fantar, the musicians ceased their toil and the great double doors at the end of the hall opened to admit a squad of soldiers dragging a prisoner. This was an old man, gray with age and exhaustion and torn and beaten from his ordeal. Lame from an old wound and bloody from a new one, he hobbled along as his captors half carried him towards the dais, then manacled him spread-eagled between the timbers at the side of the hall. The old man sagged in his bonds and his head lolled.

"Gormlath," rumbled Fantar. "I believe the honor of introduction is yours."

"Aye, Majesty, and an honor it is," said this one rising from his seat at the head table and wiping the back of a hairy hand across his wide, sneering mouth. "May I present to your Imperial Highness one Gamlarch, self-styled leader of the recent rebellion-a rebellion, I might add, that scattered like chaff before the wind once they tried to stand before real soldiers!"

There was laughter across the hall and another round of toasts to the splendid victory. Fantar tossed off his wine with the rest, but was impatient for silence. "Gamlarch," he said when it settled. "That's a name I've heard. Methinks, Gormlath, that you may have caught yourself a peacock here, masquerading in these chicken feathers. Isn't that right, General?"

The old man tried to speak, but his voice was faint and slurred by cracked and bloody lips. "Colinus," Fantar said, kicking the tiny man by his chair. "Take our guest some wine. Methinks we are honored by the presence of none other than General Gamlarch, once High Commander of all the armies of Valeria, whose bones I had long thought were buried outside these very walls. How did you escape the fate of your former master, Gamlarch? By using the same trick your men used on you today?"

A loud burst of laughter greeted this remark while the tiny Colinus poured a goblet of wine from the pitcher at his master's side and took it to the prisoner, his chain dragging from his collar behind him. Lifting the goblet, he helped the old man drink, and when their eyes met briefly whispered, "May the gods grant you a merciful death, grandsire."

"Thank you, lad," muttered Gamlarch, and fortified by the wine, made an effort to stand erect.

"Have you anything to say for yourself?" asked Fantar, draining another mug of his own.

"I have that," said Gamlarch, a sudden fire burning in his eye. "Your memory is apparently the best part of you, Usurper. I am that Gamlarch who commanded the center before these walls that day of your infamy. It's where I earned this, " and he shook his mangled right leg. "So I didn't run then just as I didn't run today. Then I lay under a pile of dead while your brave troopers massacred our women and children. And I've waited all these long years for the chance to spit in your eye!"

"Brave talk for an old hen," laughed Fantar, though his one eye had begun to smolder. "But you can't spit with no teeth... You can only drool!" The room erupted in laughter and catcalls, but the old man remained unfazed.

"I'd rather be a drooling old fool than a pig like you, Usurper," he snapped. "At least I can claim to be a man. Look at you! You're like a fat old swine who wallows in his own crap, then eats it!"

Fantar's smile became a snarl. "Keep a civil tongue, fool, or I'll make you regret it."

"I am not afraid of you, pig. But you should be afraid, oh yes, Fantar the horrible... You should fear! Soon now one comes who'll make you eat more than your own filth..."

"Who, your vaunted pretender, Valerius?" Fantar was clearly angry now, his body straining forward, his great beefy hands gripping the arms of his chair. "Ha! I have it from the Oracle Herself that I have nothing to fear from him. But you, old man... you have much to fear from me."

"You can do nothing to me," Gamlarch shot back. "You did all you could years ago when you crushed this city. All you can do now is let me go."

"Oh, you think so, do you?" Fantar rose and stalked menacingly towards the shackled, helpless old man. "You think so!"

But the old man made the first move: contrary to Fantar's assertion, he could spit, and as the latter's large, menacing hulk moved within range, he did, scoring right on the side of Fantar's face, spattering his good eye. The Emperor bellowed in rage like a

185

maddened bull and with his massive right arm, backhanded the feisty ancient.

He did not intend the blow to be fatal-indeed, he had much more unpleasant things in mind-but perhaps some god pushed his hand, for the blow snapped the frail old man's neck like a twig, and he collapsed in his chains, his head flopping crookedly like a broken flower.

Crouching by his master's throne and clutching his own chain before him, Colinus squeezed his eyes shut and whispered a quick prayer of thanks to Kala Atar, warrior god of Kantar. And had any in the room been capable of such sight, they would have seen the old man's spirit, strong and stalwart as in his youth, stride forth from the shriveled, broken thing that hung in the chains, spit once again at the gaping Fantar, and leap proudly toward heaven.

Chapter 14
A PICNIC

The island that formed the outer barrier of the harbor at Palmeria was low and sandy, covered with scrub brush and sparse tufts of dune grass. Only at the southern end did the land rise like the humped back of a whale, to form a bulbous headland that marked the entrance to the harbor. Here stood an ancient grove of olive trees, and here, Vahla and Asperides made their way one bright morning, picnic baskets in hand, and with firm instructions for their servants to remain behind with the Viceroy's personal galley.

It had been a busy couple of weeks since Asperides had agreed to Vahla's-'Vauhna's'- request to aid Valerius, and it was he who had suggested they "sneak away" and grab at least part of a day for themselves. Vahla knew precisely what he had in mind, of course, and gave every appearance of being willing to accede. Her satiny white chiton was scooped low in front to reveal a generous portion of her breasts, and she wore it belted short, like a girl, exposing her long, symmetrical legs. Asperides could not keep his eyes off her, and as they spread out their things in a shady spot, his eyes took on a glazed, hungry look.

Vahla told herself she was resigned, that this was an inevitable consequence of her plan, and that if it helped save her brother and furthered the cause, it was worth it. Any hesitations, second thoughts, or even thoughts of another, she thrust ruthlessly from her mind, a task that was not as difficult as she pretended, for in truth, Asperides' desire was not wholly one-sided. He was a handsome, charming, even at times a funny man, and she could not have so 'set her cap,' as a distant generation would phrase it, or played her hand so well without becoming involved in the game.

Asperides did not exude that raw sense of physical power Thorngere had, but he had an aristocratic arrogance that bespoke power of another kind. In the bright sun of the island, the ice blue of his eyes shown with a pale opacity that veiled his haughty face in mystery. Here, said that face, was a man who would win. He might not beat his enemy down face to face in the brute fashion of the day, but there was no doubt who would come out on top. And that, for Vahla, was a charm as potent as any in her sorceress' arsenal. It was also the source of her main hesitation, for as much as she wanted to, she could not quite bring herself to trust this man.

And she had been warned. Several days before, as she was selecting fabric in the market, a man had stopped beside her and whispered that he was sent by Bokmar. She met him that night in the alley outside her house and he told her of letters sent to Valeria, of servants who overheard Asperides talking with another-a general of the Imperial Guard-of Asperides laughing and claiming that his bread was now buttered on both sides, that either could be turned to advantage. Yes, she had countered, but letters are required and servants always talk. Servants see poison in every flask of wine. Then pray, the man had said, that a sorceress can see inside the grape.

Now, as they nibbled fitfully at their luncheon and she saw Asperides' eyes slide along her naked thigh to the hem of her chiton, she felt a rush of blood, and in an almost involuntary response, shifted herself slightly to enhance his view. Could she see the grape? Or was she dizzy from another heady brew?

Asperides grinned around a leg of chicken. "Only a few more days, my dear, and you will have my company every day for a rather long sea voyage," he said. "I hope that will not displease you?"

"I think, my Lord, that your company-and our destination-will please me very much." Indeed, Vahla was pleased with his company so far, for 'his company' was steadily growing into a substantial army, and his fleet in the harbor was steadily filling with supplies and men. To the world at large, Asperides had announced a series of training exercises, while to his superiors in Valeria-or so he had told Vahla-he had sent that he was sailing in support of Vincipius. Only to his closest generals and confidants had he told the truth, and they, he said, were solidly behind the plan.

"We will be in very close proximity. Do you think you can bear it?"

"I think, my lord," Vahla smiled, "I will bear you very well."

Asperides face flushed and his eyes seemed to swell. "You know, you are the most enticing woman

I've ever known," he said huskily, the forgotten chicken bone hanging from his fingers.

"Would you like some cherries?" she asked, leaning to offer a bowl.

"Your cherries are much brighter than those," he said, staring down her dress at her fully exposed right breast with its pert nipple.

Vahla touched his thigh and gave him a coy smile. Things were going a bit too fast. "Those are for dessert."

"I'm full!" Asperides laughed, and flung his chicken bone away with quick flick of his wrist. They both laughed then, their eyes dancing merrily together. "Did you know there is an island west of here where the women dress with their breasts fully exposed?"

"I'll bet you hate that."

"Oh, it's terrible. I have to go there periodically on inspection tours and you wouldn't believe how hard it is to get men to volunteer... to come back!" They both laughed again, drawing closer on the blanket and reveling in the sheer closeness of their bodies. "They also do athletics completely naked, boys and girls."

"I did that."

"You? When?"

"When I was a girl, in Palemia. That's the tradition. All sports are done nude there. It frees the body and the spirit."

"Don't the boys..."

"Become aroused? Well, they're usually playing with other boys, so if they do..." Vahla left the

190

thought unfinished and Asperides laughed knowingly.

"Is that where you learned to dance, then?" he asked.

Vahla stiffened. "Who said I was a dancer?"

"I thought you had said something about being a dancer at one point," said Asperides, but to Vahla, it sounded lame.

"No, I didn't."

"Oh, I'm sorry." he said and a sudden silence fell between them like a curtain.

In Vahla's mind, warnings flashed. How could he know she had been a dancer? And if he did, did that mean he also knew about her attempt to kill Fantar? How else would he know? It had been nearly a year and a half since that night in Valeria when she had danced before the Emperor and he had humiliated her and dragged her off to his bed. But, there, instead of her pleasures, he had felt only the sharp bite of his own dagger, wielded by her vicious hand. She had not danced since that night, nor told anyone her history except Thorngere and King Valerius himself.

"Did you have a good childhood?" Asperides asked, seeking new ground.

A good childhood? With Fantar's hordes scourging the land with blood and fire, crushing city after city, leaving only desolation and despair? Would she ever forget the image of her grandparent's charred remains after the palace at Palemia was burned, and how stiff and wooden their corpses were as they were dragged off to shallow graves? And was it not Asperides own father who lead that assault?

"I'm sorry," said Asperides, watching her face. "I seem to have struck another wrong chord. I don't suppose there are many nowadays who can claim happy childhoods."

"Can you?"

"Well, I certainly never wanted for anything, and obviously, I didn't suffer like many who stood against the Empire. But happy? I don't know. I never understood why there was always fighting and why we had to... do what was done." His voice trailed off and now it was Vahla's turn to see the shadows of painful memories wash over his face.

"Perhaps this is not the best topic of conversation," she said.

"Perhaps not," he smiled, then went serious again. "But I never wanted all the killing and burning, Vauhna, you have to believe that. I hated that!"

"I do believe that," she said, looking deep into his eyes. But what else she could or would believe about Asperides was destined to remain a mystery, for at that moment, two of his retainers burst into their secluded grove, followed closely by Chad. Prostrating themselves, they begged a thousand pardons, but said they were sent to inform his Worship that a large band of Scythian horsemen had overrun Kundalac, a small city to the northeast, and were even now bearing down on Palmeria.

Asperides leapt into action. Leaving the picnic things where they lay, and leaving Vahla to follow with Chad, he was off at a run, issuing orders as he went for the assembly and disposition of his troops. Chad and Vahla were lucky to leap aboard the galley just as its lines were taken in and its oars bit deep into the quiet waters of the harbor, speeding the sleek craft back to its berth in the city. During the few minutes of the crossing, while Asperides huddled with his staff and while signal flags rose and fell on the signal halyard, Chad told her what he knew of the Scythians.

They were a tribe of wild, nomadic horsemen, he said, in his halting, staccato manner, believed to come from the vast steppe lands to the far north and east. They kept no permanent homes, but lived in crude tents of animal hides. When not raiding and making war, they tended huge herds of goats that roamed the vast plains, and endured terrible winters. They were a small but hardy people, said Chad, vicious fighters who inhaled smoke from the leaves of an aromatic herb before going into battle and showed no mercy. They hated the civilized city people of the south. Normally, they raided in small bands on distant frontier towns and confined themselves to stealing sheep and grain, which they seemed in constant need of. But in the past year, a great horde of them had gathered and was carrying their depredations much further south.

"How do you know all this?" asked Vahla, as usual, surprised at the sagacity of her supposedly dim-witted servant.

"Chad listen," was all he would say.

Troops were already assembling as they reached the dock and Asperides' general, Vaxagores, sat waiting for them astride a huge black charger that pawed and reared impatiently while the dock lines were secured. Behind him, a groom held two other mounts, a brown stallion and Vahla's own white palfrey. Asperides approached her with a group of his officers.

"Vauhna the Enchantress!" he called loudly while still some distance away. He stopped with his officers ranged around him and struck an official pose. All around, men fell silent. The occasion had suddenly become very public.

"Yes, your Highness."

"As you are aware, our city is under imminent threat of attack by a large band of rabble Scythians. We march forth immediately to disperse them, and as your powers are well known to all here, we would be honored if you would ride at our side and lend your vaunted arts to our cause."

"My Lord, it is I who would be honored," she replied formally, while inside her heart was hammering, "though I hardly think any poor arts of mine will be wanted." Was this, she wondered, what Volkmir meant about being a fraud?

"Excellent! It is settled, then. We leave immediately."

Vahla was allowed a few minutes at her house to change into some more suitable riding clothes, but there was no time to pack her travelling kit. Chad was instructed to follow with that, and despite his objections, to stay in the rear with the baggage.

Vahla rode at the head of the column, just behind Asperides and alongside the scarred veteran, Vaxagores. They rode out the northern gate to a fanfare of trumpets, a column of three horses and five-thousand foot soldiers, and for several hours wound their way northeast through increasingly barren country. Land along the coast at Palmeria was verdant and lush with sprawling farms rich with grain, while inland, vegetation quickly faded. The country became hilly with barren outcroppings of rock rearing up like monoliths along the way. Beyond the hills, the land opened out into a vast desert-like prairie, the same Vahla had traversed on her journey to the Shrine at Darlung. It was as their column crested the last line of hills and the leaders looked out over the plain that they saw a rolling dark cloud of dust, which heralded the approach of the Scythian horde. Vaxagores reined up beside Asperides.

"There, Viceroy," he pointed. "See how their line extends. There are a great many of them. Let us stand here, along the high ground."

"I do not intend to 'stand,' Vaxagores. I intend to attack! We will drive this rabble like cattle." And with that, Asperides formed his line and marched out onto the plain.

Vahla was now in the center of the host, riding on Asperides' right while Vaxagores rode on his left. Extending out on either hand were long lines of men, marching behind their banners under a forest of spears. Five deep they marched, moving forward at an accustomed pace, their sergeants calling out cadence, their burnished shields, already dull with dust, locked rim to rim. It was an experienced, professional force and they were silent for the most part, each man setting his mind to the task ahead, trying not to contemplate the possible consequences. But none could ignore the fact that the rapidly approaching line of dust extended well beyond their own lines.

"We should form a square, Highness," said Vaxagores, "and protect our flanks."

But Asperides would have none of it. "They are vermin, Vaxagores. We will drive through their center like a knife through bread. They will be running too fast to attack our flanks."

Vaxagores opened his mouth to speak, then thought better of it and bowed his head in acquiescence. But the quick look he gave Vahla spoke much louder than words. It was a look she would remember for a long time.

For some time, Vahla had been conscious of a deep rumbling sound like distant thunder and now, as the raging dust cloud neared and began to resolve itself into specific shapes, she was startled to realize that the sound was pounding hooves. Asperides' army must have come to the same realization, for at that moment, without command or apparent volition, they stopped in their tracks as one man. Instead of ambiguous dust now, they could all clearly see a horde of mounted men bearing down upon them: thousands and thousands of them; a force at least four times the size of their own, and moving four times faster than any army they had ever faced.

What happened next was a chaos so wild and overwhelming Vahla was only able to remember it in snatches, like a kaleidoscopic series of still images, twisted and twirling together. There was Asperides face, suddenly drained of all color, looking to her with eyes wide and full of terror. He turned and shouted to Vaxagores but in that instant, the onrushing horsemen unleashed a blizzard of arrows and the very first shaft-she retained the image in her mind as clear and distinct as a flower you hold in your hand-struck Vaxagores in the left eye just as he turned his face to Asperides. There it was for an awful instant: the absolutely still image of the man's dark, bearded visage with its long diagonal scar, his mouth open and the feathered shaft suddenly sprouting like a branch from his eye. There was no blood in that instant, no physical reaction from the force for the blow; just that horrible still life, like a painting of death.

Then he was gone, bowled dead off the back of his horse as if he had been swept by a broom, and the army around her exploded into screams of pain and terror as the storm of feathered death descended upon them. Flight after flight were loosed by the bows of the marauding horsemen who checked their headlong charge and began circling their stranded foe, screaming as they thundered by and firing directly now at targets who cowered beneath their shields.

In the swirling madness there was Asperides' face again, close to hers now, the eyes wild, the mouth screaming. Yet she heard no words, could make no sense. An arrow whizzed between them, inches from her face. Then Asperides' horse reared and screamed and she saw him falling, arms flailing wildly, face still beseeching hers as he plunged into swirling dust. Then something large smashed into her from the other side. There was a strange sense of vertigo as the world went sideways, and then everything went black.

She awoke with the rather startling thought that she had not been afraid, that even in the midst of that whirling hell, she had somehow known the arrows were not for her, that she would not be hit. Was it possible that she had really known? Or was it simply the shock of things happening so quickly that she had no time to react? She wasn't sure. But then the realization that she was awake startled her even more and she opened her eyes.

It was dark. She was in the Scythian camp, lying near a large fire onto which jubilant Scythians were tossing the spears and shields of their Palmerian foes. Others were dancing around, waving wineskins, and yelling their high-pitched battle cries. There was a tumult of celebration, and from somewhere she couldn't see, drums and flutes lent an eerie accompaniment to the wild tableau. She sat up and was immediately grabbed by the arms and dragged to her feet. Rude hands spun her around and she found herself face to face and at eye level with a grinning Mongolian visage whose savage eyes fairly danced with glee.

He said something in a language Vahla had never heard before. Seeing she did not understand, he laughed and stroked her cheek with a filthy palm. Vahla tried to slap his hand away but was constrained by others behind her. There was more conversation and she felt several hands rudely exploring her breasts, buttocks and belly. She struggled vainly to break free, but her captors just laughed, their breath fetid with curry.

Two of them grabbed her by the arms and dragged her off, around the fire towards a group of men standing before a large tent. As they neared, she was pushed forward and stumbled to her knees. When she looked up, the other men had stepped back and she found herself staring into the cruelest face she had ever seen. Vahla was not a timid woman, and not easily frightened by men - she had learned their vulnerabilities too well, and while she respected their brute power, she easily counted herself the equal of most. But this man frightened her.

"Well," he said, holding out a hand and helping her rise, "I see our woman warrior is not dead. That is excellent! It would have been a shame to waste so much beauty." He was about Vahla's height and not heavily built, but powerful. He wore an ermine lined vest over his bare chest and as he moved Vahla could see the muscles ripple softly, like a big cat. But it was his face which frightened her. It was a flat face, like all his people, but one that seemed

199

more finely chiseled and over which the skin seemed more tightly stretched. It was a face like a painted mask, without a wrinkle, without expression, and within which shone the coldest eyes she had ever seen. Even Fantar's eye, as terrible as she knew it could be, was not as frightening. Fantar's eye was wild with madness, which, oddly, evoked as much pity as terror. This man's eyes were so sane they appeared reptilian, and there was no pity in them at all.

"I am Karghan," he said, the tiniest flick of his eyes acknowledging her appraisal. "And these are my people. Come. I think you still have time to say good-bye to your friend." Taking her arm lightly - his fingers felt hot and dry on her skin, like scales - he led her to another, smaller fire, beside which she saw Asperides, bound to a pole. He had been stripped naked and hung limply from his bonds, his wrists tied at the back, his head hanging and his knees buckled. The skin on his right shoulder had been neatly sliced and peeled halfway down his arm. He was bleeding from several other spots as well, where skewers had been thrust through his skin, and his pubic area was red and hairless. Vahla soon saw why.

"This man was your leader," Karghan said. "So we have been testing his courage. Among my people it is considered an honor for a man to die well under torture. This one, I am afraid, has not done so well."

Karghan nodded to an attendant who pulled a brand from the fire and thrust it into Asperides

200

crotch. Asperides screamed, jerking wildly against his bonds, then collapsed again, moaning, when the man pulled the brand away. Then he saw Vahla and began to cry.

"Vauhna!" he sobbed like a child. "Please, don't let them hurt me anymore. Do something, Vauhna. Please don't let them kill me!" It was too painful. Vahla could not look and turned away, nausea rising in her throat. But she saw Karghan nod again, saw the flash of the attendant's sword and heard the sickening sound as the blade was driven home. Asperides grunted once and was silent.

But now it was Vahla's turn. Suddenly Karghan thrust his hand down the back of her pants and shoved his middle finger rudely up her rectum. "This is how we steer sheep in my country," he grinned, his eyes glittering in his flat face like ice crystals. Grabbing a handful of her dark hair at the nape of her neck and using his finger as a rudder, he 'steered' her back towards the big tent, his men opening a path and cheering him on as they went.

Vahla was powerless. Karghan drove her into his tent, and before she had an instant to react, slit the back of her shirt with his dagger and ripped it from her body. Vahla spun away and backed against the tent pole, her arms covering her breasts. She was terrified. Karghan stood there calmly, her shredded shirt hanging from the dagger in his hand, his face gleaming with a quiet malevolence.

"Drop your hands, my lovely," he said, "and let me admire you." Vahla obeyed as if mesmerized, and her full breasts swung free in the candle-lit interior. He gasped quickly and his slanted eyes widened with lust. "Now the trousers," he said, his voice tightened. "I want to see all of you."

Vahla pulled off her pants and stood fully exposed before him. Karghan looked her up and down slowly, savoring every inch, his breath coming more quickly as his eyes lingered about her loins. Vahla's mind was frozen with fear. She was not even sure that she breathed. She felt like a mouse cornered by a snake, just waiting for the strike.

Karghan tossed the dagger and torn shirt aside and slowly began removing his vest. But then a rough voice called from outside. Vahla could not understand the message, but could make out his name clearly. Karghan shook himself and sighed heavily, a man recalled to duty.

"I shall return shortly, my dear," he said and abruptly left the tent.

Vahla started to tremble, then shuddered violently. Wildly, she looked about the tent for some means of escape or defense. But it was sparsely and crudely furnished and the only weapon in sight was the discarded dagger, lying where Karghan had tossed it. Almost too afraid to even move, Vahla took a tentative step towards it, her hand reaching before her.

Just then, the tent flap opened and Chad walked in.

"Chad?" she said, her mouth hanging open. "What are you doing here?"

"Chad bring extra clothes," he said casually and handed her a small bundle. "We go now, yes?"

"Go?" she asked.

"Yes, go now."

Vahla stared at him for a long moment, then, quickly and without further question, pulled on the clothes he had brought and followed him out of the tent.

Outside, she saw Karghan standing in the shadow of the tent, speaking to another man, and immediately shrank back in fear. But Chad motioned her on. "Come now," he said in a normal tone of voice. "It OK. They not hear or see. We go now."

Vahla stared, her mouth hanging, then took a tentative step after him. Karghan stood, not three feet away, totally oblivious. She took another step, then another. All around, the Scythian host continued their wild celebration, but neither he nor they paid the slightest attention as Chad lead Vahla through the camp to the picket lines where he had tethered two horses, her own white palfrey and a small pony for himself. Helping her up, he mounted himself, then turned and trotted off into the night. Vahla followed, absolutely dumbfounded.

"Chad," she asked finally as the Scythian camp settled into the darkness behind and the hills before them stood silhouetted under soft moonlight, "how did you do that?"

"Chad have ways," he said.

"Did you learn it from Volkmir?"

But instead of answering, Chad spurred his pony and trotted off ahead.

"Chad!" she called after him, "Who are you?"

He paused and turned back and to look at her with his head cocked to one side, like a bird. "Who Chad?"

"Yes, who are you?"

"Chad a servant, lady," he said, and trotted on.

"Yes," she muttered, trotting after him, "but whose?"

Chapter 15
TRANSFORMATIONS

Another morning, another fresh crop of dead sprawled on the raw earth, some already partly swallowed by the growing mound that doomed them. Morning after morning it was like this, Valerius looking out from his walls at the long night's labor-his and Vincipius'-the newly dead, some with arrows still protruding, scattered on the front edge of the slope, and the mound behind them growing ever higher, ever closer to the threatened walls of Zagorbia.

Vincipius was building a ramp. Working at night under cover of the dark, his men would plod forward in their thousands, two with a rock- and earth-filled basket between them, a third providing cover with a shield. Up the growing slope they trudged to the skidded barricade at the end, there to dump their loads and trudge back for more-unless, of course, one of the arrows lofted by Zagorbia's defenders happened to find them, in which case they themselves were tossed over the barricade, without ceremony, their remains to be covered by successive baskets of earth as they were interred in the mound they helped build.

It was, Valerius noted again this morning, a cruel, heartless tactic, but one which would ultimately succeed. Valerius could not burn this ramp, and even though he had sent out sortie after sortie, there was too much of it to tear down. His efforts only slowed its progress. Night by night the ramp grew, and when it reached his walls...

Valerius spun from the battlements and angrily stalked away, unwilling to contemplate that eventuality. The irony was this was partly his own doing. Oh, perhaps Vincipius would have come to it on his own-he was an engineer, after all-but it certainly seemed no coincidence that construction had begun very shortly after Ragnar began launching his nightly attacks from the swamp. At the very least, Vincipius had used that to his advantage, telling his men that since Valerius was raising the souls of the dead against them at night, their best defense was to stay awake and work through the night. Only that way, prisoners had reported Vincipius' words, could they bring down this pretender and forever end his evil spells.

And that was exactly what would happen, Valerius knew, if something didn't change soon. And since he had heard nothing from Grumwald and nothing from Thorngere, change seemed unlikely. What was likely was that the ramp would get close enough, and an assault would be mounted, first on the ramp itself, then all along the walls. If he were very confident, Vincipius would also support it by sea. Zagorbia's defenders would be overwhelmed, Vincipius' host would pour into the city, and they would all be butchered, including Valerius, his beautiful young wife, and his soon-to-be-born son. What was likely was that the job Fantar had started eighteen years before would finally be completed and the line of Valerius

Everreigning, High Kings of Valeria and all the Inland Sea, would be gone forever.

Valerius stopped and leaned against another battlement, his attention caught by a form at the base of the mound. Had it moved? He watched closely, but the man lay as still as the earth around him. He was a young man-hardly more than a boy-clean of face and limb, sturdy and well favored but for the feathered shaft sprouting from the hollow of his neck, just behind the collarbone. Valerius shook his head sadly. Enemy or not, somewhere a mother or sweetheart pined for this young man, yearned for the flash of his smile, the crush of his embrace. Yet there he lay, his journey over before it had hardly begun, his eye never to grace home or sweetheart more.

Besides, whether Zagorbia was doomed or not, Valerius could not see this young man as an enemy. Vincipius was an enemy. His generals and his army were enemies, but not hapless young men like this. It had been thus with Valerius of late (and more so as Eomer's belly grew full with child): he fought with implacable fury, was more than ever determined to beat off Vincipius and continue his quest to overthrow Fantar, but in between, at times like these, and especially when it involved the young, he felt an ever growing sense of remorse that it must be so. It was almost-although he knew he was not being selfish-as if he felt guilty for causing the conflict in the first place. Yes, he was the son of High Kings going back beyond memory, and yes, he was the rightful heir to an empire, which had been brutally usurped, brutally raped and repressed. But did that, ultimately, give him the right to cause the death of a young man like that, of all these men, friend and foe alike?

But wait. The hand. There, he was sure this time. It had moved. Valerius called down and in moments, a squad dashed out and carried the fellow in. Valerius climbed down from the wall and knelt beside him. He was indeed alive, though for how long was questionable. The arrow had penetrated deep into the hollow behind his clavicle. If the head dislodged when they removed it, there would be little chance: it was unlikely they could extract it from that position, and it would most likely fester there, killing him more slowly and painfully than torture. Still, it was worth a try.

Valerius followed as they carried the young man into the hall were the wounded were treated and laid him on a table. Seeing the King, an attendant scurried over, all official and comforting. He examined the wound, noting the angle of the shaft, and confirmed Valerius' diagnosis: a tricky case. Would His Majesty perhaps pull the shaft himself, the man wanted to know? The hands of the King were, after all, healing hands.

Valerius stared at the man, at his presumption, and at his evident fear that his own hands, under the watchful eyes of that very King, would prove killing hands, and nodded: this would not be the first arrow he had pulled from a wound. He remembered a particularly galling shaft he had once pulled from Thorngere; an operation so tricky he had ended up slicing the entry wider and inserting his finger to guide the barbed head out. That wouldn't work here, but it did give him an idea. Grabbing another arrow from one of the bearers, he quickly pulled off its head, ground the end smooth and round against the stone wall, then with his own dagger, carved a hook-like notch just back from the tip.

He tested the arrow in the young man's neck: it was solid, as if embedded in earth. But when he moved it, the man stirred and grunted softly. Valerius nodded for attendants to hold him steady, gently wiped the blood away from the opening of the wound, and peered closely to check the angle at which the arrowhead had entered the flesh. But he was interrupted by a light tap on his shoulder and the attendant's very apologetic, "Majesty?"

When he turned, a very white faced young man-one of his own household servants-was standing nervously before him, wringing his hands. "What is it, Bartholome?"

"The Queen, Your Majesty-begging your pardon. The Queen bids me tell you her time has come, Majesty."

"Her time?" Valerius' face clouded.

"Her water, Your Majesty, it broke some time ago now."

"Her water?" Suddenly, the fog, which had settled on Valerius' mind, was cleared as if seared by lightening. "Her water!" he exclaimed. "It's the baby! By the Gods! Yes, well..." and he turned thrice and took steps in several different directions, his heart bouncing about in his chest like a ball, before taking a huge breath, clenching his fists and forcing himself to be calm. "Yes. Thank you Bartholome. How long? How much time do I have?"

The young man shrugged. "The pains come quite quickly now, Your Majesty."

"Very well. Yes. And her mid-wife is with her? Good. Yes." Valerius looked at his hands, at the blood on them and at the dulled, notched arrow shaft he still held. "Tell the Queen I will be there as soon as I can. I must attend to this young man first. But tell her..." and here he paused, conscious of the rapt attention of every eye in the hall, "tell her our joy is boundless and that she bears the hope and future of the Empire."

The men cheered. Then Bartholome was gone and the hall emptied of sound as Valerius turned back to the still figure on the table. His working the arrow had started the wound bleeding again and a small puddle was forming under the boy's shoulder, pushing its way towards the table edge. Valerius' hands were shaking. Indeed, he felt shaky all over. He motioned for a stool, and when it was positioned behind him, sat down heavily. He closed his eyes, took another deep breath, and felt his hands relax. Gently, he pulled the protruding shaft aside with his left hand, and very delicately, began inserting the notched shaft with his right.

It seemed to take forever. Using just his fingers, he pushed his probe in and in, sliding the notched end along the other shaft, moving just slowly enough for the torn flesh to slip around the new intrusion. The young man made no movement, though four men stood ready to hold him. The wound was very deep-at least six inches-but finally, he felt his shaft butt against the arrowhead. Probing with it, he felt the tined end. In his mind, he could see the whole arrow clearly now, and pushing even more cautiously than before, slid his notched probe down the flat side of the arrow head and hooked it on the point.

He sat back to draw breath and an attendant wiped the sweat from his brow with a cloth. The young man still lay quietly, and around him, as many faces as could squeeze into a circle stared open-mouthed. Overhead, sun spilled in through the gabled end of the hall, splashing against the trussed rafters, and shimmering in the dusty air. Valerius closed his eyes, muttered a brief prayer, and with another deep breath, bent back to his work.

This would be the tricky part. Arrows tended to spin in flight and oftentimes, when they sank into flesh, the spin continued, making a spiraled path in the wound. This head, as near as he could tell, had grazed the collar bone as it entered and had only twisted slightly from there as the angle of the head at the bottom was only a few degrees off from the angle of the cut at the top. Still, he would have to guide the arrow along that very path if he was to remove the shaft without doing more damage. And with the two barbs opposing him, that would be tricky. Then, again, what if the tip of the notch broke off in the wound?

Gently, he separated the back ends of the two shafts, and keeping the tips together while maintaining a slight downward pressure on the notched shaft, began to pull. Immediately, the young man twitched and groaned. The attendants grabbed him at thigh and shoulder, but after that, he did not move: only his breath came in long, rasping gasps.

Valerius pulled again and the shaft moved. But almost immediately he could feel the left-hand barb snag on flesh. Pushing back and twisting slightly counterclockwise, he felt it let go and pulled again. Again the shafts moved, emerging ever so slowly for a fraction of an inch until a barb snagged again. This time, he pushed the notched shaft back into the wound, then slid it up along the edge of the arrow head: he could feel the flesh release the barb like a piece of cloth coming loose from a thorn. Re-hooking the point, he pulled again, and again the shaft moved.

Bit by bit, the arrow came, the wound bleeding more with every inch, and the puddle on the table spreading to the edge and over, dribbling and splattering on the floor between Valerius' legs. Slowly and steadily he worked, pulling, probing to unsnag a barb, then pulling again, while the faces in the tight circle around him watched, their features twitching with every move. Overhead, the sun's rays inched along the trussed rafters, brightening one side, leaving the other in deepening shadow.

An hour passed, then most of a second, and finally, right-hand barb first, the arrow emerged.

212

Valerius sagged on his stool, totally spent, while the room erupted in cheers and the officious attendant moved in swiftly to staunch the blood which now flowed even more freely from the open wound. On the table, the unconscious young man seemed to sense his victory and sighed contentedly.

The sigh seemed to electrify Valerius. Eomer! Leaping from the stool, he hurried from the hall and along the twisted lanes to the palace complex. Then, his armor clattering, he bound up the steps to his personal apartments, two at a time. Bartholome was waiting as he burst through the door, his hands clasped before him, his expression twisted with anxiety. Valerius stopped short at the sight of him.

"What! What is it, man?"

"At last you're here, Your Majesty!"

"What? How is she? How's Eomer? The Queen."

"You'd better go right in, Your Majesty."

Valerius hurried on through the atrium where marble fauns cavorted around a splashing fountain, and down the hallway to the bedchamber he shared with Eomer. For an instant, his mind flashed back to his first sight of Eomer the woman. She was on the double-hulled catumaran with Thorngere, sailing downwind like a gull skipping over the waves. Eomer was standing forward, drenched with spray, clinging to the mast at her back. Valerius had at first thought she was a sea nymph. She was the most beautiful creature he had ever seen.

The midwife, Beryl, and her attendants had just left the bedchamber and were pulling the door closed behind them. Beryl was carrying a bucket and the attendants, bloody linen. Valerius tried not to look into the bucket, but his eyes went before he could stop himself: it was a bloody mess of something and he looked quickly away. For a long instant, his heart stopped and he stood there, open-mouthed. Then Beryl put her finger to her lips.

"You go right in, Your Majesty. But do try to be quiet. They're both resting."

"Both?"

"Your Queen and your new son, Your Majesty." And she smiled a crooked, benevolent smile of one who had seen this a thousand times but never ceased to wonder at the mystery of it all.

Valerius sagged against the wall, relief flooding through him. Then, with a nod of thanks to Beryl, he softly pushed open the door. The curtains were drawn and the room was dark but still, he could see Eomer sitting up against the pillows in the bed. She was holding something. Softly, he tiptoed to her side and she looked up and smiled. Her face was drawn and pale, her eyes tired, and her hair still matted against her scalp with sweat.

"Your son, My Lord," she said, holding up the bundle in her arms. It was wrapped tightly in a blanket and he could see she had been trying to put it to her breast. In the shadows, he could see the tiny shape of a face, but that was all.

Valerius felt like he was suspended in the air, like he wasn't breathing. He looked down at Eomer. "I was attending a wounded man and couldn't leave.

I'm sorry. I didn't realize it would happen so fast. Are you all right?"

Eomer smiled again, a warm, happy smile this time, and patted the side of the bed. Valerius sat. "I'm fine," she said. "He came very quickly and with little trouble. Beryl said I've the hips to bear an army."

"I'll have her whipped, the impertinent hag," he said, a smile warming his own face. "And the boy?"

"That is your decision, My Lord. He is yours to accept or reject." It was the proper, formal thing to say-he did have that right-but still, the words shocked him. "Here," she said, pushing the bundle onto his lap. "I've done my duty. Now you must do yours."

Valerius shied away, then awkwardly took the thing: it was so tiny it weighed almost nothing at all. Then it moved and he looked at Eomer helplessly. Laughing, she showed him how to hold it, gently supporting the head. Like a man carrying a very full glass of wine, Valerius took the bundle to the window and pulled open the drapes. The little red face within the blanket squeezed its eyes shut against the light, then opened one, and looked directly at Valerius. Suddenly, in a profound rush of emotion, Valerius realized there was intelligence there, that; he was staring into the eye of another human being. His son.

Then the baby began to scream, a lusty bellowing that tickled Valerius as much as it frightened him. "Oh, hold on there, little fellow," he laughed. "I won't be torturing you long. We've just got to do our duty here, then you can go right back to your mother."

He laid the baby on a table beside the window, and working as carefully as he had before in removing the arrow, unwrapped the blanket. Before him, kicking and screaming for all he was worth, lay a perfectly formed, tiny, wrinkled, red-skinned little person. They had put a little cap on him and with his face all scrunched up he looked so much like a tiny gnome that Valerius laughed out loud. Then he looked him over, as was his duty, and a voice way deep in his brain whispered, "The next generation." And as his eyes passed over the boy's scrotum, the voice said again, "and the generation after that."

Valerius was rocked to his very toes. It was a sensation quite unlike anything he had ever experienced. He felt both shocked and numb, both frozen and floating, like he was either groggy from a heavy blow or giddy from a heady wine. It was like he had been standing before a blank stone wall and suddenly a door had opened before him. But it was more than a door, more than himself. It was his entire history, the history of his entire line. Suddenly, he was no longer at the end of that line. He had a successor, an heir.

Valerius put his great hand on the infant's chest and the boy quieted at the touch. Then, in a solemn voice, Valerius recited the words his father had said over him, and his father before that, back for a millennium: "I call you my son and name you Valerian, Valerius to be, and hereby acknowledge

216

you as Prince and Heir to the Throne Everreigning, High King of Valeria and all the Inland Sea. Thus I have spoken, and thus it shall be."

Chapter 16
FIRE FROM THE SKY

The next morning, a weary Valerius mounted the outside staircase to the roof of the palace. Dawn was just breaking, splashing onto the rocky peak of the promontory north of the city, and spilling dappled across the vast morning blue of the sea. But Valerius was in no shape to appreciate the beauties of the dawn. The official naming rites for Valerian and the celebration that followed had run very late-despite the continued mound building just outside the walls-and this morning his head pounded like a blacksmith's hammer, and his body felt like it had been hit with one. He was too old, he thought, to go carrying on like that.

Yet he was still ebullient over the birth of his son and thought if there ever was a morning auspicious enough for his fabled Eye Stone to reveal its powers, this would be it. He pulled the great red gem from its leather pouch, and was in the act of draping the chain around his neck when his eye was caught by something at the harbor mouth. He watched as a small fishing boat pulled around the point and made for port. There was nothing unusual about the boat, or the fact that a fisherman would be returning to port at this hour-strangely, Vincipius had made no attempt to blockade the port or interrupt its normal activities-but something about it was not right. For a few moments, he stood puzzling over it until the realization hit him: there were too many sweeps. A normal fishing boat would carry a crew of two, no more than three. Yet here were three sweeps per side, pulling mightily, and a man in the stern sheets, vigorously sculling as well. And as the boat neared, he could see other figures, too, huddled in the waist. One of them was gray-headed. It was Grumwald! Valerius fairly leaped back down the steps and raced for the harbor, his attempt to use the Eye all but forgotten.

The boat had already docked when Valerius arrived, and its passengers, including Grumwald and Ragnar, were standing in a tight knot on the jetty. But it was not Grumwald or even Ragnar who first stepped forward to greet the King. Instead, it was a well-dressed, but strange looking Kantaran with a red face and the merest stubble for hair that stepped out from behind them. When Valerius recognized him, he stopped in his tracks.

"Koltar?"

"Greetings to Your Majesty," said this worthy, bowing deeply, while behind him, the others tried to contain their smiles. Then Grumwald and Ragnar, too, stepped forward and bowed.

"Gentlemen," said Valerius, looking from one to the other as a grin spread wide across his own features, "I greet you all most heartily. You have no idea how welcome you are! I will not embarrass his majesty, King Koltar, here by asking what happened to his hair and beard. I'm sure there is an interesting story there, but let us go. There is much to be done and very little time."

Quickly, Valerius led his guests on a tour of the walls and apprised them of the situation. All was quiet on the field, but archers crouched behind battlements with arrows nocked, watching the wood line for any sign of movement. The barrier at the top of the mound loomed ominously close to the walls, and a crop of newly dead, some half buried, lay sprawled along its front. There was about the whole a lingering scent of death and despair.

At the palace, things seemed cheerier. They visited Eomer and her new babe, then repaired to the Council Chamber overlooking the pure azure sea. Food and drink were spread before them, and after toasting the High King on the birth of young Valerian, they fell to with a will.

Hunger and thirst satisfied, they settled down to business. At Koltar's insistence, Grumwald began by reciting the long story of his tribulations in the Fortunate Isles and his quest for the traitor Haradin. They had finally cornered Haradin in a deep canyon on the back side of the island. But by the time they had fought their way in, the man was already dead and his remains had been served as a banquet for his fellows. Aware by then of the siege at Zagorbia, Grumwald had left the rest of the population to fend for themselves and had sailed back to Kantar. There he had found His Majesty King Koltar and his cavalry ready to embark as well, and together they had sailed north until Ragnar had diverted them into the river on the south coast.

Ragnar's report was brief and to the point. As planned, he and several hundred of his followers had resumed their old haunts among the swamps south of the city and had been praying at night -

spirit-like- on the enemy's troops. In the old days, Ragnar said, before Valerius took the city, his men had so terrorized Tarpon's troops that none would even venture into the swamps. The same could not be claimed here, he bragged, but there were now very few among Vincipius' troops who were not afraid of ghosts.

"Ha!" laughed Valerius. "That's good. But do you think you could do something to make them afraid of shovels?"

"I might be able to help there," said Koltar.

"Yes, your majesty," said Valerius. "You've been holding back, keeping us all in suspense here: are you ready now to tell us how you managed to lose your hair and beard?"

"That was an accident," said Koltar with a smug little smile. "But when you hear how the accident happened-and how I've managed to bring along an entire shipload of similar accidents-I think you'll agree that it was quite fortuitous."

As the first glimmerings of the following dawn appeared in the east, Valerius stood again on his palace roof awaiting the final signal that all was in place. It was already hot this morning and Valerius wiped the sweat from his palms onto his tunic as he stared out into the blackness of the sea, his mind flitting among a thousand doubts and details. During the night, Grumwald had sailed around the city and should even now be in position to attack Vincipius' fleet on the beach. But what if the relay ship was at the wrong angle for him to see the signal? What if the relay ship could not see

Grumwald's signal? Or what if Grumwald's fleet was seen from shore and Vincipius launched his own ships before Grumwald could attack? What if it was a trap? Attacking the fleet was such an obvious ruse, and Vincipius had done so little to forestall it, that Valerius feared Vincipius was waiting for him, that he hoped Valerius would split his forces like this all along. Of course, Vincipius didn't know about Grumwald, but still, splitting forces had almost cost Valerius the battle of Kantar, and the subject had been hotly debated in the Council Chamber the previous afternoon.

Grumwald was not keen on the plan. His men were exhausted and dispirited after their ordeal, and after five days at sea aboard cramped galleys on short rations, he feared they were not up to the task. But, in plain truth, there was little option. Since Valerius could not launch a concerted attack from his position with the men he had, what good would the addition of Grumwald's men do? The very arrival of his fleet would alert Vincipius and eliminate the possibility of surprise. They could have attacked from the swamps, as Ragnar had counseled, but that, too, would have split their forces and would also have allowed Vincipius a way out. Pushed from the swamps by Ragnar and Grumwald, and from the city by Valerius, Vincipius could simply have boarded his ships and sailed away. Worse, he might sail around and take the undefended city in their rear, leaving Valerius and all his forces out in the swamp. Wouldn't that be a pretty turn of events for a would-be High King: to end up in a swamp!

No, it was better thus, even with the risks. And if Koltar's bit of magic worked as promised-and as his own appearance seemed to indicate it would-then he should be able to bag Vincipius' army and his fleet.

Valerius had his suspicions about the soundness of that army. Oh, they were good men, to be sure, and driven to battle they would undoubtedly fight-as they had all these past months. But neither were these the hardened veterans who had won Fantar his empire. These were their sons, or more probably, the sons of those they had conquered, and Valerius was not at all sure of their willingness to continue the fight for this particular cause.

But that was all to be seen, and would be if the signal ever shone. Hearing footsteps, Valerius turned as Koltar himself approached, a small dark figure materializing in the pre-dawn gray. They greeted each other quietly, as old comrades on watch.

"All is ready at the catapults, Your Majesty."

"Aye. All is ready everywhere, except I think the skipper of that signal boat forgot his flint and steel: the signal should have shone before now."

"We've time yet, before dawn. But I wanted to take a moment to personally congratulate Your Majesty on the birth of your son."

"Ah, thank you Koltar." Valerius bent to shake the smaller man's hand, his warm smile brightening the darkness. "You are entirely welcome. It is a wondrous thing, as I'm sure I don't need to tell you."

"I expect it might be a bit different with us," said Koltar, referring to the near extinction of his race during the time they were exiled in New Kantar. "Though I assure you, when we returned to the Old City and found our potency had returned, it too was a wondrous thing."

"Have you any notion how many sons you have now?"

"None at all, though we've so many new pure bred children the whole city looks like a nursery. But we wanted to avoid problems of lineage for the time being, so we've been rotating the women among groups of us until they get pregnant."

Valerius laughed a short, barking laugh in the still darkness. "Boy, there's tough duty!"

"You'd think so until you try it. Repopulating a city is not exactly a lark. I actually envy you with your Queen and now a son you can call your own..."

"And an army hammering at my gates? Where is that signal? But I do see what you mean, Koltar, and I tell you, it is a wondrous thing: I never thought I would react like this. The feeling when I look at that boy is like nothing I've ever experienced in this life. I can't even begin to describe it."

"Well, I wish you all joy."

"Thank you. But can you assure me again that these new contraptions of yours will work as you claim?"

"I am singed with assurance, Your Majesty."

"Ha! No man could offer more, I'm sure. But look. There it is! Let us go, my dear King Koltar, and see if we can't scorch a few of these other fellows."

Vincipius stood with his staff officers at the edge of the clearing, watching as an endless parade of men trooped out of the darkness, lugging baskets of earth between them. In the ghostly pre-dawn light he could just see the shape of the mound rising against the sky and beyond, the smudged line that marked the walls of the city. It was strangely quiet at this time, he thought, the sounds of shuffling feet and sliding earth having a muffled quality as if the grayness itself was an absorbent. It was quiet in the city, too. Usually, this was the time when the archers were their most active, when they could almost begin to aim. And it was the time when his men were most tired, the shield bearers least on their guard. Yet today there was nothing but a strange stillness that seemed almost oppressive, almost suspicious.

A sense of foreboding tickled the back of Vincipius' neck, but he dismissed it as unworthy. What could he do, this Valerius? Had he not sortied a hundred times before this and still the mound grew? And as it crept ever closer to the walls, was Vincipius not even more prepared to deal with counter measures? Even now, fanning out through the forest and along the filled edge of the swamp, there were hundreds of troops, armed and at the ready. Any sortie would be crushed before it even reached the base of the mound.

No, there was no reason for suspicion. Things were well in hand. And even though the mound moved ever more slowly as it grew, its destination was as certain as the dawn. And on that dawn, whenever it came, when ramps were dropped over those final few feet, and when his massed troops in their thousands attacked along the whole wall by ramp and by ladder, then would that city fall as certain as he stood. And when he returned to Fantar with the head of Valerius...

But, he was getting ahead of himself, a rash thing in a man who prided himself on being so methodical. There was plenty to do before that day came-if it ever did-and just as he would not allow himself to doubt, neither would he tempt his fate by speculating on glories yet unearned. The Gods alone knew in what shape his fate was fashioned and he would leave to them its unveiling.

In the meantime, they and he knew what labors lay ahead and that only by the most rigid discipline and strict adherence to plan would he succeed. He had been driving his men mercilessly since the failure of the tower assault, and driving himself harder still. While they were allowed to sleep in shifts during the day, he was lucky to grab an hour or two in the course of twenty-four, and while it was they who carried the earth, it was his will that moved them and his presence alone that held them together.

In truth, his army was as near panic and exhaustion as it was near victory, and Vincipius felt like a man walking a narrow ridge towards a distant summit. If he pushed them too fast, they would succumb to exhaustion. Yet if he left them too much leisure to think and gossip among themselves-armies were so like old women! -then superstition would overwhelm them. And the Gods knew to what end that would lead. For try as he might, he had been utterly unable to convince these rude, unlettered conscripts that the rock this Valerius so prided himself on did not have magical powers, or that these nasty sappers who stole about the swamps during the night slitting the odd throat were not in fact the souls of the dead, returned to wreak vengeance on their oppressors. And just as he was unable to teach them reason, so were there others who taught them worse, who played on their fears for whatever reason and had worked them so into a pitch of panic that the only way Vincipius could be certain they would do their duty was when they were in line, under the eye and lash of their commanders, actually doing it.

So he drove them as fast as he dared, and the mound grew with predictable precision as his force and his supplies diminished, all moving towards that singular point, the efficacy of which he would not allow himself to doubt.

The light was growing perceptibly now, and Vincipius could distinguish the shapes of men moving up and down the mound. A mist had risen from the swamps, too, cooling the air with a miasmic feeling of dampness and menace that seemed to reflect itself in the faces of the men tramping by, in the eyes of those who increasingly dared to meet his exalted gaze. Or was that, too, unworthy imagining?

This Vincipius would never learn, for at that moment, his ruminations were cut short by the thunking sound of a catapult arm hitting its stop. He strained to see the arch of the projectile, but nothing etched the glowering sky until a sudden burst of flame lit up the back slope of the mound. A scream pierced the misty air and a man-shape, wreathed all in fire, fled towards the swamps below, falling after a few steps and rolling into extinction. But then there were other thunks, many of them, and the orderly procession of mound builders quickly dissolved into pandemonium as fiery explosions erupted like tiny volcanoes up and down the slope. Other men were hit and burned like torches. The barrier at the edge of the mound erupted in flame, and burned wildly like a hero's pyre.

Screaming men, wide-eyed with fear, streamed past Vincipius. "It's Valerius!" they yelled. "The Eye Stone brings fire from the sky!" And when he tried to stop several, they fought him, kicking and clawing and bellowing like beasts. They had become a mob. He let them go and stood watching the spectacle like a guest in hell.

Then the aim of the catapults shifted and it was the turn of his massed guard troops to feel the fire. Explosions erupted among them under the trees and along the swamp's edge. In the fire's eerie glow, their orderly ranks melted away and they streamed for the rear. Vincipius stood among them like a rock on the shore when the swirling foam of a crashing wave is sucked back into the sea. He stood watching helpless as the city's gates opened and the defending troops poured forth. Among them were other catapults, small units, built up on wheels and pushed along by squads of men. These stopped as the city's troops formed around them, their long arms drawn back, and in unison another cascade of projectiles soared towards Vincipius' dissolving lines.

One landed at Vincipius' feet. It struck in a puddle of mud, which splattered his brilliant skirts and breastplate. The abruptness of it startled him, and he looked down to see a small sphere, apparently made of clay, about the size of his own head. Curiously, it did not explode. As his staff scrambled to get away and then fled with his men, he stood frozen, watching the thing warily, as one would eye a serpent. Then, heedless of his own exposed position, he knelt to examine it more closely. It was not a fully enclosed sphere, he noticed, but had an opening on one side where another vessel had been inserted. Wet clay glistened around the lip of this, apparently sealing the opening.

Vincipius reached out to grab the thing, then drew his hands back quickly. They were trembling and his heart was pounding loudly in his chest. Before the walls, the city's troops launched another fusillade, which exploded all around him, then began to advance. Vincipius reached out again, knowing he only had a few seconds. But the secret of this weapon-and this God-given opportunity to uncover it-was much too important to ignore. His fingers shook visibly as they closed around the sphere and lifted it from the mud. It was filled with some sort of liquid that he could feel sloshing about. Carefully, like a father with a newborn babe, he wrapped the thing in his arms and scurried off into the woods.

The completeness of the rout quickly became apparent when, within a half-mile, the forces fleeing from the walls ran into others of their kind fleeing from Grumwald's attack on their fleet. He had achieved total surprise and when he beached his fleet among the enemy ships, he found them nearly undefended. Most of Vincipius' men were on mound building detail and Grumwald's assault, joining with Ragnar's men from the swamps, swept them before it like chaff in a strong wind.

Vincipius was in a furious state by the time he caught up with his troops in a deep forest clearing. In this one twist he saw all his plans collapsing and with a growing sense of desperation, he mounted a large boulder to try and rally the men around him. "Look," he shouted, holding the round clay sphere overhead and shaking it, "these fireballs are no magic! This has nothing to do with the Eye of Valeria. They're simple clay pots with some special liquid inside. Listen," he yelled and shook the thing loudly.

The men around him looked up, their faces suddenly sharp and thoughtful, the masks of fear falling away. Had they been made fools of? What were these things, really? Was this man-made fire, not magic? But at that moment, fate, or the gods-or even magic if you will-played another turn. In the wildness of his demonstration, the sphere suddenly exploded, engulfing Vincipius in a shower of liquid fire.

Chapter 17
CHANGES

There are times in the lives of men when change can be as calamitous as a great storm at sea, when thunderous waves crash onto beaches and the gale drives great ships far from their charted courses. These are times of great beginnings and abrupt ends. But there are other times, middle times, when change is more subtle, when it is hardly even perceptible, yet just as significant: times when things sought long ago are quietly forgotten, when old questions cease to nag, when paths long trod disappear among rocks. Sometimes, this process can be as imperceptible as age itself, where often the only difference between this moment and the last is that this moment has not yet succumbed to the next, until at some point a boundary is past, a season is done, or you are no longer young. The great clock has ticked through that time and now you must move on, do something else, go somewhere else, start something new.

The next two weeks marked such a turning point in Valerius' life. It was not dramatic, not visible, and not even evident to him until many years later when he looked back on his course and saw here a fundamental turning.

The first thing of course was to deal with the remains of Vincipius' army. Valerius was with the van in the attack, and at the moment of Vincipius' immolation, he was at the very edge of the same clearing, about to launch yet another fusillade of firebombs. But when the enemy saw him in the flaring light of that human torch, with his huge frame etched against the dark of the trees, and the great red gem seeming to pulse on his chest, and with an avenging army on either hand, they threw down their arms and prostrated themselves before him. They were all done. A few officers tried to rally them, but these were quickly dispatched-some even by their own men-and as Grumwald marched in from the other side and Ragnar's troops emerged like wraiths from the swamps, the rest were instantly transformed from a besieging host into a herd of docile sheep.

The count of captured men was near eleven thousand and when Grumwald sailed back into the harbor, he brought with him Vincipius' fleet of more than one hundred and thirty ships and an untold amount of war gear and other supplies. The harbor was so crowded there was not room enough for all the ships to swing at anchor. Many were beached along the southwest strand and others were rafted three and four deep along the quay. The prisoners were immediately put to work tearing down the mound. They used the earth to build more land along the edge of the swamp-upon which many were forced to camp-and as the bodies of their unfortunate comrades were exhumed, each was set upon a proper pyre and sent off with appropriate ceremony. This impressed the men, who had been led to believe Valerius was in league with the evil one himself, and by the time the mound was gone, most had forsaken their enmity and sworn allegiance to the High King.

Valerius was moved by this, but not really surprised. He knew what conditions they had lived under and under what terms they served. What did surprise him was their youth. Moving among them day after day, officiating at the ceremonies for their dead, speaking here and there with those who were not struck dumb by his presence, he was struck by it again and again. There were young men among his own troops, certainly, and not a few of them. But there was also a strong cadre of seasoned veterans and a goodly number of men his own age and even older. But not among Vincipius' troops. These men were conscripted from conquered lands, and the fact of their youth told more loudly than any poet the story of Fantar's rampages. There were no older men simply because there were no older men. An entire generation had either fled or been put to the sword, and it led Valerius to wonder if these men even knew of their fathers' struggles or of what had been lost.

He was also surprised by how superstitious they were. He had expected Koltar's firebombs to be a major tactical surprise. It was, after all, a brand new weapon. But that they should believe Valerius caused the explosions by the magic of his Eye Stone, well, that was a bit hard to swallow. Even young Emaus, the man from whom Valerius had pulled the arrow; when he heard the tale after being allowed to visit among his old comrades, even he believed it was magic and would not be dissuaded by the King himself. Had not that very king brought him back from the dead, he insisted? So why not a little fire? And when the story of this resurrection spread, Valerius' reputation rose even higher.

There were other things, too, which had undermined their allegiance. Stories had spread about the camp of a horned god who had appeared in the shape of a beautiful woman and wreaked havoc among the troops guarding the eastern perimeter. These men were lucky to escape with their lives and claimed it was He-or She-who ruled the swamp demons and the souls of the dead that Valerius had sent against them. Then there was the story of the Oracle, which was apparently spreading like wildfire all around the Inland Sea. Though Valerius could hardly credit the Oracle at Cartho with taking such a political risk, it was reported that she-or again, the horned god who assumed her shape-had foretold doom for Fantar and that he, when he heard, had become fey and ranted that he now had nothing to fear. Their Emperor, the rumors whispered, was sinking quickly into madness.

All this augured well and spurred Valerius even more to launch his assault on Valeria. He had heard nothing from Thorngere or any of Gamlarch's operatives and could only assume they had gotten his messages and were holed up in the mountains, waiting. He cut short the victory celebration after the battle-telling his men that this victory was but one part of a larger triumph and that they must press on now, while the time was ripe-and even as the mound was disappearing, he was busy making preparations. There was not a moment to lose.

Within the week, Koltar's Kantaran cavalry arrived: four thousand men, near six thousand horse and another eighty-odd ships. These tiny men were the same doughty warriors Valerius had first led against the Iblis. They were too small to stand in line against outland troops, but they were as quick and agile as squirrels, and when mounted on sturdy ponies and armed with bows, they were a wickedly effective force.

But the harbor literally could not contain them. Neither could the town nor the space between the town and the swamp. All were already filled with men. Yet they needed to come ashore-the horses had already been too long afloat, and the men themselves were not exactly comfortable-and they needed the jetties to land. So a great shuffling match ensued in which Vincipius' former ships were sailed back to the strand from whence they came, and Koltar's men landed at the jetty and rode through the town to take up the enemy's old camping grounds in the forest to the east. The result, in terms of population distribution, was that the environs around Zagorbia looked pretty much the same as before Vincipius' defeat, except that now, all thirty thousand plus men crowding around were under the single command of Valerius Everreigning.

The shuffle also helped Valerius get the first news he had heard from the outside world since before the siege. And he did not like it.

The news came from a supply ship sent to Vincipius from Valeria. Seeing the fleet on the beach just as it was supposed to be, the unsuspecting captain obligingly beached his ship only to be promptly captured by the neighboring crews, hauled off to the city, and presented to the rebel king.

The captain was a garrulous old veteran named Uban who paid allegiance to whoever offered cargo. Valerius or Vincipius were all one to him, so long as his haulage was paid, and once he realized he was not in immediate danger, he was happy to fill this new king in on any number of topics. He, too, had heard of the Oracle and of the Emperor's strange response, but that was not the latest. He had lately come from the east, he reported, where a great horde of Scythian nomads had swept down from the north and invested Palmeria. The local ruler, a young Turk named Asperides, son of old general Armagon-did his Majesty ever know him? -had tried to stand before them but was utterly routed and himself killed. Now the vandals ravaged the countryside, raping and killing at will and stripping the land of grain, while what was left of Asperides' army cowered behind the walls and dared not even to open their gates to a peddler.

The people were in panic, he said. They feared the Emperor was powerless to protect them, or just too crazy to care. It was also rumored that these Scythians were in league with the Thuringians who had also tried to invade. Oh, his Majesty hadn't heard about that either? In league with some local malcontents, they were. Marshaled quite a force up by Dunlor. But Gormlath and the Guard marched out from the city, crushed them in an hour. Dragged their leader back to the city, they did, where the Emperor killed him with his bare hands... Though not, Uban chuckled, before the old bastard managed to spit in Fantar's eye.

Who was this leader, Valerius wanted to know? Oh, some old coot named Gamlarch, came the reply. Supposedly a general from the old regime. And the rest of his force? The Thuringians? Killed for the most part. They couldn't stand before Gormlath. Broke and ran like children. Bunch of wild northmen, not up to Imperial troops.

Valerius was stunned by the news. Uban, the witless captain, was dismissed without, it appeared, ever quite realizing who he was talking to, and Valerius was left feeling that something elemental in his life had been broken.

In his younger years, during all the time he wandered alone as Balazar, he had been plagued by self-doubt, racking doubts that spun him into depressions lasting for weeks at a time. But since he had reclaimed his name and gotten the Eye Stone, these had faded, and he had moved steadily forward, his eye focused on a single goal. Now, the black pit opened before him again, and High King or no, he tumbled in. Of course, he had no assurance Thorngere was dead, but grief overwhelmed him, nonetheless. And even though the rational part of his brain did point out that this loss need not impede his plans-after all, he had been planning to attack

Valeria with fewer men before Thorngere suggested his scheme, and certainly before Vincipius' men had joined his ranks-but impede them it did. Despite what his rational mind told him, another, deeper part of him was thrown off balance. In his depression, all that had seemed sure was suddenly cast in doubt, and for the first time in years, Valerius did not know what to do next.

Should he go ahead with his plans to attack Valeria, or not? He could not decide. But if not, what? He could not decide that either. He knew he had to do something-the Gods knew he couldn't stay in Zagorbia with men squeezed into every corner and consuming supplies like locust-but just what eluded him. Nothing seemed right. He was still absolutely sure of his ascendancy, sure of his right to be High King, but the thought of committing yet another slaughter before the walls of Valeria-and killing more young men like those who had served Vincipius-just didn't seem like the right path.

In his gloom, he wandered about seeking solace. He spent hours with Eomer, playing with his new son or just sitting quietly with her in their quarters. They were like the sun, breaking through the clouds of his days and he was genuinely delighted one afternoon when he was bouncing the boy on his lap and the little fellow pushed off with his legs, like he was trying to stand. "Ah, you'll be a stalwart warrior when you're grown, lad," he said. "I can feel the strength in you." But would he, he wondered? And what could his father do to ensure not only that he grew into that strength, but into his patrimony as well?

What to do? The question nagged at him. He hiked up to the promontory-somehow he lacked the energy to run-and scoured the distant seas, wondering that he had heard nothing from Colinus or any of the other resistance operatives. Here he was, he thought, free to act at last, and yet never had he felt more paralyzed. He spent hours in his map room, gazing about the Inland Sea, looking for clues. In his mind, it seemed everything had stopped. What used to be a moving drama was now a static portrait. Putting a good face on, he conferred with his advisors and wandered among the troops in training, but his presence was more often disruptive than helpful. And he tried the Eye. He tried it from the promontory at dawn, he tried it from his roof at noon, he even sat before the fire one evening, turning the stone this way and that and watching the firelight flash and flicker deep in its facets like distant signals. He wondered what they could mean.

One morning, as Valerius was nearing the tip of the promontory, the lookout yelled, and he ran up to see a huge Imperial trireme under all oars, streaming towards the harbor. At its masthead, just below the Imperial banner, fluttered a white flag of truce. Valerius ran back to the palace, but took his time bathing, then dressed in his finest robes with a mantle of purple, the ever-present Eye of Valeria, and a simple golden crown, a gift from Koltar. He received the emissary and his entourage in formal state in the throne room with Koltar and Ragnar seated on either hand, and Grumwald, Gainor and his other senior officers ranged down the hall.

The emissary himself was an oily man, gaudily dressed in gold cloth trousers and a long coat of blue with golden epaulets at the shoulder and the facings hung with fringe and gold-painted beads. As he swept up to the throne and bowed deeply, Valerius could smell the heavy scent of his perfume.

"I am Ambassador Carmen," he announced, "and I bring greetings to King Valerius from his Imperial Highness, Lord Fantar." The man had a mellow voice that seemed to match his olive complexion and he spoke in dulcet tones, almost as if he was singing. Valerius decided he did not like him.

"So, all of the sudden I'm 'King Valerius,' eh?" he growled. "What does your master want of me?" Carmen smiled graciously and bowed again, pleased that his compliment had been noticed. Then he indicated the crowded room.

"My master would have me speak privately with your Majesty about a matter of great concern to all."

Valerius snorted. "Whatever your master would say to me may be said here, before these assembled Lords and chieftains."

Carmen bowed his head with a flourish. "As your Majesty wishes. His Imperial Highness, Lord Fantar, bids me tell you he regrets the enmity that has sprung up between you, and bids me remind you that despite your differences, there is still a blood tie between you..."

"The only tie between us is the stain of my father's blood, which is on his hands."

Carmen bowed again. "Nevertheless, His Highness is now ready to acknowledge that his father and yours are one and the same."

The room gasped at this and even Valerius was taken aback. From the beginning it had been the central tenet of Fantar's policy that Valerius was an imposter, that the proclaimed heir of the old High King had been found among the women after the battle of Valeria and killed. The Oracle must have made him fey indeed if he was now ready to acknowledge the legitimacy of Valerius' claim. Or, had he some other diabolical scheme in mind?

"That is very gracious of your master. But we neither seek his acknowledgement nor desire it. And we renounce any claim he may make to our blood royal: he forfeited that long ago by the act of his own hand. But enough of these preliminaries, Carmen. What does your master want in return for this sudden generosity?"

"Simply stated, your Majesty, he wants a truce." The room erupted in laughter at this, but Valerius mastered his own incredulity and brought them to order.

"This," he said, trying not to smile, "will require some explanation."

Carmen was not displeased at the sensation he was causing. "Certainly, your Majesty. As we understand you have been much occupied of late, we are not sure how much you have heard of events in the east..."

242

"We have heard. Despite our 'occupation' as you so nicely put it, we manage to keep ourselves informed." That was not too much of a lie, he thought. "But what of the Scythians?"

"His Highness feels they represent a significant threat."

"And he would like me to conveniently stand aside while he deals with them."

"He would like to enlist your aide in a common cause."

"I see. 'The enemy of my enemy is my friend?'"

"Cannot those who face a common enemy indeed be friends?"

"Certainly, but I don't quite think that's the real question here. Tell me, Ambassador Carmen, since your master was gracious enough to anoint me a King, just what does he deem me King of?"

"Why, of Zagorbia, your Majesty, and of all the Southern Domains."

"I see. Very generous. Thank you, Ambassador Carmen, for your skilled and tactful efforts on your master's behalf. Please return to your ship while we confer with our advisors. You will have our answer very soon."

"It is a trick," snapped Grumwald. "He is as faithless as an adder, and should be treated like one. He'll make the same offer to the Scythians!" They were seated in the high Council Chamber, all the King's chief advisors. Outside, beyond the wide veranda, the sky was a cloudless blue, and the bright summer sun set the harbor and surrounding town all a-shimmer with its heat. But up here, a cool breeze wafted in from the deeper blue of the sea. Wine just up from the cool cellars had been served, and as the men lifted their cups to drink, their eyes strayed to the huge Imperial trireme, resting in the crowded harbor like a great swan among ducks.

"Aye," said Ragnar. "But he is weak now or he would not have offered. I say we slit this gilded ambassador's throat and attack. Now, before Fantar's the wiser." Up and down the table there were grunts of agreement, but King Koltar disagreed.

"I know not this Fantar," he said, his rich voice easily filling the room. "But having experience dealing with the faithless, I say that above all we must not bring dishonor upon ourselves."

"What dishonor is there in striking a serpent?" Grumwald wanted to know. Valerius held up his hand, and then sat in silence for a long moment before speaking.

"I agree with you all," he said. "Obviously, the word of Fantar is not to be trusted, as you know very well, Grumwald. And I like not this ambassador any better than you, Ragnar. But two things concern me: one, what is Fantar really planning, and two, how we craft an answer that will not legitimize him on the one hand, or signal our intentions on the other?"

"What do you mean, 'legitimize him?'" asked Grumwald.

"Well, think about it. If we agree with his terms, don't we also implicitly accept their context-that I am 'King of Zagorbia and the Southern

Domains' and he, therefore, is Emperor? That's akin to swearing fealty to the bastard. And, as Koltar says, if we agree to a truce and then attack, we'll bring dishonor upon ourselves before the Gods. Yet, if we reject his offer, we simply signal our intentions and give him more time to prepare for our attack."

Up and down the table, brows furled as the brains behind them puzzled through this logic. Perhaps Fantar was not as crazy as he seemed. "So what are you going to do?" asked Ragnar.

"Well, I'm not sure yet. That's why I want to see if we can figure out what his real plan is. Does anyone remember the exact words of that Oracle which have supposedly driven him over the edge?"

Koltar did, of course, and recited them promptly:

"'Though you look north, south, east, and west,

Oh killer of kings, you will have no rest.

You fear what your dark eye sees in the night,

Yet by he whom you half see will you die in the light.'"

"Anybody want to venture on an interpretation?" Valerius resumed. "I think the first part is quite obvious: he's being harassed from all sides. We've been the cause of a lot of that. And I think the third line, too, is fairly clear: his 'dark eye' is the one burned out by this Stone. That convinced him he is not the legitimate High King, and that's why he has feared me so all these years. But what of that last line? If it is not I who will bring him down, who must he fear?"

There was a long silence at the table until Daemon of Palmeria spoke up. He was a dark, fiery man, one of Valerius' best flotilla commanders. "I think it means the Scythians. This attack of theirs is not the first by any means. They have been raiding around Palmeria for generations. But it's always been just a few hundred or so: they sweep down from the north, steal grain and other supplies, then disappear. We've never known how many they are, but we've always feared that if they came down in force we would not be able to stand against them. I think Fantar fears he has only seen half of them."

"Interesting," said Valerius. "That would be one reason why he would want a truce. Any other ideas?"

"How about treachery from one of his own?" said Zimlait, a naval Commander from Cobanos. "He could only 'half see' him by thinking him loyal."

"Fantar has only one eye," said another. "Maybe it means he only sees half of everything!" There was laughter at this, but no more serious opinions. Valerius looked around the room one more time, then rose.

"Thank you gentlemen. I'm not sure we resolved anything, but I do have to make a decision. Let me mull this for a bit and see if a clear path presents itself."

He left them then, and wandered about the palace, ending up, as he so often did of late, in the nursery, standing over young Valerian's crib, watching him sleep. What kind of life would this one have, he wondered, his thoughts drifting? Would he become Valerius Everreigning, master of the Eye and High King of Valeria and all the Inland Sea? Or would he be like his father, an outcast, laboring for years under a name not his own, bereft of his patrimony? Would he even have a life at all? Or would he end up like poor Thorngere and so many others, as carrion on some distant battlefield? This thought was particularly galling and Valerius tried to push his wheat sack brain back onto the subject of Fantar. But his thoughts went to his own father, how he had tried to protect his son from the horrors of battle by sending him off with the women. Had he obeyed his father then, he would have died. That was another bad choice his father made, this one also for the right reasons. What if he, Valerius, made the wrong choice for his son, or for his people?

Then Valerius thought of all the generations of his ancestors stringing back into the distant past, of the young men swelling his ranks now, and of this whole new generation lying asleep before him. And he thought of Fantar and the evil he had wrought. Evil was like blood in water, he thought. It stained and spread, tainting all around it. But mankind was like an ever-flowing spring, innocent and eternal, rinsing clear the stains of the past. Fantar still spread blood and evil, but upstream, the river ran clear.

And suddenly, something clicked in Valerius' brain. Standing there, looking down at his son, he had the sudden realization that he was not the end point of all history, but a single link in a greater chain. He was not the owner of his crown or the Eye, but a steward. And no, he could not undo the bad choices his father had made, or avenge all the evils Fantar had wrought. He could not do anything about the past. All he could do was look to the future, look upstream where the water flowed clear and the current ran strong.

Knowing now what he must do, Valerius reassembled his staff and summoned Ambassador Carmen. "Tell your master," he called out before that worthy even had a chance to approach the throne, "that he is a vile dog and I will not treat with him! Tell him from me that his life is forfeit, but that I will not bother with him just now. And tell him two more things: one, that Valerius Everreigning, High King of Valeria and all the Inland Sea, sails east to deal with the Scythians! He may do as he will, but if he stands against me, now or later, I will crush him.

"Two, I am this day declaring an amnesty for all who have innocently struggled against us. If they join with us now in our campaign against the Scythians, and if they stand guilty of no blood crimes against us, we shall welcome them into our ranks and they shall be free!"

"You told him your plans!" Grumwald blurted when the startled ambassador had scuttled away.

"Two can play this amnesty game, Grumwald," said Valerius. "Besides, if I am to be High King, it's high time I started acting like it."

Later that afternoon, Valerius went back to the roof of his palace and stood watching as the great ball of the sun slowly settled towards the western sea. Now that his mind was made up, his depression and confusion had cleared like the summer sky when a sudden change of wind blows storm clouds out to sea. He felt calm and at peace, clear in his perception of himself and of his place. That's when it happened.

He had taken the great gemstone from around his neck and was weighing it idly in his hand, as one would heft a rock before hurling it. But as it caught the westering rays, a light flickered deep inside, and as Valerius looked down into the stone, it flickered again, then flashed and began to glow. Startled, Valerius' eyes hardened and his frame stiffened as the stone began to pulse and throb like a thing alive. Mesmerized, he watched while in his mind, a troop of wild horsemen thundered across an arid plain, and the stone-hewn image of a strange god toppled to the ground.

Chapter 18
THE PROGRESS EAST

Having anointed Ragnar as King of Zagorbia, Valerius sailed east. And though he did not realize it, he gathered with him as he went the largest amphibious force to range the Inland Sea in many generations, perhaps in the history of that epoch. Point to point across the sea, it was just less than 1,600 miles from Zagorbia to the harbor at Palmeria. By land, it was near 2,000. A fast galley, sailing with a fair wind and staying in touch with the shore (for the sea itself was as trackless as a wizard's mind) could make the run in under ten days. But an army marching along the shore could take months, even years, depending on the impediments-or inducements- encountered along the way. In his ascendancy, Fantar had spent the better part of fifteen years conquering his way clockwise around the Inland Sea, the majority of it from Palmeria onward. Valerius now intended to counter that movement in the space of a few months.

He had assembled a sizeable armada. Including the small, sleek galleys of Kantar, the troop transports and galleys Vincipius had commanded, his own galley fleet with his mighty flagship, the trireme, Valdator, as well as a miscellaneous assortment of captured or stolen war galleys, stubby merchant vessels, and even a few fishing smacks, more than three hundred sail spread their wings before a promising southwesterly breeze that morning, rounded the towering promontory at Zagorbia, and headed east. Valerius ranged his fleet into three flotillas under the overall command of Grumwald. The first of these were the fast Kantaran war galleys. Small and highly maneuverable with Koltar's fore and aft rigs and wicked bronze-sheathed rams projecting from their fore-keels, these ships could sail virtually into the wind and had proven themselves more than a match for conventional galleys in the fighting around Kantar. They fanned out before the fleet to act as a screen, while a small squadron of them was kept in reserve as messengers and consorts for the flagship. Behind them came the bulk of the fleet, full-sized war galleys, biremes, and even a few of the newer triremes, all crammed to the gunnels with men, equipment and animals. Last, and struggling to keep the pace, came the heavy transports, also crammed with men, the supply ships and other miscellany. Ranging far and wide and servicing the fleet like a mobile city, was the fishing fleet.

It was Valerius' intention to cover the first stretch from Zagorbia to Cartho entirely by sea, then land his cavalry and proceed in consort from there, beaching the fleet at night to cook and camp. Still, it was a long run from Zagorbia to Cartho and conditions aboard the ships quickly became deplorable for men and beasts alike. There were no cooking facilities for that many people, and not enough room for even half the men to lie down at one time. So the men subsisted on prepared rations and spent large portions of their time trying to find a place to sleep or just waiting to use the head platforms built out fore and aft. Fortunately, there was very little seasickness. The seas stayed calm and the breeze fresh from the southwest as day and night, the massive fleet forged eastward, keeping in sight the distant sands of the desert to their south.

On the morning of the third day, the foothills of Cartho appeared silhouetted against the rising sun on their starboard bow, and by noon, the fleet stood at short anchor. The harbor was much too small to contain them all, so they stood inshore as close as possible, overlapping harbor and city from east to west. Only Valerius on the massive Valdator and his immediate consorts ventured inside the harbor, and here he stood, the royal banner of Valeria fluttering at his masthead, while what appeared to be the entire population gathered along the waterfront to stare.

Finally a single barge put off from the town pier and made its way towards the flagship. Gaudily painted and propelled by a dozen uniformed oarsmen, it carried a group of official-looking dignitaries on an awning-covered platform amidships. Civil affairs in Cartho were managed by a mercantile arm of the Guild, consisting of a management board of leading burghers, and headed by a functionary akin to a mayor or burghermeister. It was this group that occupied the barge. Their departure had been preceded by a hastily convened council in which several members were replaced as political factions rather abruptly realigned.

As they approached the huge ship, board members stared open-mouthed at the royal banner flapping lazily in the mid-day sun-a sight they had not seen in a generation-and wondered at the incredible spectacle of the vast armada confronting the town. Some questioned openly what this all portended. Others-those who had perhaps been a bit less circumspect in their support for Fantar-feared for their lives, while the newer members waited quietly in hopeful expectation. The pragmatic majority, however, including the chief magistrate himself-a rotund, congenial fellow by the name of Quamous-relied on the long held tradition that things worked differently in Cartho, and was fully prepared to welcome any new opportunity.

Tying off at a landing stage rigged on the side of the great vessel, the officials made their way up the steep sides, and to their surprise, were welcomed on board with considerable fanfare. Drums rolled and trumpets blared, and neatly uniformed side boys saluted as they stepped onto the deck. Rank upon rank of brilliantly armed men stood to attention on either hand, while across the deck a large group of senior officers stood at ease, their helmets tucked under their left arms and welcoming smiles on their faces.

Ever the salesman, Quamous stepped up to the foremost of these with a broad smile of his own and his portly hand extended. "Gentlemen," he announced loudly, "Let me be the first to welcome you to the city of Cartho."

"On the contrary," said Grumwald, taking Quamous' proffered hand while nodding quickly to another just behind him, "let me be the first to welcome you, and your city, to the new reign of Valerius Everreigning, High King of Valeria and all the Inland Sea. Come. His Majesty is expecting you."

They were led into the stern castle and down a narrow passageway to Valerius' private quarters, which had been hastily cleared and set up as a throne room. He sat in state before the broad stern windows, a golden circlet on his brow and the great red gem glittering on his chest. When they saw him, the delegation fell to their knees and prostrated themselves before him.

"Arise, gentlemen," said King Valerius, "and let us face each other as free men."

For Quamous, the word 'arise' was something of a euphemism. Still, he managed to regain his feet and delivered a flowery welcoming speech to "His Highness King Valeria," then introduced the members of his delegation. Valerius made particular note of one.

"Bokmar," he said, rising and taking the man by the hand, "how glad we are to see you again. Quamous, you should be aware that Bokmar here is an old comrade of ours. Once we are reestablished in Valeria, he will act as our representative here in Cartho."

"We will honor him," said Quamous with a slight bow that was echoed by the rest. "Then Your Majesty returns to Valeria?" Quamous asked, the question larger than the words that framed it. Valerius returned to his throne and surveyed the group in silence for a moment, choosing his words carefully.

"Quamous, gentlemen of Cartho, let us be under no illusions here. We come, not to conquer Cartho, but to release her. I'm sure Our appearance here today has come as something of a surprise-perhaps more to some than others-but I am also sure you are aware of Us and our situation. So let us not deal in innuendo, but in plain truth. Here is my truth: I am no imposter but the real Valerius, heir to the title, Everreigning, and Rightful High King of Valeria and all the Inland Sea. I am Master of The Eye of Valeria, vision stone of the Kings Everreigning and symbol of the high power. Where I stand shines the light of that Empire which has existed for a thousand years, and the idea of freedom that sustained it. We travel east, and those who choose to stand with us enjoy that light. Those who do not, remain in shadow. But we do not conquer-we merely proclaim, and offer freedom to those who can bear the light. Of Cartho we require only two things: water to replenish our casks, and some space at your jetties for a time that we may disembark our cavalry. After that, we will be on our way. In return, I offer you this," he said, and unfolded for Quamous a red and white banner embroidered with a golden lion, symbol of Valeria. "Fly it if you will. It may even prove good for business."

"Then Fantar is not...?"

"Dead? Deposed?" Valerius laughed. "I know not and care less. Fantar's time is past. We look to the future. But isn't this Cartho, Quamous, city of prophecy and divination? You should be the one telling me!"

Watered and lightened of some six thousand horses and men-Koltar's men augmented with new volunteers-the fleet beached a mile or so east of Cartho and the army went ashore. The men enjoyed their first hot meal in days, and then stretched out in delightful luxury upon the sands along the shore. Valerius met late into the night with Bokmar and his people, and when he again ascended the quarterdeck of Valdator to sail east in the bright morning sun, he was pleased to see the Royal Banner of Valeria fluttering over the town.

With the fleet travelling in concert with the cavalry ashore, the progress east became something of a procession. The cavalry trained their new recruits-thundering and wheeling across the plain in their formations like great flocks of crows, spilling novice riders along the way like bird droppings-and the army, relieved of the press of men aboard, settled into a comfortable routine. They made excellent progress, covering forty or fifty miles in a day, but word traveled even faster, and the next few towns threw open their gates in welcome. Cheering citizens lined the streets, strewing the path with palm fronds as Valerius rode in on his great white warhorse. At night they beached their ships on the soft sand of the southern coast and camped ashore, being careful to fortify their positions, and feasted on roasted sheep and bullocks, and wine purchased from local vineyards. In each town, Valerius declared his amnesty, and assisted by the resistance, placed whatever remained of the old order back in power. He had no wish, he said, to rule as a tyrant, but only to provide a greater state, to guide a league of cities. As for the small garrison forces they encountered-none of whom even offered token resistance-unless they were charged with specific crimes, any who had enlisted with Fantar but were now ready to swear fealty to King Valerius were forgiven outright.

Most swore willingly and many immediately enlisted with Valerius' forces. Those who were charged-and there were not a few among the people willing to make such charges-were placed in the hands of the newly reinstated local authorities for justice. If their crimes were particularly severe, Valerius rendered judgment himself. Executions were swift and merciful, the condemned beheaded in the public squares, their remains dragged away to the pyres, and the stains of their blood as quickly washed away. Against tradition, there was no retribution on families, and the heads of the deceased were not piked for public display, much less stacked outside the walls, as had been a favorite decoration of Fantar's. Valerius said he did not want to revel in the blood of the past. They should put the past behind them, he said, and look instead to the promise of the future.

But not all was goodness and light. Three weeks out they approached Falkan, the first real city in their path. The former seat of the Viceroy Vincipius, it was from this city and the region just passed that he had drawn most of his forces. The night before they reached the place, a delegation from the city approached the camp, seeking audience with the High King. Valerius met with Curio, a sharp, quick-featured man who had been left in charge by Vincipius.

He had come, he said, to beg King Valerius to spare his city. Did his city intend to resist, the King wanted to know? Oh, most certainly not, came the immediate reply. How could a pitiful town such as Falkan hope to stand before such a host as this led by the High King? And especially against a High King whom the gods so obviously favored with auguries and prophecies.

Then, said the king, you need have no fear.

Ah, gushed Curio, all but kissing Valerius' feet. His Majesty was so merciful, so clear in his vision, so forthright in justice. But still, the city trembled in fear because of its former-and unwilling-association with Vincipius. If His Majesty truly meant them no harm, could he give them a sign, a royal banner that they could fly over the town when he entered, to reassure the people?

Valerius gave him the banner and the next day, as his fleet came to anchor inside the breakwater that formed Falkan's broad, shallow harbor, the banner indeed flew over the palace. But Valerius was still cautious and had made his own preparations. He moved into the town in force, arms at the ready. Curio met them amidst a large crowd on the steps of the palace, his senior staff, all smiles, gathered about him. They knelt as Valerius ascended the steps and humbled themselves before him. At the High King's side was Emaus, the young soldier he had rescued from the mound. Emaus' mother was in the crowd, her heart leaping with joy at the sight of him.

"Emaus," said Valerius, his parade-ground voice carrying across the square and through the streets like the sound of a great horn. "What manner of man is this Curio, and these, his confederates here kneeling before us?"

"They are snakes, Your Majesty," said Emaus flatly.

Valerius nodded and turning to the crowd, called out, "Is there a man called Nickelamous here?"

"Aye, Your Majesty," said a stout, middle-aged man stepping out from the crowd. "I am he." He was dressed in ragged robes and carried the staff of a shepherd.

"Nickelamous, you have worked with Lord Thorngere for years and are known and trusted among many here. Is what young Emaus says the truth?"

"It is, Your Majesty," said Nickelamous, his voice clear and strong. "With my own eyes I saw that man, Curio, slit the throat of old King Caramon when Fantar first took the town."

"This is as I thought. Commander Gainor!" Valerius snapped, turning to the battalion commander on the steps below him. "Place Curio and his associates here under arrest and take a squad of men to secure the palace. Nickelamous, is there any scion of King Caramon yet living?"

"There is, Your Majesty-a man called Fargo, his nephew. He has been living in hiding all these years, tending the shaduf at the well south of the city, serving water to shepherds and their flocks."

"And what manner of man is this Fargo?"

"He is a good man, Your Majesty, wise and humble in his station. He tends to the poor and has been of great support for those of us who know him."

"My lord Grumwald," Valerius called out again in his best parade ground voice, "send forth an honor guard to this well south of the city, and escort this man Fargo hence, for he shall no more draw water for shepherds, but be anointed himself to tend the flock of his people."

Grumwald stood with a file of impeccably dressed guardsmen at the side of the square, already set and rehearsed for this task. "Your Majesty," he called back, "It shall be done as you say."

By the time the honor guard returned, the entire population of Falkan had packed themselves into the square and along the street leading to the southern gate. Fargo himself had been amply prepared as well. He had been bathed and trimmed and dressed in robes suitable to his state. His long hair had been combed out and was drawn into a queue at the back, and his beard was braided into a double fork, the fashion of old Valerian aristocracy. He entered the town on a white pony, flanked by

Nickelamous and his associates, and all surrounded by Grumwald's honor guard. Cheers echoed and re-echoed from the white adobe walls as the procession made its way to the square. But as Fargo ascended the steps and knelt before the waiting High King, the crowd hushed in breathless anticipation. Few present ever thought they would witness such an event in their lifetimes.

Two attendants draped Fargo in an ermine robe and a third brought forth the ancient crown of Falkan in a jewel-encrusted case. Valerius held up his arms and total silence descended on the square like a curtain.

"Nearly a dozen years ago," he began, "I stood before these very walls with the men of Falkan as Fantar's hordes descended from the eastern hills. King Caramon lead us that day, a brave and wise leader, and Fargo here was a stalwart captain. I was a common man-at-arms, bereft of my name and patrimony, and without hope of anything other than striking another blow against the tyrant confronting us. At the end of that day, Caramon and a thousand more lay dead, the rest of us were fugitives, and Fargo here was as dispossessed as I. Fantar was ascendant then, rising on a great tide of murder and mayhem, and we were swept aside like wrack in the sea.

"But today that tide has turned! Today, I stand before you with my true identity revealed-Valerius Everreigning, High King of Valeria and all the Inland Sea-and I hold before you this Eye of Valeria, Vision Stone of the High Kings of Valeria and symbol of their power for a thousand years. Now I take up this crown, symbol of the free city of Falkan, proud confederate and ally of Valeria, and I hold it above the head of this man, Fargo Cimmeon, nephew of Caramon, King that was, and a scion of all his line. And I ask you now, shall Falkan again be free? Shall this man Fargo be your King?"

To both questions, the crowd let out a tumultuous cheer, and as he lowered the crown, the noise reached such a crescendo that the naming rite and anointing were done in dumb show. Even Valerius could not hear his own voice.

That evening, while the great feasted in the palace and the city was ablaze with celebration, young Emaus spent a quiet evening reuniting with friends and family. Still convalescent, the excitement of the afternoon had exhausted him and he lay on a pallet in the single room shared by his widowed mother and three sisters. Several others, close friends and neighbors hovered near as well as Emaus recounted the tale of his adventures and all the wonderful things this magical High King had done. He told them how the king had brought him back from the dead, how the spirits of the dead fought for him and how he brought down fire from the sky to defeat Vincipius, how the gods sent huge demons and tiny Halflings to fight at his side. And he told them how, in spite of his greatness, this King knew the name of every man in the army, and most of all, how his face and eye shone with such a light of gentleness and peace that enemies threw down their arms before him and begged him to lead them. And as young Emaus drifted off to sleep and the neighbors sought livelier entertainments, these tales went with them, and spread through the night like pollen on a soft spring breeze.

Chapter 19
BEYOND THE GREAT RIVER

The High King's grand procession ran into its first roadblock at Telos, a long six hundred miles east of Falkan, where the Great River spilled into the Inland Sea and where the shoreline of the Sea turned northward. It was also the beginning of a new military district; one of four Fantar had defined to control his Empire. The first was the area around Valeria, ruled by Fantar himself, with Gormlath, head of the Imperial Guard, as his close second. Next was the area around Palmeria and Bangorum, formerly ruled by Asperides. The third was this at Telos, and last was the area from Falkan west to Zagorbia, just liberated by Valerius. Telos was one of three cities in the southeastern district, and the principal naval port south of Palmeria. Many of the ships Vincipius used to attack Zagorbia, in fact, had their homeports in Telos. The other two cities comprising the district were Cobanos, also on the Great River, but some hundred miles upstream, and Durumkai, another two hundred miles up the coast to the northeast. The whole was under the command of an aging Viceroy, one Zenemahr, who had been one of Fantar's chief mentors in crime even before his rise to power.

East of Falkan, the desert again intruded upon the shore, and for vast stretches, sand lay like a dull brown blanket across the earth, or piled in rolling dunes that walked with the wind. It was a hostile stretch and the sand stung the faces of the men, gritted their teeth, and choked their throats. There were few villages, except where an occasional subterranean stream broke from the desiccated earth to form a small pool or make a mad rush to the sea. In these spots, a few hovels might stand against the elements, their inhabitants scratching a bare living from the sea and from a few hand-irrigated fields. There were no military garrisons, no reason for Valerius' forces to tarry, and many reasons for them to hurry on. And with even the novice riders now able to keep their seats, hurry on they did, making fifty and more miles a day, and ferrying water ashore at night for horses and men. Only once did they stop for several days when they came upon an oasis large enough to water the fleet.

On the fifteenth day, they were some forty miles west of Telos when they ran into Zenemahr who had marched out from the city to intercept them. Valerius had stayed ashore that morning and was riding with Koltar and the cavalry when they saw the dust from what could only be an approaching host. Signals from the fleet soon confirmed that an army was indeed blocking their path. Valerius had himself rowed out to Valdator for a hurried conference with Grumwald, then returned to the shore. Just before noon, they came up to them, a full army of at least twelve thousand infantry, all brightly arrayed in battle lines and spread, rank upon rank, across the flat sands before them.

Valerius was cautious. Why would a commander lead his men so far from his base to confront an enemy, especially one supported by a fleet? Were they on their way somewhere else? If so, where? Was there some other plot afoot, and if so, what? There was certainly no place in this vast expanse an enemy could stage an ambush. Bidding his men dismount and rest their horses, he and Koltar rode forward for the ritual parley.

"Have you lost your way?" Valerius called out as the elderly leader marched out from his lines, senior staff, attendants, and standard bearers in tow.

"Not in the least," the old man shouted back. "We've come hunting for trophies, and I'm thinking your head will make a fine one-almost as good as the one we took from your father before the walls of Valeria!"

"Then you are Zenemahr himself?" said Valerius, reining up and towering over the old warrior.

"I am that," said Zenemahr, his white-whiskered chin jutting in defiance while his attendants eyed the tiny Koltar with amused disdain.

"And you've marched all this way to confront us?"

"We have that! And you, my young friend, have come a long way to reach the end of your road."

Valerius found it hard to credit the situation before him, though he had heard before of Zenemahr that he was not the greatest of thinkers. Still, it was difficult to answer the man. He almost felt sorry for him.

"Look, Zenemahr," he said, trying to sound conciliatory, "you don't seem to realize the position you've gotten yourself into here. You really don't have a chance, you see. I've got eight thousand troops on fast horses over there, and another thirty thousand aboard ship just out there. You're hopelessly outnumbered and nearly forty miles from your base. Why don't you just surrender now and spare the lives of these fine men here? We'll treat you fairly, you have my word."

But if Valerius words had any effect on Zenemahr, he didn't show it. "Ha!" he snorted, " I've twelve-thousand here at my back and you'll be in hell long before your ships even reach the shore!" And he turned to stalk off.

"You men!" Valerius called to Zenemahr's attendants. "Surely you can see your position? Your commander has lost his wits. Put him under arrest now and lay down your arms! You will not be harmed. You have my word!" But though some of their expressions showed willingness, and some even hesitated, none made a move to stop the old man. Instead, they followed him meekly back to their own lines.

Valerius made one more try. Riding out along their front, he shouted so the whole host of Telos could hear: "Men of Telos! Hear me! Hear the words of Valerius Everreigning, High King of Valeria and all the Inland Sea! None of you has to die! I offer you peace! Right here and now. Forsake this fool Zenemahr! Lay down your arms and none of you will be harmed. Surrender now and you will have peace!"

But though he rode up and down the front for several minutes, shouting out so all could hear, none moved. "So be it!" he shouted then. "Now you will die needlessly! And you will keep dying, so long as you follow this old fool's path! But remember that Valerius offered you mercy!" And he trotted back to where Koltar still sat, a tiny figure facing an army.

"Any other suggestions?"

Koltar shook his head. "None that would be of any use, I'm afraid."

"Well then, let's take a ride," said Valerius and they turned back to their own lines.

Valerius gave the signal to mount and trotted off to the south, leading his troops at an easy canter right around the Zenemahr's flank. The old commander tried to block them, but in vain: his men could not outrun horses. The riders proceeded unhindered, leaving the old man confounded and furious in their wake, and his subalterns with the sudden realization that there was now an army between them and home.

Valerius and his men rode on until late in the evening, entering the lush and fertile river basin unopposed, and with the dawn, appeared on the western bank of the Great River just as Grumwald fell upon the undermanned fleet of Telos and captured it almost without loss. By the next morning, when Zenemahr's host made it back to the river, not only was the city on the eastern bank secured, but a large portion of Valerius' infantry had been landed on the western bank, and stood in fortified lines against him.

Valerius again tried to parley, but an enraged Zenemahr immediately threw his men into the attack. But his men no longer had the enthusiasm they had shown a few days before, and it faltered quickly. Zenemahr then tried some maneuvering of his own, marching off to the south in an apparent flanking movement. But it was not to be. Valerius marched in parallel, keeping his men between Zenemahr and the river, while a good part of the fleet sailed along in easy support.

Zenemahr's flanking movement soon became a mad dash inland. Short of both water and provision, his only remaining hope was to reach Cobanos, where he could cross the river and reach sanctuary in the city. But he didn't make it. Valerius sent his cavalry dashing out ahead. They easily circled Zenemahr's army, and harassed the straggling column with vicious archery attacks. The tiny Kudanim warriors galloped along just out of javelin range, and fired arrow after arrow into the terrified and bewildered host. Zenemahr's column soon lost all order and cohesion, the men rushing pell-mell to avoid the stinging arrows one moment, then bunching up the next like cattle before a gate, all the while leaving an ever growing trail of dead and dying.

With darkness, the host collapsed in it tracks, only to wake to another day of hell and fury. Mercifully, Zenemahr himself was brought down just after noon and the remainder of his men surrendered quickly.

Grumwald danced a merry jig on the deck of Valdator when he heard of Zenemahr's demise, and Koltar glowed with visible pride at the performance of his pint-sized warriors. But Valerius was disgusted by the whole affair and could take no joy from the easy victory, or from the fresh influx of men and material, which was becoming the pattern of this campaign. Instead, he moved quickly to consolidate control of Telos and reinstall what he could find of the old regime.

And he was impatient of delay. Reports had come in that the Scythian hordes were growing larger. They still had not made a direct attack on Palmeria, which was shut and barricaded against them, but their growing numbers filled the plains to the north and east, and more were arriving every day. No longer were they just warriors now, but women, children, old folk and all their belongings. It appeared the invasion had become a migration.

Reports also indicated that Fantar was on the move. He had left Valeria and was also marching east, gathering forces as he went. Unlike Valerius, however, he was keeping to the land with little naval support, and seemed to be in no particular hurry, evidently dallying to let Valerius reach Palmeria first. This was fine with Valerius, who decided to bypass Cobanos for the time being and move on instead to Durumkai. If his luck held and he had as easy a time there, he thought, he would be able to continue right on to Bangorum and then to

Palmeria itself, though what he would do there remained a very large question.

Still, Valerius knew he could not be too hasty. Military victories were only one part of the equation: if he was to rebuild his empire, he must also win the hearts of the people. So, before announcing his plans, he ordered a major feast to be held in Telos. He wanted, he said, to thank the gods for their favor and honor the new leaders of the city. And in keeping with his policy for the new Valerian Federation, he especially wanted to honor the local gods who, after all, had been most responsible for driving Zenemahr mad and securing the release of their people.

The feast was held over three days, and as it happened to coincide with the feast of local God Balam-hc, it was said, who had given the gift of winemaking to mankind, and whose mysteries, it was reported, embodied the spirit of life-Valerius was invited by the sect's chief priest to celebrate its secret mysteries in a sacred glade south of the city. He attended in state, accompanied by Koltar, Grumwald, his Queen, Eomer, and several of his other senior commanders, and very quickly regretted it.

As a young prince of Valeria, Valerius had been schooled in all the major deities worshipped around the Inland Sea. The region around Telos, he had learned, principally worshipped Aman, the god of the Great River, and Re, god of the sun, along with a host of lesser deities. But the cult of Balam was new to him. It had grown out of the hinterlands,

271

he had been told, spread by a handful of wild priests, and in the years since Fantar's ascendance, had achieved a certain respectability as its message was a balm to people in bondage. Other gods were not replaced under the influence of Balam-they were merely anesthetized.

The mysteries themselves were secret, of course, and open only to the initiated. But arrangements had been made for the High King and his retinue to visit the glade along the river where the rites were held, and to join in the celebration after the mysteries were concluded. Thus, Valerius was expecting to see a crowd of reverent worshippers, benign faces still aglow with divine inspiration. But the scene that confronted them was anything but benign. Even as they approached along a wooded path, they could hear the revelers in the distance, and at first they thought some insurrection was underway. But as insurrections are seldom accompanied by wild flutes and chanting, they kept on. Then, at the edge of the glade, Valerius nearly tripped over a pair of bodies half sprawled across the path. They were fornicating.

The scene in the glade stopped them cold. Lit by the eerie red glow of torches, a hundred or more worshipers congregated around a marble, phallus-shaped statue of the God, which stood in the center of the glade. Behind it stood a small chapel made of poles and palm fronds from which came the sounds of flute and drum. A chorus of bare-breasted women-some quite matronly-danced around the statue, chanting and leaping and waving their arms in wild abandon. They had been scratching at their breasts and arms, and some were quite bloody. Around them, a larger group of both sexes swayed and undulated in an urgent, though seemingly aimless accompaniment. From these came a low murmur, like the surge of distant surf upon a rocky shore, or the frightened lowing of cattle spooked by an impending storm. Above the whole, the eerie, invisible music swirled and pulsed. As Valerius and his party watched, one of the dancing women let out a shriek and rushed off into the shadows, followed by several of the men. Her place was immediately taken by another woman from the crowd who as she danced, ripped open her garment and began clawing at her neck and exposed breasts. About the glade, wine skins and amphora, and crumpled bits of clothing lay everywhere, and among them, couples writhed in pairs and small groups.

"By the gods!" said Koltar, staring. "What is this?"

"Looks like one hell of a party!" said Grumwald, his eyes glistening.

Valerius said nothing. The scene before him was totally outside his experience. His first instinct was to shield the young Eomer, his second to turn and leave. But political considerations gave him a moment's pause, and that was enough. One of the maenads spotted the king's party and let out a shriek. She rushed over, followed by a goodly portion of the crowd, and in moments Valerius had become the center of attention, with celebrants dancing and chanting before him. There was no one present with any apparent authority to guide him, and he stood there smiling awkwardly, with Koltar and a much too curious Grumwald by his side, trying to shield Eomer, not understanding the words of the chant, and having no idea what the crowd expected, or what he was supposed to do next. That's when one of the women leapt at him.

She was one of the younger maenads, very attractive, with sharp features and a full, large-breasted figure. But her long hair was twisted and snarled, her face and breasts smeared with blood, and her eyes glazed and wild. She pounced on him from a distance of several feet, like a cat, and wrapped her arms around his neck, her legs around his thigh. In his surprise, he caught her in his arms for a brief moment, they looked like a pair of entwined lovers, staggering in the flickering torchlight. Then she sank her teeth into his neck.

Valerius howled and tried to throw her off, but she clung tight against him, and it was not until he was able to wedge his arm up between them and shove against her chin that he was able to dislodge her. He pushed her away violently, then, and she landed in a heap several feet away. But she bounced up like a ball and flew at him again, wailing now a high-pitched, inhuman scream. Koltar and Grumwald interceded as well, and between the three of them, they threw her off again. Yet, again she came at them, wild and flailing, and this time Valerius struck her hard with his fist and she staggered back into the arms of several other celebrants.

"Aiiiiieee!" she screamed. "Valerius rejects the God! Valerius rejects Balam! Kill the unbelievers! Kill them!"

Suddenly, dancers became attackers, crouching and snarling where an instant before they had been leaping and singing. Sticks and clubs appeared, along with knives and a few swords. There were only eight in Valerius' party, one of them a woman, and all unarmed except for their daggers. Pulling these now and backing into a tight circle with Eomer in the middle, they began edging away, back down the path towards the river and the safety of the flagship Valdator, nearly a quarter mile away. But the woman's screams were taken up by others now and the crowd circled them, chanting. "Kill the unbelievers! Kill the unbelievers!"

Still, lightly armed as they were, Valerius and company were a formidable foe-trained professionals well versed in their craft-and the drunken revelers around them were reluctant to actually attack. Again, it was the women who leapt into the breach. Screaming wildly, three of them flew at Valerius, clawing and scratching like fiends. Valerius threw his arms up in defense, exposing for an instant the huge red gem on his chest.

Perhaps it was the firelight refracting within the peculiar crystalline structure of the stone that did it, or perhaps it was something else entirely, but in that instant, the stone seemed to explode. A bright red beam flashed out and struck the first of the women flush in the face. She screamed and fell back into crowd like a tossed rag.

Stunned silence fell like a blanket. Faces that were twisted in anger suddenly stared agape. The two other women scurried quickly out of sight, and the one who had been struck lay stretched full length on the ground, senseless. Valerius straightened to his full height and thrust out his chest, the gem upon it still seeming to glow and smolder. The crowd began backing away and suddenly, Valerius got angry. Very angry. It started deep inside him and burst upward and out like a volcano.

"Down!" he screamed, his voice seeming to shake the very earth, his form seeming to swell and grow. "Down on your knees!" And now he rushed at the crowd, grabbing the men by the shoulders, thrusting them down. One by one they dropped to their knees, then in groups, then the entire crowd followed and knelt before him.

"How dare you?" he boomed. "How dare you insult the High King of Valeria and all the Inland Sea? Is this how you treat a king and his queen? Is this how your god treats invited guests? Is this the will of your god?" And he raged among them, like an angry schoolmaster marching up and down the aisles, berating and chastising. The crowd, like frightened students, averted their eyes and bowed their heads before him, not daring to face that wrathful face nor tempt the power of that pulsing stone upon his chest. And none dared answer him. Even his own party, his own queen, watched in awe.

"Answer me!" Valerius demanded. "Is this how your god bids you treat guests? By attacking them like dogs? Is this the spirit of Balam? Come, answer me, someone. You!" and he grabbed a poor fellow, several ranks back, and yanked him to his feet by the dirty collar of his tunic. "Is this the will of your god?" But the man was terror stricken and could only tremble and moan. Valerius dropped him like a sack.

"If you won't answer, what about the God himself?" Valerius roared, and stalked to the center of the glade where the phallic statue gleamed like wet obsidian. Furtive eyes followed him as he stood before the statue and spread his arms wide. "Balam, god of the desert, god of the secret spirit," he called, "I, Valerius Everreigning, High King of Valeria and Master of the Eye stand before you. We came, I and my queen and my people, in peace to honor you. We came at the behest of your own priests, to celebrate your name, and express our gratitude for your help in defeating Zenemahr, our enemy. Yet your people have profaned themselves before us and attacked us like dogs. Is this your will? Is this what you would have them do? All the other gods hold guests as sacred. I ask you, Balam, god of wine and spirit, do you repudiate them? Or have the people mistaken you? Have your priests lied to them?"

For a full minute Valerius stood in silence before the gleaming black statue, waiting. Then he turned and looked out over the kneeling crowd, their faces now lifted, expectant. "There is your answer," he said, his voice somber, filling the glade like the sound of a cello. "Balam has forsaken you. You have shamed him and he has turned his face away.

277

You have twisted his spirit, profaned his name, and shamed him before all the other gods in heaven. Here," Valerius said and suddenly gave the statue a great shove. It toppled easily and broke into several pieces. "Your statue is empty! There is no god here. Balam has gone, and now you must deal with the pieces." And he turned and stalked out of the glade.

"How did you know the god would not answer?" Eomer asked later as Valdator glided back down the great river and she lay beside Valerius in their great stern cabin. She lay propped up on her elbow, looking at him, a little further away than normal, her eyes still bright with what she had seen.

"I didn't know what the god would do. I only did my part." Valerius was exhausted and wanted only to sleep. From the moment he left the glade a great weariness had settled on him and it was all he could do to get back to the ship.

"But did you know that was going to happen?"

"No, I didn't know any of it was going to happen. I would never have taken you if I'd known something like that was going on."

"Would you have gone yourself?" she teased.

Valerius smiled and rolled to face her. "Why would I seek out old hags like that when I have such as you right here?"

"Well, wouldn't it be your duty as King?"

"I don't think so. I even wonder now whether I should allow the practice."

"Was the Eye attacking Balam, do you think, or just protecting you?"

"I don't know," said Valerius, suddenly weary again. "I'm not even sure it was the Eye. It could have just been a reflection: that's happened before, you know. But I do think next time we'll find out a lot more about any such 'mysteries' before we agree to participate."

But if Valerius was unsure whether the Eye had attacked Balam, the population was not. Word spread like wildfire of the High King's battle with the god and in the way of such things, a single woman fainting was soon exaggerated into a battle royal of immortals with Balam, wounded and stricken, driven from the field. His priests and acolytes, who had the day before trod the streets of Telos in lordly fashion, suddenly returned to their humble status as shoemakers and shepherds, and the wild women who bared their breasts with such abandon went quietly back to their baking and their looms.

Nor was the defeat of Balam the only consequence of the episode. Several days later, Cobanos sent an emissary to the High King in surrender, and within a week, Durumkai did the same. In one three-minute incident, the last remaining obstacle along the southern coast was cleared away and Valerius was free to move on Bangorum and Palmeria.

Chapter 20
THE SERPENT'S TAIL

In the midst of his host on the northern shore of the Inland Sea, Fantar sat in his tent, the remains of a half-eaten roast chicken and a flagon of wine scattered across a small table by his side. Chained to his chair and scavenging the remains, was his tiny Kantaran captive, Colinus, while before him, their heads bowed in submission, stood two operatives, one recently arrived from Telos, the other from Palmeria. They were respectable looking fellows for their sort, either one of whom would as soon slit a throat as look at it. Fantar, however, was not happy with them. Indeed, he was not happy with much of anything these days. But these men, he thought, were special fools.

"Does he know?" Fantar demanded.

"We do not believe so, Highness," said the one from Telos. "Inquiries were made afterwards, of course, but the crowd dispersed so fast that our people were not even questioned, and the woman herself has been secreted away."

"Well, it was a damned fool idea anyway... having the man attacked by women at some religious ceremony. I should never have countenanced it. What about the woman who was struck?"

"Happily, Highness, she was not even one of ours... Just got caught up in the moment."

"She must have had a snoot-full, eh?" said Fantar, suddenly mirthful. "To attack a High King with only her bare tits!" And he laughed loud at his joke. The others joined with hesitant, coughing sounds. Colinus ignored them, picking avidly among the chicken bones with tiny, greasy fingers.

"And all it cost me was an entire sector!" Fantar roared, his single eye snapping with sudden fury. The two officers ceased their sniggering and stood still, once more abashed. "Fools!" Fantar spat. "What of the other matter, in Palmeria?"

"That seems to be progressing nicely, Highness," said the other. "Of course, we can't be sure he will occupy the palace, or that he will not replace the entire staff..."

"Well, I hope you produce something a little more effective than tit-slapping this time!" The men started to laugh but Fantar interrupted them. "Guards!" he called and instantly, two burly fellows appeared from outside the tent flaps. "Seize this man," he said, nodding towards the operative from Telos whose face twisted in terror as the two held him fast.

Fantar then turned to the other operative. "You will produce something more effective than tit-slapping, won't you?" he asked, his voice quiet, almost plaintive.

"Oh, yes, Sire! You have my word," said this man, fright etched plainly on his face, as well.

"Your word," mused Fantar. "Your word. And just what might your word be worth?"

"It is worth my life, liege," said the man, trying to sound bold and forceful.

"Is it worth his life?"

"Sire?"

"This one, too, pledged his word. Such a pledge must be redeemed, don't you think?"

The man had no choice in his answer. "Yes, Sire," he said, but the attempt at boldness was gone.

"Well, redeem it, then," said Fantar. "Here," and he handed the man the dagger he had been using on the chicken. "Show me how you would have your pledge redeemed, should you fail."

The man looked from Fantar to his compatriot, then back again. He knew the other fellow well, had worked with him, on and off, over fifteen years. They were friends. But there was plainly no choice here, either. Grabbing the dagger, he turned swiftly and drove it into the other's chest. Yanking it free, a gush of hot blood soaked his arm. He looked away as the guards dragged the sudden weight of the corpse away, its feet leaving twin bloody furrows on the earthen floor.

"So," said Fantar, accepting the dagger back and spearing a piece of chicken with it, "what about the Scythians?"

"They appear to be unapproachable, Highness," said the man, trying to recover his voice. "We've sent several men, but none have returned."

Fantar glowered at this. "Well, what are they doing out there? Why haven't they attacked the city?"

"We don't know, Highness. They've not even invested it, and we haven't been able to get close enough to their camps to see if they're building any siege equipment. All we know is that there are a lot of them out there, with more coming south all the time. As for why they haven't attacked, no one knows. There are some unfounded rumors..."

"Rumors of what?"

"I hate to trouble your Highness with talk that may only be some old man's imaginings."

"You will if you have any hopes of becoming an old man yourself," said Fantar. "I didn't get this far in life by avoiding trouble."

"Yes, your Highness," said the man, and glanced quickly at the track left by his former friend. "It was a shepherd, out in the hills tending his flocks, who gave the report, Highness. He said he saw a large band of Scythians approaching. Knowing he could not hope to save his flock, he hid in the hills and watched. As they came, he said he saw a beautiful young woman step out before them on an outcropping of rock. He said he had heard of her before but thought it just someone's fancy. But she stood there, he said, and as the riders approached, she suddenly raised her arms and began to keen in a high-pitched, wailing voice. Then, before his very eyes, she transformed into a huge beast-like creature. The Scythian horses reared and screamed and would not approach, then they all turned and fled. It is said she is a warrior goddess, Highness, come to protect the city."

"A Goddess, eh? There seems to be a lot of that going around these days. Has anyone approached her?"

"Not that I'm aware, Highness."

"And you didn't think to..."

"No, Sire."

"Even though she may be our strongest ally yet."

"No, Sire."

Fantar shook his head in disgust and waved the man away. "Leave me, now! And see that your little affair in Palmeria works better than religion!" Then he turned to Colinus: "You see the quality of my servants?"

"At least the one had sense enough not to march out with your Viceroy, Zenemahr," said the little man, not looking up. "Though it doesn't seem to have done him much good, long term."

"Sense, you say? But what you mean is cowardice."

"The two often masquerade as one another."

"Aye! 'Tis true. You are a clever little one. Much more clever than my old friend Zenemahr, I'm afraid! But tell me, what think you of all these gods and goddesses running around, and the Eye Stone knocking old women off their pins?"

Colinus sat on his small stool and considered this, then looked up with clear, surprisingly youthful eyes. "In my country, it is said that the gods only appear to witness great events."

"And what great event do you suppose that would be? Me disposing of your vaunted Valerius?"

"I hardly think the gods would deem 'tit slapping' a great event. Actually, I was thinking of the other way around."

"Of me being deposed? Oh, aren't we witty today! You little imp. I suppose you also think it cowardly of me to have Valerius assassinated."

"I think it makes sense to you, Highness."

"Ha! Another pun! You'd rather see him kill me in open combat, I suppose?"

"I would," said Colinus, crossing his arms and nodding emphatically. "It is the warrior's way."

"Then why do I have to chain you beyond the reach of my bed at night? Tell me that, you little bastard."

"I suppose, because that also makes sense to you."

"Aye, it does that! And despite the wit of tiny fools and wizards, I am not a fool. Dead in bed is as dead as any, I say. The means are incidental. And that's why I may yet have a surprise for your vaunted Valerius one of these nights as he lays his curly head down to sleep. Eh, my little man?" Fantar laughed again, deep in the back of his throat. "And in the meantime, you can sleep on the dung heap!"

"If it will make me fitter to serve you, my Lord," said Colinus, and ducked away to avoid a blow.

Directly north of Fantar's encampment, the land rose abruptly to a ridgeline that formed the first step of the northern mountains. Here and there along this ridge, the underlying rock broke through the surrounding forest in a series of naked bluffs. Atop one of these that afternoon, lying on their bellies just back from the edge and surveying the host spread out below, was a party of Thuringian warriors. They were busy counting: picking the standards of individual units in the haphazard chaos that was the camp, then estimating the number of men nearby. It was easier to count an army on the march, but this was the best vantage point they had had in weeks.

Their leader, Thorngere, stood back among the trees, staring out over the vast blue of the Inland Sea to the south. He had seen enough of the camp below-and enough of Fantar's growing host over the past few weeks-to know there were more troops down there than his paltry force could handle.

Thorngere and his troop of Thuringians had been dogging Fantar since he had marched out of Valeria, staying to the rough trails in the hills to the north and watching for an opportunity to strike. But the opportunity had consistently eluded them and with Fantar's force swelling at every town and village along the way, the chances for such an opportunity were growing slimmer by the day. This camp, it was thought, might present that chance. Apparently heedless of any threat, Fantar had positioned his camp just below these dominating heights and when Thorngere's scouts had rushed back to announce that news, his leadership council had insisted on a reconnaissance in force.

But a single look had told Thorngere there was no opportunity here. There was no way his men could attack from these cliffs, and to try and insinuate his force between the base of the cliffs and Fantar's camp would only serve to get them trapped and annihilated. From here they might loft a few flights of arrows into the camp, but what end would that serve? No, they either had to find a spot where they could launch an effective hit and run raid, or do something else entirely.

And it was this something else that arrested Thorngere's thoughts as he stood atop the cliff, looking out over the Inland Sea; that and the thought of Vahla, way over the other side of that water, high in the mountains south of Zagorbia. For more than a year he had been trying to get away from Vahla (and even thoughts of Vahla), but now, with the revelation from Panella that she was not his sister, he was consumed with thoughts of getting back to her. Now, the thought occurred to him that there, out over the sea, was a spot at the very end of his vision that was closer to Vahla than any spot he had been able to see since he started his return. It was a silly notion, he knew, and another part of his brain chided him for it even as he thought it, but he liked the notion nonetheless, and his mind probed that spot for some sense of her presence.

But there was nothing. Then his commanders were around him, their faces questioning, and duty reclaimed him.

The consensus was between twenty-five and thirty thousand troops in the camp below, compared to just under five thousand of their own. Many of Fantar's troops were, like Thorngere's, new recruits, untested by battle. Given the element of surprise and a hard assault, they might be driven to panic. But the core of Fantar's force were the battle-hardened veterans he had garrisoning all the towns along the Inland Sea, the same men who had won him the Empire in the first place. They would not run. What were the chances they could break through and get Fantar himself? And what then if they could?

Thorngere walked again to the cliff's edge and surveyed the camp. Fantar's Wild Boar standard was there, dead center, flapping lazily atop a tent that could sleep a battalion. Surrounding it, on other tents, large and small, were banners Thorngere had seen on a score of battlefields. No, he thought, there was no chance here to knock off the head. But the heart?

His decision made, he turned quickly and stalked off into the woods, his commanders falling into hasty formation behind him. "Mount up," he said as he passed through them. "We march west."

Hours later and far to the east, Vahla left her camp at dawn and with Chad in tow, rode out among the grassy plains north of Palmeria, scaling the low hills and outcroppings and scanning the horizon from their heights. As the sun climbed, high clouds began filling in from the northeast, blocking its warmth and sending huge shadow wraiths sailing across the empty plains. Soon, she had been told, the rains would come, but for now the long grasses were brown and parched, waving stiffly in the fitful breeze. She rode at leisure with no apparent destination, tracing an arc north and west around the city. It was a path she had been following for some months now, and her goings and comings, her climbing and watching, had become a matter of routine.

About mid-morning, from the top of a particularly rugged outcropping, she spied a small dust-cloud in the north and watched as it headed her way and resolved itself into a group of Scythian riders. Cautioning Chad to stay out of sight, she walked out into full view on a shoulder of the ledge and waited. She might have been relaxing in her own garden for all the concern she showed.

The riders pulled up about a quarter of a mile away and began an animated conversation amongst themselves. One was apparently urging the others on, but they were having none of it. Finally, he waved them off and rode forward slowly himself. Stopping again about a hundred yards out, he dismounted and proceeded forward slowly on foot. As he neared, Vahla started as she recognized Karghan, the Scythian leader. He stopped about twenty feet from her ledge and dropped to his knees, spreading his arms in supplication.

Twenty miles to the southwest, the great fleet of Valerius entered the harbor of Palmeria amidst fanfare and wild rejoicing. Over four hundred sail strong by now, and bursting with lusty, victorious warriors, the fleet made its stately way to the many piers lining the harbor, and disgorged its soldiery into a tumultuous city. Like Bangorum to the south, the Palmerians had no thought of resistance, but only cheering acclamation at this appearance of a savior. Formed on the docks in their thousands, the army of the High King paraded through the streets, while at their head, Valerius himself rode with his beautiful queen, Eomer, adorned by the crowds with flowers.

Once inside the palace, Valerius quickly got down to business, conferring with his advisors and local resistance leaders, and rapping out orders to ensure the security of the city. They met in the same inner courtyard where Asperides had entertained Vahla for lunch, but the place was far from serene now as the command structure of a sizeable army set up shop. High on the agenda, after the quartering and disposition of troops and a number of internal security matters, was the whereabouts of the Scythians. Information was difficult to come by since their horsemen precluded any near approach, but two things seemed sure. One, they continued their depredations of the countryside, and two, they continued to increase in numbers as more and more migrated down from the north. But the central question remained, why had they not attacked the city?

It was the goddess, ventured several, she who roamed the hills north of the city and intercepted their war parties. She had been seen several times, swelling and transforming into a horrible, horned creature. The Scythians ran from her.

But one disagreed. "I don't think they care about the city," he said. He was Kundar, the chief scout for the resistance organization, and the one man who had perhaps been closer to the Scythians than any other. An excellent horseman himself, he had not only fled for his life from them a number of

290

times in recent weeks, but in his youth he had traveled in the north and spent some time among them, learning their habits and a smattering of their language. In Palmeria these days, he wore the airs of an expert and was not shy about offering his advice even to the new High King.

"They are a nomadic people, Highness," he explained. "They live in tents out on the plains the year round. They know nothing of houses and would not know what to do with a city if one dropped in the middle of their camp. As for laying siege, why they know less of that than of sailing the sea."

"Then what are they doing here?" Valerius wanted to know.

"They want the land, Highness. Even when I was young, the Mitani were pushing them from the north. They come south for land."

"Well, goddess or no, nomads or no, they'll not have this city or this country," Valerius pronounced. "If it's land they want, let them go back and fight the Mitani for what they had."

Several nights later, Valerius shooed away all his commanders and advisors, made sure young Valerian was comfortable with his nurse, and sat down to a quiet dinner with Eomer. They had not had any time together in months. They had either been too crowded aboard ship, or too busy when they got ashore, or before that, too besieged to relax. Indeed, there had been no truly private time, no intimate time, since well before Valerian was born, and Valerius was as eager as a boy to rectify that situation.

This particular evening seemed like an excellent opportunity. He had achieved his stated goal of reaching Palmeria, over half the empire was now under his sway (though he was under no illusions how fast it could sway back the other way if he should falter), and while Scythian hordes still roamed the plains outside the city, and Fantar still lurked somewhere to the west, he was, at the moment, facing no imminent threats. For him, that felt like a holiday. And when you added the fact that he was sitting in the glow of the same candle as the beautiful Eomer, he did not need wine to elevate his mood.

Eomer looked elegant, wearing her hair piled high to expose the slim stem of her neck, and a simple white gown that set off her bare shoulders and the swell of her full, maternal breasts. She was still very young, this Queen of Valerius, not yet nineteen years, and the added weight of pregnancy had slipped off her frame like last winter's heavy cloak, leaving her with the same slim, girlish figure she had before. Only her eyes seemed to have changed. They were deeper, fuller, and the lines of her face had softened and matured with a mother's grace. She was the daughter of King Reuters of Dulcai, and Valerius had known her since she was a stripling, indeed, even before he himself was known as Valerius. After the battle for Dulcai, when he had seen her again for the first time in several years, sailing down the wind with Thorngere on Koltar's catumaran, he had tumbled head over heels in love. But he had never seen her more lovely than she was at that moment, in the light of a single candle in the palace of Palmeria.

"You are so lovely tonight I can hardly eat for looking at you," he said.

"Indeed?" said Eomer, her eyes flashing with good humor. "Then what happened to that plate of food that was in front of you?"

And it was true. All that remained on Valerius' plate were a couple scraps of fat and a stray stem of boiled broccoli. He popped the stem in his mouth and grinned sheepishly. "You see," he said, "you've quite driven me out of my wits!"

Eomer laughed, but was not to be so easily seduced. "This 'goddess'," she said. "Do you think she's your sister, Vahla?"

"I can't think who else," he said, pushing aside far more pleasant thoughts. "It was known she left here with Asperides force, and Bokmar told me she used the same trick when she played the Oracle in Cartho. She must be a very fast learner, or old Volkmir is a better teacher of magic than he was of ciphering."

"But what's she doing here?"

"Saving the city, according to some. But other than that, I don't know. Bokmar said she had tried to get to Zagorbia during the siege, then after Cartho, had set sail for Palmeria in royal state. He spoke of her in very hushed tones. Whatever trick she pulled, she clearly frightened him."

Eomer smiled at this, pleased that a woman could have such power: especially one who had suffered as much as Vahla. "Are you going to send for her?"

"Well, certainly. But I suspect she'll turn up when she hears we're here. A little more wine, my dear? I was hoping to avoid talking business this evening."

"I'm sorry dear," said Eomer holding out her glass. "But I don't get to talk to you very much either, you know."

"Yes, I know. And I'm sorry, too. It's been a very hectic few months."

"What are you going to do about the Scythians?"

"Do? Why, fight them I suppose. Unless they are very obliging and pack up and leave on their own."

"But didn't you say they were homeless, driven from their own lands?"

"That's what Kundar says. But even so, that doesn't give them the right to take our lands."

"Well, certainly not. But might you not reach some accommodation?"

"So far they have wiped out an army of several thousand, killed an indeterminate number of other people, decimated the countryside, and stolen a year's worth of grain. Seems to me like the accommodating ought to start on their side."

"Well, of course. But I was just thinking that if there was some way you could help them get their lands back, then you'd have an ally to the north instead of an enemy."

Valerius stopped his glass halfway to his mouth and looked at his wife with pleasant surprise as this thought settled into his mind. It was an excellent one, and he told her so. "But," he added, "at the moment, I'm afraid that would be a little like a sheep trying to convince a lion to go eat a goat. And before anything like that is even possible, we've got to convince them we're not sheep."

"Are you confident you can do that?" Eomer asked, a quick shadow of fear crossing her face.

Valerius considered this. Until that moment, it had not occurred to him to question his confidence. "Yes," he said finally, "I am confident. I mean, militarily, I am certainly confident of our troops..."

"That's not what I mean."

"Do you mean have I seen the future? No, I have not. Nor do I know how to explain it, but ever since we left Zagorbia, I have felt more and more confident in myself, more and more comfortable that things were moving as they should. That's surprising in a way, because, gods know I have never had command of such a vast enterprise as this, never had so much riding on every move. But I am very confident. I don't know if it's that the gods are guiding me, or the powers of the Eye, or the fact that I am descended from a thousand year line of kings and have been raised to this, but I feel that I am the High King and it feels right to be the High King. For once in my life, I actually feel like I am in control of things."

Eomer's eyes were large and luminous in the flickering candlelight. She set her glass down and reached across the table and took Valerius' hand. "It also feels right that I am your Queen, my Lord," she said, and Valerius' heart began to pound like a drum.

Their private chamber was just down a short hallway, but before they could traverse it, Valerius was interrupted by a very anxious adjutant. He was very sorry, the man said, but if his Majesty could spare just a moment, there was a matter...

Valerius excused himself and told Eomer to go on ahead. He had only just stepped back into the courtyard when her scream sent him running.

She was on the far side of the room when he burst in, standing in terror with her back against the wall. On the bed, where she had just pulled down the sheet, lay a serpent. Without even thinking, Valerius snatched it by the tail and whip-snapped it viciously against the wall, spattering blood and venom. Dropping the thing, he turned to his wife.

"Are you all right?" he said, rounding the bed.

Her eyes were wide and her mouth opened in a silent "O." Her left wrist was clutched in her right hand. She held it out and he could see the two puncture wounds on the fleshy part of her thumb. Then, just as he reached for her, her eyes rolled back in her head and she slumped to the floor.

Chapter 21
THE REUNION

When Vahla rode into the crowded streets of Palmeria early the next morning, she rode in a circle of silence. Guards at the gate, citizens, groups of soldiers along the street, artisans in their shops, children at play, shoppers and vendors in crowded market stalls, mothers standing in windows, even the elderly hobbling along or resting in early spots of shade, all fell silent at the sight of her. People left the street, clearing the path before her. Many knelt, bowing their heads as she passed. Some prostrated themselves completely. And in her wake, groups congealed, eyes glued to her back, whispers rustling like leaves in distant trees.

Indeed, the Vahla who reentered Palmeria seemed a very different creature from the pampered, suspected consort who had left with Asperides some months before. Many, perhaps, did not even associate the two, but even if they did, the desert had wrought remarkable changes. This was a lean, sinewy, hardened Vahla, one burnt near bronze by exposure to the desert sun. In place of her court gowns, she wore a simple muslin robe with a hood and long, wide sleeves from which extended slim, brown wrists and holding the reins, callused, capable hands. Instead of her plaited, perfumed hair, her black mane now flowed free, sweeping up and back from her face as if set that way by hot desert winds. But it was in her eyes where the difference showed most. These were eyes that had grown used to the vast scope of desert spaces, long-seeing eyes, as dark as coals, that flashed now, falcon-like, as she gazed about her.

Vahla had always been remarkable for her beauty, but now, after months in the desert, that beauty had deepened and matured. There was about her now a serenity that was at once austere and haunting, and, in her erect carriage and determined look, a sense of strength and resolve. She bore a distinctive aura of power and mystery, and those along the street knew instinctively that here, in the flesh, was that rumored goddess of the desert to whom they most probably owed their lives and their city. She was not challenged at the gate, nor at any of the intersections along the way, but rode quietly in the silence that surrounded her, followed by the inevitable Chad, and made her way towards the palace.

She knew, of course, that Valerius had arrived, but even if she had not, the signs of his military presence were everywhere, from the troops along the streets to the masts crowding the harbor. The palace especially seemed fortified and busy, but again, she was not challenged as she and Chad handed their mounts to a waiting groom and climbed the steps to the broad portico. Here, at last, was she met, and to her surprise, by none other than Valerius himself. The High King rushed out to her like a man desperate for water. He looked wild-eyed and disheveled, like he had not slept, and there were dark rings, like stains, beneath his eyes.

"Thank god you've come!" he said, and grabbing both her hands, dragged her into the palace.

They went immediately to his private chamber where Eomer lay upon the bed, as pale as the linen sheet that covered her. In a jerky, disconnected voice, Valerius sketched the events of the night before, and then his voice trailed off plaintively as Chad went to the bedside and placed his finger on Eomer's throat. She was unconscious, her breathing light and shallow. Under the linen coverlet, her left arm was swollen and bandaged, the site of the wound still bleeding slightly. Chad inspected the dressing and the wrapping, which was quite snug and extended halfway up her forearm.

"Who bandage arm?" he wanted to know.

"One of the attendants," said Valerius, fresh alarm starting in his eyes. "She said she knew about snake bites. Is it all right?"

"Yes, very good," said Chad. "Queen lucky. Where snake?"

"Snake?" For several seconds, the question did not register. Then Valerius shook his head clear and motioned to the corner where the remains of the serpent still lay: in the confusion following the attack, no one had thought to remove it.

Chad went over and inspected it closely. "Horn viper," he said. "Very poisonous." Then he pulled a small lancet from a pouch at his waist, stretched the snake on its back in the angle between wall and floor, and began slitting it open from the gullet down. Valerius watched with a look of revulsion on his face. Vahla stood at his side, watching him.

"Ah!" exclaimed Chad. "Look. Look here!" Valerius and Vahla bent and looked where Chad was holding open the viper's innards. They saw a congealed mass, matted with fur. "That very good," said Chad. "Very good!"

Valerius looked at Vahla, his face blank. "Explain to him, Chad," she said.

"Snake just eat when he caught," Chad said. "Use up venom on rat, not Queen."

"Does that mean she'll be OK?"

"Mean she not dead," said Chad and went back to the bedside.

Vahla took Valerius by the arm and lead him from the room. He followed meekly and flopped down beside her in an adjoining chamber.

"Will she be all right?" His face was desolate. Vahla put her arm around his shoulder.

"I don't know," she said. "It's a good sign that the snake ate recently, and the swelling doesn't look too bad, but there's no way to know. Chad will give her something to help her sleep. Beyond that, it's in the gods' hands."

Valerius leaned his elbows on his knees and shook his head slowly. "I don't know what I'll do if I lose her. I just don't know. All these years I've been fighting Fantar, and now when it seems I'm so close... I just don't know."

Vahla saw that his hands were trembling and when he looked up, a large tear was running down his cheek. He did not look like a High King to her then, just a large boy, and she folded him to her breast and held him. He recovered quickly, however and with a great sniff, sat back and rubbed his face. "I'm sorry," he said.

"Hey, what are sisters for?"

"Well, thank you. I'm glad you've come. If she has any chance at all, I know you and Chad can save her."

"Do you know who planted the snake?"

"No, but I've got Grumwald on it. He'll get to the bottom of it if anyone can." They sat in silence for a few minutes, and then Valerius changed the subject.

"From what I hear, you've made quite an impression around here yourself. Is Volkmir with you?"

"No. I'm sorry to have to bring you more bad news, but Volkmir is dead."

"Ah!" said Valerius softly, his body flinching as if from a blow. But then again he settled his elbows on his knees. "I should not be surprised: he was old when I was a boy. May the gods grant him peace. Did he go easily?"

"Very easily. Like he wandered off into a dream."

"Yes, he would arrange things like that. I shall miss him."

"As do I," said Vahla and again they lapsed into silence, the noises of the palace and the surrounding streets drifting past unheeded.

"That makes you the Mage, then," Valerius said at last.

301

"I prefer Enchantress," she grinned. Then, more seriously, "But I'm a long way from being able to fill Volkmir's shoes."

"From what I hear, you've already outgrown his and fashioned your own. No one ever accused that crusty old curmudgeon of being a god! Tell me what happened."

"No, first you must introduce me to my nephew, Prince Valerian."

Valerius smiled broadly at this, despite his troubles, and after checking in on Eomer again-she was sleeping peacefully now with Chad by her side-took Vahla to the nursery where young Valerian, unaware of how close he was to becoming motherless, was yelling up a storm and giving his nurses no end of grief about being changed and dressed for the day: it seemed that the young prince much preferred going naked. He quieted when his father took him, however, and when handed to the eager Vahla (she practically snatched him from her brother's arms!) he lay still as could be, staring up at her face with utter fascination.

"I see even the young are unable to resist your charms," Valerius chuckled.

"He's beautiful, Valerius!" she said. "I can see both you and Eomer in his face. He's going to be a strong and wise king, I just know it."

When they returned to the day room, Valerius called for food and drink, and they exchanged stories. She told him about the visions in the fire, the wreck of Colinus' catumaran ("I've often wondered what happened to that lad," said Valerius, shaking his head sadly. "He was a rare one.") and about the passing of Volkmir. She told of the journey through the swamps with Chad as her guide, of her encounter with the sergeant, the events in Cartho. She embellished nothing.

"The versions I've heard of those things are a bit different," said Valerius archly.

"People see as they believe," said Vahla.

"Yes. And as wizards will. But go on. How came you here?"

She told how she had sought Asperides' aide for Valerius in Zagorbia, how he had agreed and gathered his army, but how the arrival of the Scythians had cut short her plans and his life.

"Did you trust him?" Valerius wanted to know.

"No. He was playing both sides. But I believe I could have managed him."

"And since then I hear, you've been riding the desert, impersonating a goddess and frightening whole armies," Valerius chuckled. But then, more quietly, "Did you love him?"

"Asperides?" Vahla laughed. "The man was a fool, Valerius, a poppycock. Besides, you already know the answer to that question." Then, more quietly herself, "Is he here?"

"No, I'm afraid not, my dear. We don't know where Thorngere is, or even if he's still alive." He held up his hand at the alarm that sprang to her face and continued. "We have no indication he's dead either, mind you. We just don't know." He explained how the plan to attack Valeria had been interrupted by the siege, and how after the defeat of

Vincipius, the trader Uban had brought news of the Scythian invasion and of Thorngere and Gamlarch's defeat.

Vahla took the news quietly. Wrapping her arms about her knees, she hugged herself tightly and tried to let the pain flow past. Then, as suddenly as Valerius, she pushed the grief aside and straightened up.

"So you came east," she said.

"Yes. Fantar sent an ambassador offering a cleverly worded truce recognizing me as one of his under-kings in exchange for help dealing with the Scythians. There was no way I could have anything to do with that, of course, and then I got to thinking, 'what would I do about the Scythians if Fantar wasn't around?' The answer was, I'd head east, gathering forces as I came, and deal with the situation. Then I thought about all the support we had been getting from all around the Inland Sea, and Thorngere's network, and about the state of Fantar's popularity generally, and I thought, 'Why not just go for it? Proclaim myself High King, head east offering amnesty to all who repudiated Fantar-except the most guilty, of course-and see what happens.'

"So, that's what we did, and the results have been remarkable. It's been like a victory procession. We've had very little fighting, and our forces have swelled at every step."

"Well, it certainly looked like the High King was in town when I came through the gate."

"You know, it's a strange thing. It's not that just saying something will make it so, but believing it is certainly the first step. I don't know if I've ever told you this, but when our old friend Volkmir returned the Eye to me, he said something similar, that before you can become a king, you must proclaim yourself one."

"Or an Enchantress..."

"Or an Enchantress." They sat in silence again for a while, each musing on their own thoughts. Then Vahla looked at him from the corner of her eye. It was a calculated look, as if she were weighing something in her mind.

"So now you're here," she said, "what do you intend to do?"

"Well, it's not as if Fantar has really gone away, you know. He's been moving east as well, and from what I hear, has also gathered a considerable host. So what I need to do is deal with these Scythians as quickly as possible, then finish things with him. That part has never really changed."

"But what about the Scythians?"

Valerius gave her a narrow look. "What about them? What are you driving at, Vahla?"

"All right. I guess my 'charms' don't work with you. There is another reason I came to Palmeria. I mean, I would have come to see you anyway-and I'm delighted we came in time to help Eomer-but there is something else."

"Which, I gather, has something to do with the Scythians."

"Yes, I'm acting as their ambassador."

"Ambassador!"

"Well, that's a bit strong. Let's say intermediary. I agreed to speak for them. But let me explain..." Vahla went on to describe how Karghan had approached her in the desert (though she omitted to mention how he had fallen to his knees in supplication.) She had gone down to speak to him, she said (though, again, she did not say how he was almost worshipful in his deference). He had matters of the utmost importance to discuss with her, he had said, and would guarantee her absolute safety if only she would accompany him back to his camp.

"And you went with the fellow?" Valerius was incredulous.

"Of course. I was in no danger: I know when a man is telling the truth." So she had ridden with him, hard for the better part of the day until they came upon the Scythian camp. This was a sprawling affair of brown, hide tents that filled a broad, grassy valley. There were thousands of tents, she said, extending the entire length of the valley, and the smoke from their cook fires floated over the valley like a flat gray roof. The surrounding slopes were littered with herds of sheep and goats, and when Karghan lead her down into the valley and among the tents, the stench was very strong. But she had followed her flat-faced host as he meandered his way slowly among the tents and their inhabitants prostrated themselves before them. Karghan was seemingly intent on letting her see as many of his people as she could (or, she thought, letting as many of his people see her with him).

And people there were, thousands upon thousands of them. And not just warriors. Women, children, the sick, the aged-the population was as large and mixed as a city. Surely, she thought, this was more than a raiding party. This was a migration. Finally, Karghan stopped before his own tent (the same she had walked away from on that other night), and once inside, offered her his own chair, and served her wine and figs (and oh, how different his demeanor this time!).

"Now that you have seen my people," he said, spreading his open hands before her, "I hope you can begin to understand." They had been driven from the north, he said, and were in search of a new homeland. But wherever they went, they were met with hostility. Now his scouts had told him, a huge fleet was approaching the city, filled with soldiers, and he feared for his people. He did not know where else they could turn, and appealed to the goddess (Vahla just said 'to me') to intercede with the leader of this great army.

"He said," Vahla concluded, "that the land here was broad and good, and the needs of his people were few. And he asked, 'could we not share the land?'" (But again, she omitted certain other, more personal inferences.)

Valerius watched Vahla's face as she spoke and absently stroked his beard. "It's curious," he said, "but Eomer was speaking in just the same vein last night. She said the Scythians might make a better ally than an enemy."

"And might she not be right?"

"Allies are always better than enemies. But I'm not even sure the question has relevance. Look at the situation: These are people who have invaded our lands-who have been raiding our lands for years. Now they have slaughtered an army, pillaged the countryside... And they ask that all be forgiven and that they be left in peace to consolidate their gains? I think any ruler who even considered such a thing would soon lose his crown."

"You mean you will not even consider the plea of this people because of your own political situation?"

Valerius' eyes flashed darkly at this, but he answered calmly. "No, Vahla, it's a question of justice. They must pay for what they have done."

"Even if they had no choice? Even if they acted in self-defense and to feed their children?"

"The people of Palmeria, too, have children. They, too, must be fed. And defended. Did the Scythians consider this when they stole their grain and killed their fathers?"

"So your heart is closed," said Vahla, with more of an edge to her voice than a question.

"No, but we don't have a lot of time and we must look first to the security of our own people. Look, I've got your Scythian friends on one side and Fantar closing in on the other. He'd like nothing better than to catch us between the two armies. Or better yet, fall on us immediately after we've beaten them. Whatever we do, I need to act fast."

"Even at the expense of innocent lives?"

Suddenly, Valerius' eyes narrowed with suspicion. "This is not like you, Vahla. What is it you are not telling me?"

Vahla sighed and dropped her eyes, suddenly shy. "All right," she said. "Karghan has asked me to marry him."

"Marry him! But...," and he fell silent, seeing the anguish on her face and recalling the enormity of her situation. "Do you love him?" he asked softly.

Vahla looked up sharply and opened her mouth to speak, but at that moment, Grumwald burst into the room, shouting, "Valerius! Your Majesty!"

Valerius jumped up, but at the sight of Vahla, Grumwald stopped in his tracks. "Oh, I beg your pardon! I didn't know the Princess Vahla was here," he said, his eyes never leaving her. "Your servant, Your Highness," and he bowed deeply.

"What have you got, Grumwald?" Valerius snapped, forcing the man's eyes away from Vahla.

"We got him, Your Majesty! Found him hiding in the grain bin under the stairs in the stable..."

"And?"

"As we thought, Your Majesty, He's a Scythian!"

Blood rushed to Valerius' face and his nostrils flared as a great rage rose up within him. Eyes flashing and hands clenched into fists. "Scythian! Sound the alarm, Grumwald. We march immediately."

"Valerius, don't do this!" Vahla cried. "They are not guilty of this, I know."

Valerius turned on her. "You know, do you? You ask about my heart! Yours is the one that has been blinded, treacherously so! Your lusts have turned you against your own flesh and blood. Well, I'll tell you this: we'll let those Scythians share our land, all right-with their bones!"

Vahla's dark eyes turned to obsidian and her color rose to match her brother's. "Beware, Valerius Everreigning," she spat back, "that the brilliance of your vision does not blind you!" And with that, she stalked out of the palace.

Chapter 22
THE SCYTHIAN HORDE

Now unfolded the grand spectacle that was ancient warfare. With fanfares from scores of trumpets atop the walls, the host of Valerius Everreigning issued from the gates of Palmeria, marching to the beat of a thousand drums. Over fifty thousand strong, they spilled from every portal onto the surrounding plains like water from a fountain, and with their burnished arms glistening in the sun, congealed into a massive stream that flowed north onto the steppes in search of Scythians.

At their head rode a grim faced Valerius, resplendent in plumed helm and silver inlaid armor, his buckler hung over his shoulder and his great falchion slung by his side. Flanking him were Grumwald and the tiny Koltar, the latter also ornamented as befitted his kingly rank, the former, uncomfortable on his spirited mount, in plain, serviceable plate, only his red cloak of office and the gray tangle of his beard distinguishing him from the officers that followed.

The organization of the army in the field mirrored the organization of the fleet with Grumwald as general-in-chief controlling the center under Valerius, and Gainor and Zimlait commanding each wing. Lower command structure was by squadron, ship, and crew with newer forces either augmented as units or dispersed among existing units in whatever fashion made the most sense. Troops from Zenemahr's army had been spread among a number of galleys, for instance, while ships from the fleet at Telos were absorbed with crews-and even captains-intact, but the ships were spread throughout the fleet. The most recent additions, a squadron of ten new galleys from Durumkai, which had sailed out with their commodore to join Valerius' fleet, served now as a single squadron.

All these men in their thousands, their dress and arms often reflecting the style of their towns, now slogged along behind their banners into the dusty hills, their spears sloped against their shoulders. Many also carried lumpy packs, and among them-an oddity for an army on the march-rolled many hundreds of curiously built carts.

Koltar's cavalry paced along on either side of this great column, with small squadrons ranging far and wide in search of the enemy, while other units stayed behind, riding herd on the vast collection of baggage and supplies that trailed the host.

Among these troops, too, there were differences. It had long been held by Valerius' high command that the tiny Kantaran horsemen could not stand against full sized infantry. But Koltar's success against Zenemahr, and reports of similar tactics used by the Scythian horsemen had caused the leaders to reevaluate whether these troops might be used to better effect in the coming battle. To this end, his force had been nearly doubled with the addition of nearly every man who had ever ridden a horse, and even with a number who thought it might be better than walking. But they were not all archers. The force had been divided roughly in two, the first group composed mainly of Koltar's veteran Kantaran archers. The remainder-all full-size troops-was much more heavily armored, sporting extra-long spears, and slung at their waists, curved slashing swords not unlike Valerius' own falchion. These were designated as shock troops, their mission to charge in under the Scythian archery and break up their attack.

Soon the walls of the city faded into the dust cloud behind them and the men fell into the mind-numbing rout-step of the march. Hour after hour they trudged through barren hills and rocky, scrub-covered vales: heads down, one foot going before the other, watching out for the man's heels ahead. Overhead, the sun climbed slowly to its zenith then passed and began sliding into the west. Only then did Valerius call a halt for water and a brief rest.

The column was spread over several miles by this time, and while they waited for the rear units to close up, one of Koltar's cavalry squads rode in to report a disturbing find up ahead. The three leaders rode out with them, and topping a line of hills, saw the remains of Asperides force spread across the plain below them. Valerius, Koltar and Grumwald rode down among them.

Scythian pillagers, desert sun, vultures, and hordes of jackals-some of which the king's party interrupted-had all done their work, but what remained was still a gruesome sight: colored rags of cloaks and clothing fluttered about, torn leather packs, the contents strewn, skeletons of men torn partially or completely apart, occasional bits of dried flesh still clinging. Here was a skull with the face half eaten, its teeth white in a brown, shriveled jaw, its remaining black hair splayed against the white sand. There was an intact foot still laced in its sandal, the well-gnawed ankle and shinbone protruding bare above it. Broken spears and arrows lay everywhere, among the bones and between (here was a skull with an arrow still sprouting from its eye), but every trace of usable weapon or armor had been removed. And over all lingered the faint, sickly sweet smell of long-rotted flesh, of death that had visited and then passed on.

The sight was neither new nor surprising for Valerius or his companions, and they viewed the remains dispassionately, reading in their configuration the progress of the conflict. At the far edge, where Asperides' line had stood when the Scythians first hit them, Valerius stopped and looked back at the line of hills and then out across the level plain.

"That man, Asperides, was a fool."

"Aye," said Grumwald. "And it doesn't look as though the Scythians ever really closed. I see no skulls split from sword or axe, only arrows."

Valerius scanned the remains around him again and grunted in agreement. But just then, Koltar touched his sleeve and pointed: out in the desert a dust cloud was visible, like a small brown ball rolling towards them across the sand. As they watched, another cloud rose low on the horizon

314

behind it. But this one was not a ball and not small. It was like a dark bar and spread wide across their field of vision.

"Looks like one of your scouting parties has had some luck," said Valerius.

"Aye," said Koltar. "And they'll have better luck to get here with their hides intact!"

Valerius and Grumwald laughed, short, barking laughs, then looked back again at the line of hills behind them. "What say you, General Grumwald? Could you find a better spot to defend?"

"Not without walls, Your Majesty. And I also say let's recruit these fellows here to act as skirmishers. They may be dead, but they're not beyond use!"

"I had that thought myself, my friend. I had that thought myself."

There was no parley before this battle. When the Scythians attacked, they did not bother with the formal niceties of so-called-and self-proclaimed-civilized peoples. Rather, they attacked with all the ferocity of the wild dogs that roamed their native steppes. They came with all the force they could muster, and they came fast.

Valerius had just time to deploy his line along the hills and his men stood waiting as the Scythians fanned out into their attack positions. An afternoon breeze had set in from the sea, cooling the men as they stood behind their shield wall and blowing away the dust cloud that obscured the oncoming horde. From his new position with his cavalry on the far right, Koltar immediately saw that this time the Scythians did not have a numerical advantage. Rather than overlap the defender's lines, the Scythians were dwarfed by them, and as this fact became apparent to them, he could see their battle line almost hesitate.

It hesitated even more when they encountered the remains of their previous foes. As if the waiting dead stretched their bony hands up from the desert sands and grabbed them, the whole center of the Scythian line came nearly to a halt as they picked their way carefully among the bones, dried flesh and debris. And they were just again spurring their mounts towards the hills before them and their waiting enemies when Valerius beat them to the punch.

It was a repeat of the tactic used so successfully at Zagorbia. During the long months of the progress east, carpenters aboard all the galleys had constructed small catapults on carts, several thousand of which now lined the hills immediately behind the front lines. Each soldier had carried one or two of Koltar's bomb canister parts-separately, so as to avoid accidents-and now, at his signal, they unleashed a barrage of assembled bombs which arced out overhead and down onto the horsemen below.

The Scythians saw them in the air overhead as they themselves were preparing their first volley of archery. But they never got it off. In an instant the curious round canisters crashed into flames all around and among them. Men were hit square and burst screaming into flames, horses reared and screamed. Flaming liquid splattered everywhere, and in an instant the air was filled with smoke and confusion. Some bombs even reached Asperides' former lines, setting fire to the scattered equipage and releasing a few of the trapped souls there with purifying fire.

A second volley followed the first and the wild horsemen from the steppes suddenly turned and fled in panic.

That's when Valerius released his cavalry. Koltar saw the King turn in his direction, saw the deliberate nod, and with a yell from his own outsized voice, sent his troopers clattering down the slopes in pursuit of the fleeing Scythians. From the left, the heavy cavalry charged down as well, smashing into the Scythian flank just as another volley of firebombs hit their center. The southerners were larger and more heavily armed than the leather-plated Scythians, and their long spears impaled men left and right, knocking them from their saddles. Then the heavy sabers came out, hacking and slashing the confused foe whose lines had folded back on themselves and were now a jumble of panicked horses and men.

Koltar's troops kept to the tactics that had served them so well against Zenemahr, the same the Scythians themselves had used against Asperides. They kept well off, streaming along the opposite flank of the fleeing foe, firing volley after volley from their short, powerful bows. Within minutes, the initial panicked flight of the Scythians turned into a complete rout and as the desert horsemen fled to the northeast, first the heavy cavalry, then Koltar's men veered off and let them go. Behind them, strewn over a long mile of ground ending at the still smoking remains at the base of the hills, were hundreds of Scythian dead and wounded, mingled with the bones of Palmeria's former defenders.

Koltar was elated. He knew the tactical situation as well as Valerius, and for them to have disposed of the Scythians this readily-and having sustained hardly a scratch themselves-was a great victory and a great relief. Now they could turn all their attention westward to where Fantar lurked, and deal with what just might possibly be the last barrier standing between Valerius and the complete reclamation of this throne. A dream that seemed so impossible only a few months ago would now become reality. And Koltar could go home. As exciting as all this travel and high adventure was, and as much as he had dreamed of just such things all his life, there was much yet to be done in his Hidden Valley, and he was homesick.

So as he trotted back towards Valerius' lines, he was surprised to see the army marching down the slopes and starting out across the plain. At first he thought it only to put the wounded Scythians out of their misery. But as he neared and saw the look on the huge king's face, he changed his mind. And when Valerius curtly ordered him to resume his positions on the wings, he knew for certain: they were marching in pursuit.

318

They marched for days. Koltar's cavalry scouts located the Scythian camp near the end of that first day, but by the time the army reached it next morning, the Scythians had packed up and fled, their trail clearly visible in the churned and increasingly desolate earth. The trail did not go north, but east. That meant the invaders were not returning to their homelands, but only avoiding Valerius. And Valerius would not be avoided. He would follow them, he said, until he could corner and crush them.

Koltar had not seen this side of Valerius before and as he walked his horse along beside his, he kept stealing sidelong glances at the High King and puzzling over it. It was just not like him. Valerius rode along, staring straight ahead, with this look of grim determination on his face. He hardly spoke, even at night, and when he did, it was only to issue necessary orders. The rest of the time, he was dark and silent, a presence so brooding and fearsome that not even Grumwald dared break in on it. When questions needed to be asked, the two senior leaders coughed politely and said his name hesitantly, as if they were not sure he would answer to it. And when he turned his baleful eye upon them, they blurted their questions, like raw boys, and most often received only a curt nod or a shake of the head in response. Then that face would resume its implacable watch forward and the army would plod on and on.

It was a monotonous march, and hot. As they moved east, the land flattened out, vegetation became more and more sparse, the earth drier and sandier. But Koltar became more and more restless. He was not used to plodding along at the infantry's pace, not used to this much forced inactivity, and his mind wandered. He worried about Fantar, off somewhere in their distant wake. What was he doing while they chased away eastward? Would they return to find the city taken and held against them? And while he did not like to doubt Valerius- he and his people owed the man a debt loyalty alone could never repay-he did question the insistence of this pursuit. Drive them from their camp, certainly; chase them one or two days beyond just to make sure they got the message, sure. But this? A week and more into the desert with an active enemy in their rear? Yes, the Queen was still lying near death at Palmeria, and yes, there were strong indications the Scythians had a hand in the attack. But was that enough to justify this? Why was Valerius so insistent that they be punished?

Koltar remembered the first time he had ever seen Valerius-who was called Balazar, then-and Thorngere. They had thought them great stupid brutes of men, he and Queen Salonis, and she had ordered him to concoct a poison that would immobilize them in battle. Fortunately, he had misjudged exactly how large they were, but that was not the worst of it: he and the queen had misjudged the entire situation, including their generations long war with the Iblis. It was a matter of perception: things seen from one side, or one direction, appeared different when seen from another. But the same logic could be applied to both. If you started from one, the logical progression was two, three and four. But if you started from four, or ten, the progression, and the conclusion drawn, was very different.

Koltar looked again at the huge figure riding beside him, at the great red gem suspended on his chest on its golden chain. What was Valerius' perception in this matter? Had he seen visions in that stone of his which impelled him on this course, or was it, as it appeared, simple rage at the injury to the Queen? And if he had seen visions-and Koltar was never completely sure whether even Valerius believed in the power of the Eye-how could he be sure they were the correct ones? If the power behind the stone was sentient, was it not also capable of misleading?

Koltar, King of Kantar, was nothing if not loyal, but as he plodded along beside the High King, something in his gut told him to beware, that the High King was marching beyond bounds.

Valerius finally cornered the Scythian horde on the plains of Darlung, trapping them between the high spurs of the mountain in the vicinity of the old shrine. He deployed his battle line to the north and stationed his heavy cavalry to the west and south, blocking them in. They were all there, men, women and children, in a pitiable state after nearly two weeks of flight. Their flocks had run wild along the way, the supplies of grain and other foodstuffs they had carried were nearly gone, and starvation threatened. Already, many of the children stared about with the round, haunted eyes of hunger, and their empty bellies protruded perversely. The warriors formed a defensive perimeter around their families, and prepared to die.

But it was late in the day. By the time Valerius' lines were set, the sun was already low on the western horizon, its fading rays setting the slopes of the mountain aglow with a soft red light. His own men were also exhausted. They had been pushing hard for days, knowing they were fast closing with their prey. Now they needed rest nearly as much as the Scythians. He ordered the army to make camp where they stood, but forbade any fires: he did not want to ruin the men's night vision or show the Scythians the extent of his lines. Besides, there was not that much to burn.

Refusing even his own tent, Valerius sat on the barren sand with his senior officers and watched as darkness settled over the plain and the last light slowly worked its way up the mountain. For a time, only the very tip was visible, floating eerily in the darkened sky as if it was, indeed, the home of the gods. Then it too was gone, and the whole scene plunged into darkness.

But at that moment, from the center of the Scythian position, came a quick flash of bright light that caught the attention of every soul on the plain. In an instant it was there and gone, a bright flash that left the darkness darker than before. Then it came again; another flash, as bright as before, but green this time, and seemingly closer to Valerius' lines. Then came another and another, pink, green, and blue. Then another white. All across the space between the armies the flashes moved, proceeding in stately progression towards the High King's lines. All eyes were riveted upon them and all across that plain, among the many, many thousands on both sides, not a sound could be heard.

The flashes stopped about twenty yards out. Then a white light flickered, flared quickly, then steadied and grew brighter as it was hoisted aloft. Beneath was revealed a figure on horseback, a white horse, draped with cloth of gold that glimmered softly. It was a woman, robed in silks and precious stones, a woman whose hair swept upwards in the shimmering light and mingled with the darkness as if it were the darkness itself that bore her. For a few moments, her face remained lost in shadow, but there were those later who swore that in the darkness of that visage, the eyes glowed green. Then she lifted her face and the light flashed off the dark eyes of Vahla.

"Valerius Everreigning!" she keened, her voice high and prophetic, flowing out over the darkness with such force and clarity every man in the army could hear it. "Valerius Everreigning, High King of Valeria and all the Inland Sea-beware! Beware this sand lest it turn quick beneath your feet. Beware this path that will lead you down. Beware your pride lest it cost your crown. Look, Valerius Everreigning, oh Master of the Eye! Look to your vision, lest you stumble blind, and die."

With that, Vahla quickly doused her torch in the sand before her, plunging the scene into utter

darkness. And by the time Valerius struck a light of
his own, the Enchantress was gone.

324

Chapter 23
FIRE AND WATER

Valerius ordered his tent pitched well behind the lines and summoned his senior counselors. They sat on camp stools, staring into a small fire. They ate dry bread and washed it down with wine that had seen too much sun and been jostled over too many miles of desert. Valerius looked from one face to another, but no one looked back, no one spoke. Even Koltar would not meet his eye, but looked down quickly when Valerius turned his way. What none of them would say, and what Valerius knew without saying, was that right or not, inspired or not, prophetic or not, Vahla had succeeded in spooking the entire army, and that for him to order an attack now, without some remedy for this magic she had wrought, would be to invite disaster.

He looked down at the great red gem hanging on his chest and made his decision. "Let the men sleep in their places tonight," he said softly. "In the morning, have rations issued up and down the line, but make no move towards the enemy until I return. As our sister Vahla has suggested, we will go up on the mountain and seek our vision."

Taking only a small guard, Valerius made his way around behind his own lines to where the northern spur of the mountain thrust its way out into the plain. This, according to the legend, was one of the twin streams of lava that had encircled the Valerian and Palmerian armies of old. Stripped to his toga and sandals and leaving his guard with instructions to stay out of sight (which they promptly did by crawling in under the loom of the rocks and going to sleep), he clambered atop the flow and made his way up the slope.

The way was smooth at first, but grew increasingly steep, and by the time he reached the bulk of the mountain proper, he had worked up a good sweat, and paused to catch his breath. A gibbous moon had risen, casting a pale luminescence along his path and out over the sands where his battle lines extended into dark shadow. On the southern side, a few small fires were visible in the Scythian encampment, but over the entire panorama floated a strange, almost surreal silence, the kind only experienced on quiet nights in high places, bathed by moonlight. As he resumed climbing, his footsteps crunched loudly on the hard scrabble.

The way was steeper now, the path zigzagging back and forth among boulders and around outcroppings, and the dark, volcanic rock of the mountain was curiously warm. In places, he was forced to scramble on all fours. Sparse vegetation sprouted among the rocks. It was a place where occasional goatherds grazed their flocks and the thought struck him that he felt more goat than king on this mission. But he put it aside and focused on the climb, trying not to think at all but to keep balanced in his mind, that hard, implacable ball of fury that drove him. His goal was the crown of the mountain where the last rays of the sun had lingered, that spot, which had seemed for one fleeting moment, like it could indeed be the home of gods. If any place was fitting to undo magic of the kind Vahla had worked, that would be it.

It was well past the end of the mid watch when he staggered into a small hollow atop the mountain, and flopped down onto the hard, hot stone. Despite his fury, the past two weeks had drained even his reserves of energy, and now, filthy and exhausted, dripping sweat, and with his tunic torn and his knees bruised and bleeding, he curled up against the eastern side of a large boulder, and fell asleep.

He stirred as the first rays of the sun spilled over the rim of the eastern mountains and splashed against his face. Shying away from the light, he tried to shift into a more comfortable position, but the hot rock poked him in the ribs and prodded his mind towards wakefulness. His first thought was of Eomer, lying so still on their bed in Palmeria. Was she better this day? Would she mend? Then he thought of Vahla and full consciousness-and the reality of his situation-rushed upon him. He sat up and opened his eyes, squinting into the early glare.

Down on the plain, the dawn was still gray as Koltar, too, stirred and rose from his sandy bed. Looking to the mountain as he made his rounds of the watch, he saw the rosy glow as first light touched the peak and wondered where Valerius was and what was in his mind. Vahla's appearance had been a blow to him, he knew. He had been running headlong and she had stopped him like a wall. And had done it very well, Koltar thought with a wry smile. She was not a woman to be taken lightly, the

327

Princess Vahla. But what did it mean? Grumwald had told him of their argument at the palace, but was she speaking for the gods, or simply for herself?

Koltar managed a cup of last night's wine and some hard, black bread, and as the sun spilled daylight down onto the plain, he rode the lines with Grumwald. But he kept thinking of the Iblis and the story of their appearance in the Hidden Valley in the old Chronicles he had found in the cellars of the palace at Kantar. They, too had been refugees, just like these Scythians. As the ancient scribe had reported, they had straggled into Kantar from the mountains to the north, a few bedraggled survivors, totally bereft. Their leader, a man named Chubar, had told King Corinon, Koltar's ancestor, that his people had been numerous and prosperous in the north, that they had homes and fields and counted their wealth in many herds of cattle. But, he said, there arose a king in the far north who exacted tribute from all the peoples. He sent emissaries to the Iblis, demanding their cattle, and when the emissaries were killed for this offense, the king set his armies against them, killing them and driving them from their homes.

"Who is this King who so abused you?" Corinon had asked. "He is called Valerius," the other replied, "Valerius Everreigning. And may the curse of the gods descend upon him and all his line."

Surely, Koltar thought, there could be no connection between the Iblis and these Scythians?

Or between that ancient despot and this Valerius who already carried more than his share of burdens? Surely, Valerius had expiated any vestige of that curse when he resettled the Iblis in the Fortunate Isles? But as Koltar watched the men forming their ranks, and saw them nervously glancing up at the mountains as they adjusted their helms and shields, he could not help but think there was a similarity. Was Valerius replaying that same ancient sin? Had he gone too far, violated some sacrament? Was Vahla correct that these people-who had been raping and pillaging with impunity-now deserved mercy? Were these Scythians favorites, somehow? Or were the gods, as so often seemed to be the case, simply being frivolous?

On their side of the Plain of Darlung, the Scythian warriors, too, donned their arms, mounted their ponies and took their places in line between their women and children and the vast host of Valerius that confronted them. Lucky were those few among them who found some bread or dried meat to break their fast, and luckier still those who managed wine or even water. Karghan took only a small cup of water, sending the rest of his share to the women and children, even though his advisors insisted he needed strength to win the day. "The strength I need will come from the gods," he said and wheeled his mount into the front ranks.

He could see the dark line of the foe across the intervening mile or so of desert, a dark, shimmering line running from the northern spur of the mountain right around in a great semi-circle, locking his people between the southern spur and the bulk of the mountain itself. In the center, between the two lines, stood an ancient stone cairn, commemorating some event or other. 'Let us hope it does not become ours,' he thought.

Karghan would have attacked before now, in the first gray light of dawn when surprise and panic could have multiplied his numbers. But the Enchantress had forbidden such a move. Wait, she insisted, there were portents in the wind. "Let the gods' will rule," she told him and so he waited, reining in his eager pony, and watching the mountain for some sign, while she had gone off again, as mysteriously as she appeared.

When the sun was full up over the eastern mountains, Valerius rose. Facing the light, he took the Eye stone from around his neck and held it cupped in the palms of his hands. How many times had he stood thus, he wondered, seeking visions from the sky? And how many times rewarded? Surely, too few of the latter. But today felt different. Perhaps it was just the after-effects of Vahla's magic, or perhaps it was the heat rising from the mountain, but the morning air seemed charged with power. Curiously, he bore Vahla no ill will on this morning, as he had in the dark of the previous night. In this light, her actions appeared as fated as his own.

Holding the stone so it would catch the light, he bent close and peered into its ruby depths. It looked liquid in there somehow, as if the stone were filled with a viscous fluid that slowly began to move like current in the murky depths of a river. As light filled the stone, the current turned and began to swirl, almost imperceptibly at first, then slowly accelerating. As he bent closer, the edge of the stone facing the sun began to glow softly and behind it, the swirling current spun faster and faster until the infinitesimal specks that defined it began to blur, trailing tiny streaks of light like comets. Then the stone began to pulse and surge, and Valerius' hands began to tremble. He could feel the power of it building, pulsing through his arms and shoulders, raising the hairs on his neck and chest, puffing out his beard.

Never had he experienced anything like this before. Involuntarily, he began stretching out his arms and leaning away from the thing, his eyes growing wide, not so much with fear as from the force of it. Yet still faster did its inner current spin, still more wildly did it throb, like a great glowing heart. And a sound began, a low humming that increased in frequency until Valerius bared his teeth, and clung to the stone as if he was being dragged through space. His hair blew back, his cheeks distended; his eyes seemed to swell in their sockets. Louder and louder the thing wailed. Then it blew.

Koltar saw it from down on the plain. They all saw it: a huge red flash that lit up the morning sky and seemed to engulf the entire shoulder of the mountain. It was like the flash from one of Koltar's firebombs only a thousand times brighter. On both sides, soldiers cringed in their battle lines. Some ducked. Some tried to flee. Then came the sound. Not an explosive sound, but a deep rumbling that seemed to come from the very earth beneath them and rise up through the mountain. The ground began to shake, and as they watched, small avalanches of dirt and debris began cascading down the mountain.

The force of the blast blew Valerius into the air and he landed on his back in the middle of the hollow. He lay there, dazed, his head spinning, his sight blasted into shadows and suffused with a misty afterglow. He was not unconscious, but neither was he awake. Rather, he hung somewhere in between, in a spinning, blank world where there was neither thought nor sound, just a thick murky fog that seemed to swirl like the current in the stone. There were faces in it, indiscernible, yet there somehow, like spirits. There were thousands of them, thousands upon thousands, their faces insistent, their features grim. He felt small and mean, like a guilty child. He had presumed, and the Eye had denied him. Then the mountain began to shudder and he sat bolt upright like one startled awake from a nightmare.

Unsteadily, he climbed to his feet and made his way to the rim of the hollow. It was difficult walking. The ground rocked back and forth beneath him and he moved in a crouch, like he was crossing a high, narrow ridge. From deep inside the mountain came a rumbling sound like heavy, distant thunder, only it was larger than that, heavier, and he could feel it beneath this feet. It felt like the mountain would suddenly collapse beneath him.

Crawling to the edge, he looked down and out over the plains of Darlung, at the two hosts, one backed against the southern spur, the other circling it like a long dark ribbon. Just below him, a huge boulder broke loose from the side of the mountain and tumbled down in a shower of debris. Then the whole mountain surged and shifted and he fell flat, stretching his arms and grasping handfuls of earth for support. There was a great rending sound and as he watched, the very base of the mountain cracked and then exploded outward with a horrific roar and a great gush of steam and water.

It was as if a damn had burst. A great wall of water surged from the base of the mountain and out onto the plain. Karghan was closest to it and saw the base of the mountain erupt. He had heard stories in his youth of mountains that belched fire, and for an instant, he thought they were surely all doomed. Then he saw it was just water and laughed. But again, only for an instant. As the torrent began inundating the plain, he realized the danger was as great as fire and spun his mount around and spurred back along his lines, yelling and waving wildly for his people to run. They didn't need encouraging. Within minutes, the entire horde had snatched up their infants, their food, and whatever possessions they could grab and headed west, towards higher ground.

On the other side of the plain, the army of Valerius was more disciplined in its reaction, though the faces of officers and men showed no less shock and amazement. Still, they held their lines-many instinctively locking shields with their neighbors as if that could stem the flood-and waited for orders. These were not long in coming, despite Valerius' injunction to hold their ground, and with Grumwald and Koltar directing, the whole force began to shift laterally to their right, towards the west and higher ground.

For his part, once the immediate tumult of the earthquake had subsided and he could regain his feet-though he was still trembling in every limb-a badly shaken Valerius Everreigning wasted no time in clearing out of that hallowed hollow and getting himself down off that mountain.

Although the Plain of Darlung appeared level and flat to the naked eye, it was in fact, a huge basin whose base, which ran from the shrine for about three-quarters of a mile to the base of the mountain, was a good thirty or forty feet lower than the surrounding rim where the two armies stood. It was this that saved them, for after the initial surge flooded this base to a depth of several feet, the waters rose more sedately. The initial panic among the Scythians also subsided and while the two groups were still forced to move westward, they were able to do so in a more deliberate and orderly fashion, maintaining their guard and each presenting a respectable front to the other.

The waters were, in fact, just beginning to stretch along the base of the northern spur when Valerius completed his descent. His guard had been washed out of their overnight encampment, but they had not forsaken their duty or been forced too far along the spur, when he came dogtrotting down the lava slope. Battered, bleeding, filthy, and disheveled, he looked as if he had taken a serious beating, or had himself just crawled out from underneath the mountain. It took half a skin of wine to clear the caked dirt from his throat so he could talk. One of the guards held his breastplate and greaves, another his horse, but before he touched either, he looked at the steadily approaching waters of the lake, then down at himself, and plunged in.

"It's great!" he yelled, scrubbing himself in the still muddy waters. "It's like a huge warm bath!"

As Grumwald and Koltar directed their march around the spreading shores of this sudden lake, they tried to press southward as well, so as to keep their quarry penned against the mountains and not let them escape. The Scythians, on the other hand, tried to make as much distance westward as possible in order to do that very thing. But such was the lie of the land-and hence the flow of the water-that neither was fully able to attain their objective. As the Valerian army moved, so rose the waters, and even with his heavy cavalry, Koltar was not quite able to turn the Scythian front. And even though they had the shorter line of travel, neither were the Scythians quite able to outpace the flood or their opponents.

The result was two opposing lines, moving along parallel tracks in a large arc towards the southwest, with the rising waters flowing constantly between them. At the head of the two columns, a race began, with Karghan on the one shore leading his wild warriors, and Koltar on the other, a tiny figure on a splendid mount, racing along at the head of a mixed force of Kantaran and outland cavalry. Between them, and managing to stay in the lead by a hundred or so yards, was a new river, forging a channel for itself towards the Inland Sea.

In the middle of that channel stood Vahla and the ubiquitous Chad. The river was the first to reach her, and as she sat calmly atop her horse, the first shallow springs splashed about his ankles, then swirled swiftly up to his withers. Karghan and Koltar saw her at the same instant, and in mirroring movements, hauled on the reins of their horses and nearly skidded to a halt on opposite sides of her. Their riders quickly congealed around them, and in moments the shores on either hand were thronged with thousands of staring warriors. Swords were drawn but Vahla sat imperturbable, looking quietly upstream as if she were expecting her lover to come drifting down in a canoe.

Who came was Valerius. Shouldering his horse through the quickly parting crowd, he dismounted at the river's edge and waded several feet out into the stream. "Vahla!" he called. "Sister Princess and Enchantress of Valeria, I greet you!"

"And I greet you, Valerius Everreigning, High King of Valeria and all the Inland Sea. Have you done as you were bidden?"

"I have, my Sister, and I stand ready to serve the Gods' will."

Nodding solemnly, Vahla motioned for Valerius and Karghan, who had also waded several steps into the stream, to come together before her. "And what of you, Karghan," she called as they approached? What of your pledge, Warlord of the Scythians?"

Karghan dropped to one knee before Valerius, the water swirling up to his chest, and spoke in a loud, clear voice: "I pledge fealty, my Lady, to this Lord and this land, for myself and my people, now and forever. And I beg for his mercy."

"And what say you, Valerius Everreigning, High King of Valeria and all the Inland Sea?"

"I accept his pledge, for such is the will of the Gods. With this water"-and here, Valerius poured a handful of the warm, running river onto Karghan's bowed head-"I wash clear the deeds of the past, and offer to any of his people who will follow him through this stream, all of the lands to the north of this river and east of Palmeria, unto the boundaries of our realm, to have, hold and defend from this day forward unto the end of time."

Vahla's stern, official expression broke into a wide grin at this, and her eyes sparkled with delight. "Valerius, my brother," she said quietly, "You are a wise and gifted king. May the Gods grant that your line does indeed reign ever until the end of time."

Chapter 24
THE WAY HOME

And so it was that the Scythian tribes passed to the north and into their new homelands. Valerius sat his horse on the bank of the newly dubbed Darlung River beside Karghan and Vahla, and the army stood to attention, as files of armed Scythians waded the stream with their women and children. Each group stopped before the trio of leaders, dropped to one knee, and splashed water on their foreheads in obeisance to the High King. Beyond, as the people trudged back along the path they had come, riders fanned out to recover their wandering flocks and herds. But the bulk of the warriors and their sturdy ponies formed up beside Koltar's men, as enemies became allies.

But Valerius was not quiet in his mind and sat his horse impatiently as the seemingly endless stream of Scythians knelt to acknowledge him. He had been too long away, had strayed too far from the main path of his duty, he knew, and it had been too long since he had heard any word from Palmeria or beyond. What had Fantar done while he was chasing away east? Was he close enough to strike? Could he move that fast? And what of Eomer, his queen? Was she better, or worse, living or dead? His heart burned to know, and as soon as the last of the Scythians-a withered crone who flashed him a toothless grin-had passed over, he formed his men and drove them west and south, following the track of the new river, whose waters soon flowed clear and sweet enough to drink. A squad of Koltar's troops was sent ahead to scout, and a trio of the fastest was sent directly west to Palmeria for news.

Early the next morning, one of the riders returned, nearly exhausted. It was Kundar, the scout. They were unable to get through, he gasped, because Fantar had moved south and gotten between them and the city. Had he invested the city yet, Valerius wanted to know? No, Kundar thought, they were too far to the east. Besides, he ventured, Valerius was the target, not Palmeria. Yes, Valerius thought, that may be true, but my Eomer is there.

Valerius convened a council of war in his tent with his senior leaders. They all stood in a ring in its dark confines, Koltar and Grumwald, Karghan and Vahla (with Chad at her back) Gainor, Zimlait, and a half dozen of the newer battalion commanders. In the center, by the remains of last night's fire, stood Valerius and the scout, Kundar. Valerius had him repeat his tale and from the questions asked, it appeared most likely that Fantar was moving east, just south of the track they had followed.

"What is the ground like to the west and south of here?" Valerius wanted to know. "I do not want to fight him on his ground."

"There is a large valley away south and west of here," said Kundar, "about two days march from the city. For all I know, this river may well pass through or just south of it. But it would seem to me- if I may so venture, Your Highness?"

"By all means, Kundar. We all venture here."

"Thank you, Highness. It would seem to me that if this river runs true and we follow it, this Fantar will learn of it and move to head us off. Stop me if I presume..."

"No, you speak sense."

"Well, an army moving down from the north would see this valley as an ideal place to pounce. Now, I am no general, but it would also seem to me that the southern rim of this valley would also make an ideal place to defend."

"He speaks true," said Vahla, stepping into the center of the circle. "I know the place well. And I can well see Fantar taking to the northern heights, thinking you would have to attack him there or be hit on your flank as you tried to pass."

"I, too, know the place," said Karghan. "My people would have camped there, had there been water. But I also think this Kundar is right that the southern heights might be even better to defend... if we can take them first."

"Well, we're throwing rocks at shadows now," said Valerius. "But where there's shadow there may also be substance. Are there any other suggestions? All right, then, here's what I propose: Koltar, you take your men and follow Captain Kundar, here,"-at which the erstwhile scout's face broke into a ragged grin-"and see if you can take the southern heights of this valley. We'll march like hell and try to come up with you in time. If not, or if he's already there before you, try to draw him east to us. Any questions?"

"A request, Majesty," said Karghan. "I have seen these tiny men ride and fight: my warriors would be honored to fight by their side."

Valerius hesitated, and though he tried to disguise it, his eyes narrowed with suspicion. Did he dare trust the Scythians this far, this fast? He looked to Koltar who met Karghan's eye, then nodded. Then Valerius looked to Vahla. She, too, nodded. Then Grumwald, Zimlait and Gainor all nodded in their turn. Then Valerius met Karghan's eye, and seeing no flicker in the flat, smooth planes of his face, clasped his hand. "Karghan," he said, "we are honored to have you at our side."

The march was grueling. Valerius' men were nearing exhaustion before, but now he called on them for even greater efforts. "Men of the Inland Sea," he addressed them, the great bassoon of his voice floating out over the flat sands, "yesterday you followed me into a burning hole in the desert. And the Gods there created a lake and a life-giving stream. They turned enemies into friends. Now you are tired and hungry, I know. And your feet are burned and sore from marching on sand. Yet all I can tell you right now is that the road ahead is worse than the one behind. With blood and battle with Fantar himself at the end. But follow me again, I ask you. And trust in the justice of the gods. For if we persevere now, this road will lead us to victory!" Tired as they were, the army cheered, and stepped out willingly. But the cheers faded fast, for all their breath was soon needed for the march.

They marched west and south all through the heat of the day and long into the night. They left their baggage far behind. There was little food and without the river beside them, many would have faltered. But on they went, at a killing pace, into the small hours of the morning before finally Valerius called a three-hour halt. Then, at dawn, they were at it again, stumbling along, half asleep, driving their legs at nearly a run. By mid-morning, they had covered nearly sixty miles, but it was clear they could not keep up that pace much longer. Already men were stumbling out of line and falling onto the hot sands.

But they were also nearing the valley. Riders came back from Koltar telling them they had secured the southern slopes, but that Fantar was already forming to the north, that they needed to move fast. Valerius drove them harder, dismounting and trudging along at their head himself, waving his great falchion before them.

The new river did not pass through the valley, but skirted it to the south. As Valerius approached, he could see the massed cavalry mounts in the distance, crowding the back slopes of the hills that defined the valley, and along its rim, Koltar's dismounted battle line. They looked thin and ragged, etched against the clear blue of the sky. Another rider spun from the crowd near the top, his mount rearing up, then plunging down the slope and clattering across the intervening distance. The man waved his arms, shouting as he came. "Hurry! Hurry! Fantar has begun his advance!"

Valerius remounted and charged up the slope, Vahla, Chad and Grumwald right behind. He pulled up beside the tiny figure of Koltar and looked out over the valley, spreading a mile and more in breadth before him: there descending the northern slopes in orderly ranks, was an army of forty thousand or more, and floating at its head, the hated Wild Boar, Imperial banner of Fantar. The sound of their drums floated up to him on the quiet air with a sound of foreboding. Looking back, he could see his own force spread out now over several miles along the river and straggling towards him with agonizing slowness. They looked spent and tired, more like they had just escaped a desperate battle than were advancing towards one. Back and forth between the two forces Valerius looked, gauging time and distance. Was there any way his men could reach the crest in time? And if they did, would they even be able to swing their swords?

Fantar marched at the head of his troops, his great bulk jouncing with every step as he descended to the floor of the valley. Resplendently dressed for the occasion, he wore a gold-inlaid helm with a huge purple plume and matching purple mantle, a gold-plated breastplate large enough to fashion a shield for two men (though, if truth were told, it was made exceedingly light and flimsy, for its owner had no intention either of bearing the weight of a heavier one, or of needing it in battle), and gold-plated greaves whose leather thongs had to be lengthened to fit around his enormous calves. In his right hand, he waved a great jeweled sword high above his head, urging his men onward, while in his left hand, he held the chain of his Kantaran captive, Colinus, who bobbed along at his side like a mastiff. Colinus was similarly armed, in fake, ceremonial stuff, and the sword he bore was a mere child's toy, carved from a thin slat of wood. Behind this duo marched the Imperial Standard Bearer, and behind him, flanking out to the right and left, the commanders and staff of the army.

Fantar was in fine fettle this day for it was clear from the rag-tag line opposing him on the opposite heights, that he was very close to winning the game. The usurper Valerius had obviously miscalculated, and now Fantar would be able to engage him piecemeal, and once he had disposed of the rabble before him, he would totally command all the approaches to Palmeria. Marooned in the desert, Valerius would have little choice but to spend his remaining force in fruitless assaults on Fantar's soon to be impregnable defenses.

Yes, it was a fine day, despite the heat and the sand fleas that seemed to have infested his tunic. For years, now, this Valerius had survived every effort to eliminate-even assassinate-him. Now it would all end here. Valerius would leave his bones in these hills outside Palmeria, and he, Fantar, would be fully vindicated and his rule legitimatized at last. A fine day, indeed!

But then, several figures on horseback broached the skyline above him, and just behind them, a standard bearer unfurled a flag: it was white and red with a golden lion leaping, the Royal banner of the

344

High Kings of Valeria. Not for nearly twenty years had Fantar faced this flag in battle, and despite himself, he stopped in his tracks.

Unaware that his master had stopped, Colinus plodded on, his head sunk into his own private misery, until the chain on his neck stopped him short, and a quick yank from Fantar toppled him over backwards. When he looked up, a slender, dark skinned man was bending over him, smiling. Sure that the fellow had not been there an instant before, Colinus looked back and around, but neither Fantar nor any of his attendants seemed aware of him: all their attention was focussed on the line of hills before them. But there he was, nonetheless, holding out a hand and offering to help him up. Colinus took the proffered hand.

"Who are you?" he said, his voice a hoarse whisper.

"Chad a servant," said the fellow. "Help you get free." And he held out to Colinus a pointed dagger, its hilt gleaming with jewels.

Colinus gasped, then quickly looked back at Fantar who still stood, oblivious. "What is this?" he breathed.

"This a weapon," said Chad. "You a warrior. Take it."

Colinus took the weapon and stood, looking down at it in disbelief. It was heavy and solid in his hand, the jewelled hilt lumpy and too fat for his small fingers.

"Try it," said Chad. "It even cut chain. Make you free."

Colinus pressed the blade against the chain trailing down from his collar. It cut it like string and the loose end crumpled to the ground with a clinking sound. But to Colinus, that sound was like a great bell, which rang in his ears and swelled the chambers of his heart. He was free! He was a man again. And a warrior! He turned to face Fantar.

"Fantar One-Eye!!!" he screamed, his small voice swelling to fill the valley. "I am Colinus, Commander of the Royal Guard of Koltar, King of Kantar, Vassal of Valerius Everreigning, High King of Valeria and all the Inland Sea. I challenge you!"

Fantar shook his head as if he had momentarily dozed off and looked down in surprise at his former captive. But as the words sunk in and he saw Colinus standing before him, snarling like a small terrier, and brandishing a dagger, his surprise quickly turned to anger.

"Oh, you challenge me, do you, you little bugger?" he snarled. "Well, I'll take that challenge. I should have killed you long before now for all the good you've been, you worthless little bastard." And with that, Fantar lunged at the smaller man, swinging his sword down at his head in a vicious arc.

But Colinus was faster. Darting inside the stroke, he plunged the dagger deep into the huge man's chest, right through breastplate, tunic, corselet, skin and bone. Fantar grunted once, a deep "Ugh," then collapsed forward onto his assailant, blood gushing from his mouth.

Colinus knew nothing. He neither felt Fantar collapse on top of him, nor felt the crushing impact as their two bodies hit the ground. It was all nothing: just a deep, black silence. Then there was that hand again, seeming to emerge from a sudden pool of light, and the slender, dark-skinned man offering to help him up; then his smiling face in the light as the two stood there beside the grotesque body of Fantar in a seemingly motionless valley.

"Come," the man said softly. "Chad take you home now," and they turned and Colinus followed him towards the light.

With Fantar's death, resistance quickly collapsed in the rest of his army. Many units deserted, some fleeing in droves towards Palmeria, others switching sides entirely and marching to help their former foes surround their former comrades. Only the central core of Fantar's host-a group of less than a thousand-remained stubbornly loyal. These were men who had been with him for years, many part of his Imperial Guard, the bulk of which had been left to defend Valeria. These men had heard about the justice of the High King and knew they had no option. Facing death either way, they chose to die fighting.

But while Fantar's demise disheartened his host, it positively electrified the exhausted men of Valerius. The sight and portent of that obese body, crumpled on the sandy floor of the valley with its purple mantle spread over it like a pall, was unmistakable, and the charge it sent through the battle lines gathering on the southern hills flashed

347

through the rest of the straggling host like a burst of energy from the sun. Even men who had fallen by the wayside, too exhausted to move, struggled back to their feet and joined the throngs that flooded towards the valley. Koltar's cavalry and Karghan's Scythians quickly resumed their mounts and attacked from the heights, surrounding Fantar's die-hards. Deserting troops supported the horsemen, and soon, Valerius' own men swelled the enclosing ring and escape was beyond question.

The fight was short but vicious. Valerius called on the die-hards to surrender, but he was answered with a hurled spear. Keeping his own troops in a tight cordon, he directed Koltar's archers to pour volley after volley into the ring. Two attempts were made to break out, but these only stretched the edges of the ring as the surging forces shifted this way and that. Their only real effect was to present more opportunities for the archers as troops shifted fronts. In a very short time, the majority of even these troops reconsidered the 'death now versus justice later option,' and threw down their arms.

Valerius and his leaders met in a ring around the purple-shrouded hulk that had been Fantar. Drawn to it irresistibly, they stood in silent contemplation for a few moments; each absorbed the enormity of the moment. Then Valerius nodded and the crowd gasped in unison as two men rolled the huge corpse over.

It was Fantar, all right. There was no mistaking that savage visage or the burned out eye-socket staring blankly from under its dislodged leather patch. But there was another body too, that of a small Kantaran whose twisted neck had obviously been broken as Fantar fell. He wore a heavy leather collar and a long chain that was attached to Fantar's wrist. And as they rolled the great body over, the smaller one's hand slipped away from the splintered hilt of a toy wooden sword that protruded from Fantar's chest.

"It's Colinus!" said Koltar, kneeling by his side.

"Yes," said Vahla, the ubiquitous Chad standing quietly by her shoulder. "I saw a vision of him in Volkmir's fire before I left. He was wrecked at sea on a catumaran. I thought him dead, but he must have been captured."

"Aye," said Valerius, "I doubt not that some sorcery played a hand here. It was he, whom the prophecy said Fantar could only 'half see,'" and here several eyes turned towards Vahla. "But he was always a doughty little champion and now he shall be honored as the greatest warrior of this generation." Freeing him from his collar at last, they bore the small body of Colinus off to be prepared for the pyre.

Chapter 25
THE FALL OF VALERIA

It took more than a week for the exhausted army of Valerius to make its way over the remaining sixty miles to Palmeria. They followed the waters of the Darlung, which twined its way through the countryside, conjoining with the natural watershed and even forming a series of small lakes and ponds along its way, before pouring into the Inland Sea just south of the city. In after years, the lands along its course bloomed with vegetation. Its waters fed lush gardens and broad fields of grain, and its lakes and ponds abounded with fish and wild fowl.

But Valerius could not wait for his troops, so anxious was he over the condition of Eomer. Leaving Grumwald in command and riding ahead with Vahla, Chad and a small escort of Kantaran horsemen, he drove their mounts nearly to collapse before allowing any rest, then pushed on again at first light. He himself could not sleep at all, such was the state he was in, and even entering the city he was deaf to the cheers and applause of the crowds lining the walls and streets. Somehow, it had gotten into his head that Eomer's plight was his fault, and that his march eastward had only exacerbated her illness. He said nothing of this, even knew on another level of his consciousness that it wasn't so-couldn't be so-yet guilt galled and gnawed at him like a canker and would not quit until he reined up before the palace and saw Eomer

350

herself waiting to greet him with young Valerian in her arms.

Sweeping her into his arms, he carried them both to his chambers where, after a hot bath and a warm meal, he collapsed and slept for two days.

When the army did march into Palmeria, Valerius prepared a Royal celebration to greet them, with his queen and heir, his official Enchantress and all the rest of his entourage decked out in their finest splendor. The army was too large by far now to be entirely accommodated within the city, but they all marched through, even the Scythian warriors who could barely keep their lines for looking about in awe. Such were the numbers of Valerius' host that it took an entire day for their parade, and afterwards many there were in the city who could not speak from cheering. The army entered the northern gate and exited to the south where a great military camp was set up near the new river. The feasting and celebrating that followed went on for days.

When things quieted, Valerius called all his commanders to council. There were several issues to decide, not least among them their next moves. There were still a number of towns along the northern shore which had been garrisoned by Fantar that had to be dealt with-though few expected these would put up any resistance-and, of course, there was Valeria itself, left under the command of Gormlath, the head of Fantar's Imperial Guard, and the man, many felt, who had been the real power behind the power for the past several years.

But, it was apparent to all that taking Valeria would not require a multitude, and that there was much work yet to solidify the High King's regime in all the cities around the Inland Sea. So the army was reassigned, with many units returning home and others sent to a number of potential trouble spots. Valerius, of course, would move on to Valeria with his core divisions, his intention being to take the city in a quick move, then deal with the northern shore cities one at a time.

In all, however, these discussions seemed perfunctory. With Fantar's death, the whole struggle seemed less a war than a police action with little doubt of the outcome. The various dispositions were arranged as a matter of course, and the talk quickly turned to other matters which had suddenly assumed importance: matters of policy, protocol and trade. And in these Valerius, for the first time in his adult life, found himself considering matters of peace.

This notion left him with a heady, almost giddy feeling as he relaxed on the veranda after luncheon with Eomer and Vahla. And when Eomer, her left arm still bandaged, left to check on young Valerian, Valerius thought it an appropriate time to discuss some future issues with Vahla as well. They had not really spoken personally since before the march to Darlung, but now he looked at her again with his old warmth.

"Vahla the Enchantress," he murmured to himself, as if he were still getting used to the title. Then, "Are you planning to accompany me to Valeria?"

"I haven't decided yet," she said, unsure of his intent, unsure still, how things stood between them.

"Well, you've won the hearts of the army, you know. They'll fight much better knowing the power that struck down Fantar is with them."

She looked at him sharply. "You know I had nothing...," but he cut her off with a raised palm.

"Vahla, you don't need to explain to me. No one knows better than I how right Volkmir was when he said we do not rule the Powers that guide us. The best we can do is serve their will. But whether you come or not, you must understand that you have become the Mage of Valeria. You have a place at court aside from being my sister, the Princess... So, I guess what I'm really asking is whether you intend to marry Karghan."

Vahla looked down at her hands folded in her lap. "I don't know." Then meeting Valerius' eye again, "I told him I had to have your blessing."

"Well, that was proper. But surely you know my blessing follows your desire."

"Thank you for that... I could do worse than Karghan, you know. He's an extraordinary man."

"Yes, he is. But, do you love him?"

"Is love all that important?" she asked. But seeing the answer plain in Valerius' eyes, she dropped hers again and for a long moment, they sat in silence. When she raised her face again, he could see moisture in her eyes. "There is no love for me, Valerius. Whether Thorngere is alive or dead-and I pray fervently that he is alive-I cannot have him, and there can be no other. And if I come to Valeria

353

with you, I will only be reminded of that day after day. I can't face that. And I don't want to spend my life in a cave like Volkmir. But if I marry Karghan, I may still do some good. His people are nomads; they know nothing of our ways. I can help them."

But Valerius was not so easily deterred. "You could still help as Mage of Valeria-or Enchantress-whether or not you came to court. So, why marry Karghan?"

Vahla flashed him a hard look, but her eyes burned with pain now, not fury. "Because then," she started and then stopped as a tear spilled down her cheek. "Because then maybe I can forget!" she spat, and quickly wiped the tear away. But before either could say any more, a herald interrupted them.

"Your Majesty!" the man snapped, in the way such creatures have of announcing themselves. "A trading scow has entered the harbor and its Master, one Boltar, sends to seek an audience with the High King. He says he has news of Valeria."

"Boltar!" Both Valerius and Vahla started up as if electrified. "It must be the Elusive! Yes, by all means, man. Tell Boltar we will receive him in the Audience room immediately."

The news that word had come from Valeria spread like wildfire, and the audience chamber was packed when Boltar entered, followed by two seamen bearing a small cask. Valerius sat on a raised dais at the far end of the hall, flanked by Eomer and Vahla, and surrounded by his senior advisors. Boltar approached the throne and bowed low.

354

"Your Majesty," he announced with a good deal more poise than he felt. "I am commanded by the High Chieftain of Thule to bring you tidings of Valeria."

"You are welcome, Boltar. What are these tidings that you bear?"

Boltar nodded and the two seamen set down the cask and pried off its lid. Boltar reached into the preservative brandy and pulled out by the hair a gruesome, dripping, twisted thing that once had been a face. "Here, Valerius, is the head of Gormlath, former Head of Fantar's Imperial Guard, and late keeper of Valeria. Your Majesty, the city is yours!"

It was some time before order could again be restored in the hall, but when the cheering subsided, Valerius gave answer. "Boltar, you have brought me my heart's dream and shall be suitably rewarded! But tell us how this came to be? What forces? How went the battle? It is wondrous news, man-tell us the story!"

"That is the second part of my errand, Your Majesty. The High Chieftain of Thule bade me ask your leave for him to present an embassy from Thuringia. As it was the Thuringians who took Valeria, he himself would like to relate that tale, and to offer their allegiance."

"Boltar, I can only say we would be most honored to receive him."

At that, the doors at the back of the hall were thrown open and in marched Thorngere, attended by several of his warriors and wearing the formal

mantle of the High Chieftain of Thule. At sight of
him, another furor broke out in the hall. Vahla leapt
to her feet and then with a physical effort, sat
herself down again. But it was some time before the
hall quieted, and when it did, Thorngere knelt
before Valerius and offered him the hilt of his
sword.

"Valerius Everreigning, High King of Valeria
and all the Inland Sea, along with the city of Valeria
which I now relinquish to you, I Thorngere, High
Chieftain of Thule, here proffer you my sword and
the fealty of my people, now and forevermore."

Another round of cheers filled the hall, but
Valerius, grinning broadly, was unable to keep
within the bounds of formal protocol. "Thorngere,
my brother!" he exclaimed. "Your loyalty has never
been questioned and while the allegiance of
Thuringia is assuredly most welcome, why do you
dissemble? It is great show, certainly, but surely..."

"There, Majesty, I fear I have dire news to
report," said Thorngere, retaining his formality of
manner but rising to his feet. "I have only recently
discovered that a great fraud has been perpetrated
upon you-upon us-which I deeply regret, and for
which I must now seek your absolution."

"What is this?" said Valerius, his face growing
dark and resuming its formal expression. In the hall,
not another sound could be heard.

"Your Majesty," said Thorngere, "the simple
truth is, I am not your brother. In fact, I am none of
your blood at all."

Stunned silence filled the hall, except for Vahla, who gasped audibly and half-rose again from her seat. This time, she hung there as if suspended by wires.

"Well!" said Valerius, his high, formal visage beginning to crack again with just the slightest hint of a grin. "This is a most serious thing indeed, one we must surely get to the bottom of. But in the meantime, there is only one way I can think of to absolve you. You, Thorngere, High Chieftain of Thule, must immediately become by brother by accepting in marriage the hand of our sister, Vahla, the Enchantress of Valeria. What say you Thorngere? Will you accept our judgement in this matter?"

But Thorngere looked not at Valerius. Nor, in fact, were any in that room looking more at the High King. He was but a spectator himself as all eyes went to Thorngere and Vahla, whose eyes were locked so tightly together that a palpable force emanated between them. Vahla was on her feet now, her whole body poised, and as Thorngere said, "My lord, that would be my greatest honor," she flew into his arms.

End of Book III